LOST

Jennifer Davis

Copyright © 2017 Jennifer Davis
All rights reserved.

ISBN: 1544077939
ISBN 13: 9781544077932

For my love,
who has always loved and believed in me, even when I did not

PROLOGUE

I glance up from my book and see him walking toward me. *When did he get on the plane? I thought he was going to New York?* My heart starts racing. I look over and Jack's sleeping soundly next to me. My eyes meet the object of my lust and he nods, wanting me to follow him. *But should I follow him? What does he want with me?* I sit in my seat, undecided for a moment. Curiosity wins. I jump up and walk down the aisle, glancing behind me to be sure Jack is still sound asleep. *Where did he go?* I walk toward the galley, expecting him to be in there. I peer around the corner and see no sign of him. *Is this some kind of game?* A forceful hand on my shoulder startles me. I whip around to see Mr. Lust discreetly holding open the door to the lavatory. *Seriously?* He extends his hand and my intrigue forces me to follow him inside.

He shuts the door and I shift uncomfortably. "What are you doing here?" I question him, both scared and excited by the situation.

He lets out a sigh. "Bella, I'm just"—he pauses—"fuck, I'm finishing this." He pulls me toward him and our arms immediately wrap around each other. He grabs my head, pulling my chin toward him. Our lips meet and I feel a burning throughout my body. I never thought we'd share another kiss, especially not trapped in the confines of this tiny bathroom, just feet away from my boyfriend.

We kiss each other hard, our tongues wrap around each other's while he pulls my head, tugging my hair in hungry passion.

He turns me around and we grasp for air to catch our breath. I stand in front of him, our bodies still pressed against each other from the tight quarters of the bathroom. We both stare into the mirror in front of us, and he slowly pulls down the top of my dress, exposing my bra. His fingers slide across my shoulders, and my body is electrified, with every little hair standing at attention, wondering, waiting for his next move. He leans forward and kisses my neck, taking small nibbles as he moves along. His hands slide across my breasts, and my nipples immediately harden, begging for more attention.

His hands continue downward, grabbing my hips and then lifting up my dress enough to slide his hand beneath the fabric. His left hand is wrapped around my waist, holding me close to him, and his right hand slips into my panties. I watch his face in the mirror, so focused and entranced by me. I'm still barely breathing, releasing only short shallow breaths as the pleasure and anticipation move through me, waiting and wondering what he'll do next. I reach my hand behind me, grabbing his belt, and feeling his arousal through his pants. I remove his belt and slide my hand inside, finding his massive muscle ready and waiting. I gently massage him, feeling the sheer size as I move my hand up and down. He lets out a groan of pleasure just as he slides his finger inside of me. I nearly lose it right then, feeling myself tighten and excite with his expert stroke. His fingers are long and strong, giving me a preview of the mystery object waiting in his pants.

"I need you now," Mr. Lust commands, both telling me and asking me at once. I nod my head with approval, desperate to feel him inside of me. He slides my panties to the side with his finger, and without removing them, he pushes forward and I feel him inside of me. We groan in unison, and our bodies start moving in synchronous rhythm. Our hips rock in succession and I feel myself tighten around him. I grab his head again, kissing him so that our tongues are moving in the same sweet sequence as our bodies. He slides in and out of me, quickly but fully, teasing me with each movement, bringing me closer and closer to the edge. I reach around and grab his ass, feeling how taut it is as it flexes over and over again. My climax begins to build inside of me, and he instantly starts moving faster and faster, somehow sensing that I'm near the edge. The explosive need keeps building and building, and I know I won't make it much longer. I feel my body reaching the point of no return and I grab his neck and deepen my kiss just as my climax explodes through my body. His body responds to my vibrations and I feel him tense, then watch his eyes close as he finds his release with me. I sit with him still inside of me, lost in his eyes. I study his face, trying to tell what this practical stranger is thinking.

Then, my own thoughts return, and I realize what I've just done. *Did I really just betray the man I'm falling in love with for Lust?*

CHAPTER ONE

The jetway is cold from the winter air, and Jack leans his body into mine, sweeping his arm loosely around me to keep me warm. "Will they be greeting us with a hot toddy once we board?" Jack laughs. I smile back at my handsome boyfriend, just steps away from our first holiday together.

"That would be nice! But we'll probably have to settle for champagne." I giggle, feeling nervous but excited. Today marks only six weeks of dating, yet here we are, about to embark on our first trip together. And not just any trip, a holiday in Paris, the city of love, on the weekend of love. *In what fantasy world am I living? Love doesn't just come this easily.* I force the negativity from my mind. *I am deserving of love.* I remind myself of the words of my childhood therapist, still wanting to believe in love despite never having experienced it.

"Welcome aboard! Which seats are you in?" A sweet, southern flight attendant, clearly hailing from my hometown of Atlanta, greets us as we enter the business class cabin. She smiles at us and soft wrinkles form around her face, showing her age.

"3A and 3B," I reply.

"Great, you're right this way." She points to the aisle in front of us and we make the short walk to our seats. Always the gentleman, Jack takes my suitcase from me and lifts it into the overhead compartment. I smile to myself, enjoying the view of his flexing muscles. His sky-blue eyes sparkle with the evening sun that shines through the windows. He wears dark jeans with a gray mock neck sweater zipped down to reveal a peek of his navy blue and white checkered shirt. Standing six feet tall with a strong linebacker build allows him to easily toss our bags above us.

"Window or aisle?" I turn to ask him, catching an excited grin on his face.

"Wow, babe, this is awesome! Are these really our seats?" He glances around the business class cabin, taking it all in.

"Yes! Just one of the perks of my job," I nonchalantly respond, while secretly gloating that *I* have finally managed to impress *him*! He's spent the last month and a half wining and dining me with opulent dinners, but thanks to my job I can get us business class to Paris!

"Well, this is awesome, thank you. And I'll take the aisle...unless you want it?"

"Nope it's all yours." I slide into the window seat, setting my red Longchamp purse and matching tote bag in front of me. I catch a glimpse of myself in the window and smooth my medium-length blonde hair. My hazel eyes are complemented by my dark brown mascara and curled lashes. Light pink blush gives color to my otherwise pale complexion, with a similar tint on my large lips.

"Can I offer you two some champagne?"

"Yes, please!" Jack nods at the request. He takes the glasses from the flight attendant and hands one to me. "Cheers, baby. Here's to a wonderful Valentine's Day weekend that we'll never forget."

"I'll drink to that!" My glass clinks with his and he leans over and gives me a quick kiss. Even the brief graze of his lips makes me squirm inside, reminding me of my wicked weekend plans for him. After forty-four days with my perfect-thus-far boyfriend, we've gotten to know each other in many ways, except one very obvious and intimate one. This weekend, I will be handing him my v-card. *You're not technically a virgin, Jess,* my subconscious quickly reminds me. *Will may not have been good in bed, but you did still sleep with him.* I internally roll my eyes at the thought of my ex-boyfriend. Fine, if women were allotted two v-cards, Mr. Jackson Clarke would be the lucky recipient of card number 2.

The thought of giving myself to him has been on my mind since we first met, thanks to my impromptu enrollment in an online dating app, under the guidance of my dear friend Sarah. The stars were aligned for me and Jack; we met after just one day on the app, which gave me the push I needed to officially move past my boring and loathsome relationship with my college boyfriend, Will. A relationship that at times gave me glimpses of lust and even love, but never warranted true feelings or release of the L word.

"This champagne is fantastic!" Jack says, leaning into me. "Almost as fantastic as kissing you," he says in a deep, quiet voice. *Oh, my.* Jack's oversized lips quickly entrap mine, and I melt into the fantasy that awaits us just hours from now. Knowing what lies beneath his fitted dark jeans makes me squirm, imagining his sexiest muscle inside of me. *Looks can be deceiving, Jess. Will looked the part but didn't have the talent, remember? And do you really think that you've met the perfect guy and you can just fall in love and live happily ever after?* "Mmmh," Jack groans into my mouth and it's just what I need to squash the negativity resounding within.

As the plane accelerates forward, I say a quick silent prayer to my non-denominational god. Thank you for my job at Global Airlines, which has given me the ability to fly to Paris in business class, with Jack. Thank you for Jack, my perfect, all-American boyfriend. And thank you for the mind-blowing sex that hopefully awaits. And maybe, one day, love.

After a five-course dinner with wine pairings, two movies, and a short, buzzed nap on the plane, we arrive à Paris. Brisk, snowy air greets us as we walk out of the subway tunnel onto the Champs-Élysées. The famous street is a beautiful sight even on the dark winter morning. White lights decorate the trees that line the wide street. Parisians ride bicycles through the crowds, making their way to work. The sidewalks are bolstered by the most amazing designer stores: Chanel, Burberry, Christian Dior Couture, Louis Vuitton, Dolce & Gabbana. And the list goes on.

Jack sees me bundling up, and he outstretches his right arm, pulling me close to his body. I take the cue and wrap my arms around him, holding him tightly. His black puffy jacket squishes against my arms and I giggle as he deflates in front of me. His gorgeous eyes scan ahead to the street in front of us. He has a slight rim of red around his eyelids, a telltale sign of the sleep we missed on the plane. His dark blond hair is a little rumpled, but despite his airplane bed head, he becomes even sexier as snowflakes decorate his short mane. His cheeks are rosy from brisk air, and it reminds me of his post-orgasm glow.

"Oh, don't worry baby, I'll warm you right up once we get to our room." *Yes!* My body starts craving the post-breakfast dessert, a hot Americano sliding down my throat.

"Oh yeah? Maybe I'll warm *you* up." My frisky comment draws his attention.

"I'd like to see that. Come on, the Sofitel is just up ahead," he nods.

We're finally alone. I hear Jack bid adieu to the bellman and the door to our hotel room close, signaling my heart to beat faster, thinking of what comes next. I stare back at myself in the mirror, feeling my erotic anticipation overriding my incoming jetlag. I quickly splash water on my face and gargle some mouthwash in a sixty-second attempt at freshening up. I pull the towel to my face and sense Jack is just a few steps behind me.

"So," he says, posting himself up in the bathroom doorway, looking unbelievably sexy in his wrinkled undershirt and eighteen-hour stubble.

"So," I respond back with a giggle, unsure if I'm ready to make my move or not.

"So, Jess. You kidnapped me and forced me to come to Paris, and now you have me here. In your hotel room." He pauses, sauntering slowly toward me. "So..." another pause, this time a wicked grin spreading across his face, "what are you going to do with me?"

Oh, fuck me. Literally. I lunge at him, stopping him dead in his tracks. I grab at his belt and pull it furiously as I kiss him hard. "I'm going to have my way with you," I moan the words, and as he grabs my head, I feel his divine mouth move into an approving smile. My lips quickly part, wanting to taste him. All of him. My fingers quickly find the button on his pants and I undo it using my thumb and two fingers. I unzip him in one easy movement, then use both of my hands to push his pants to the floor. Jack reaches his left arm around my back, then grabs the fabric of my sweater dress and lifts it up, resting his palm on my bare ass.

I fumble with the buttons on Jack's shirt, and I have only undone three of them before I feel a warm finger circling my clitoris. "God, baby, you're so wet for me." He groans into my ear as his finger slides deeper inside of me. "I want you, Jess." His words radiate through my desperate body and a small squeak falls out of my mouth. Jack pulls me to him and I feel his long, hard cock through his boxer briefs. Our eyes meet, and we stare deep into each other as we both pant, knowing what's to come. *Hopefully me!* Jack guides me backward a few steps before he stops to lean his back against the side of the sofa, then slides a second finger inside of me. My body gyrates with his hand, responding to his touch. He withdraws his fingers and moves both of his hands around my back, finding the zipper of my dress. His hands are warm and strong, and they move purposefully, teasing me as he goes painstakingly slow to remove my dress.

My thoughts are pleading with him to get it off. To get me off. *Please, Jack, fuck me already!* His breathing is heavy, and he groans into my ear as I step out of my dress. "I can't wait any longer, baby. I need to have you. Now." His eyes stare into mine, looking for my approval before he continues. *Finally!*

"I want you too, Jack," I respond with a whisper of approval. He kisses me with need and scoops his hands below my ass, lifting me up to him. My arms are wrapped around his neck, my legs holding tightly around him. I balance myself against his body, and Jack slowly kneels, taking us both to the ground. My bare bottom lands on the plush rug beneath me. Jack scoots me forward as he leans me on my back. I feel his warm man muscle slide across my clitoris, and my body nearly explodes. I will myself to wait for him to be inside me before letting go. I lie on my back and slide my hands down Jack's strong arms. I feel him inching toward me, and his body slowly lowers onto mine as our eyes lock. He leans down and my mouth meets his, our tongues lingering passionately.

Finally, I feel his throbbing manhood against the apex of my peach and I wiggle my hips, trying to push him inside of me. It slides against my wetness and Jack gives me a quick thrust to push his body inside of mine. We both groan as our bodies connect for the first time, and I relish how he fills me completely. Our bodies begin to grind together in perfect rhythm and Jack wastes no time further exploring me. His mouth moves to my neck, sending erotic tingles through every millimeter, making me suddenly aware of every nerve ending in my body. His lips move down to my right breast, and he pauses, gently sucking it, and I feel the need swelling inside of me. My left breast is his next target and my back arches, allowing him to take more of it in his mouth. His hot mouth sucks, and nibbles, and then sucks it some more. His tongue swirls around across my nipple in torturous rhythm until I can't take it any longer. My legs begin to shake and Jack's eyes stare wickedly into mine. He grabs my hair and kisses me hard while moving his hips faster and faster, forcing me to let go, my body exploding around him. *So, this is what I've been missing!* The feeling is so intense I can barely breathe; I inhale oxygen only through my shallow moans that I can barely control.

"You ok, baby?" I nod my head as I focus on my ruggedly handsome boyfriend. Jack continues thrusting inside of me, but slows his pace as I catch my breath. My fingers move across his back, holding him tightly, and I feel the orgasm growing inside of me again. The muscles in his back and arms begin to tighten and his rhythm increases. Each movement massages me inside, bringing me closer and closer to another climax. *I didn't know I could do this once, much less twice in a row!* The intense feelings overtake me as the explosion rises to the edge of the surface once more. I see Jack's face twist as he edges closer to his release. Then, his muscles tighten further and his body vibrates across mine as he comes, grabbing me tightly. Feeling him lose control extracts my second orgasm. Our bodies shake while we clutch each other's skin. *My. Mind. Is. Blown.*

CHAPTER TWO

I open my eyes, bleary and tired from the amazing and passionate morning I shared with Jack. I turn my head to the other side of the pillow, and a smile forms on my lips as I feel his warmth next to me. *How could I be this lucky?* The combination of mental and physical attraction is something I haven't felt before. Literally, I realize, considering my one and only prior sexual partner was never able to give me an orgasm from sex. *I guess I wasn't the problem!* It's like everything about Jack just matches perfectly with me. The hopeful part of my heart tries to reassure me that this feeling is more than just a postcoital fantasy. *It's the beginning of something real.*

I nuzzle my head into Jack's chest, feeling it gently rise and fall as he sleeps peacefully. I begin running my fingers through his chest hair, a feature that makes him even manlier and sexier to me. As I twirl my fingers, I watch his body begin to twitch, recognizing my soft touch. His eyes open, staring back at me with the intensity I have come to enjoy. I know exactly what this look means, even this early in the morning. His fiery, hungry stare pulls my innermost desires right up to the surface. Jack swiftly grabs me, pulling the rest of my body on top of him. Despite the frigid winter morning, I feel the heat run through me, anxious and excited for his next move.

"How'd you sleep?" Jack breathes, his voice cracking slightly after our sleep. He clears his throat, allowing him to find his deep smooth sound. My eyes peel open at the sound of his savory voice.

"Never better," I whisper, nuzzling my lips across his ear and onto his neck. "You managed to successfully wear me out this morning," I giggle. "Should we get dressed and get something to eat?" I playfully kiss his neck and nibble his ear, unable to keep my hands off of him.

"Oh I'm hungry all right," he says naughtily. His tone instantly tells me that he's not looking for a meal just yet, but another piece of me. *Again? I'm not sure my body can take any more of this!* He tucks a piece of my blonde hair behind my ear as he moves his lips across my neck. He slowly works his way down my neck with soft kisses, nuzzling his nose into my body, and then uses it to push open my black satin robe. I feel Jack Junior growing even more excited as he inches down me, enjoying the easy access to my body. My legs fall on either side of his and I rock forward onto my knees, leaning down to bring my body closer to his. My robe cascades off my shoulders with the help of Jack's eager hands, pooling the fabric around my waist. I raise myself up a few inches so I can reach down and slide off his boxer briefs, all the while Jack's hands continue to work their way down my body. His Calvin Kleins shift down his strong legs, and his rabid animal is released from its cage. I lower myself back down onto him, using my body to push his sex stick flat against his stomach. My body sits against him and Jack moves his hands around to my back, holding my hips. I sit up straight, placing my hands on his chest to support my body.

"What an amazing view!" Jack looks up at me eyeing my body. "You're unbelievably sexy, Jess." I blush at the compliment, wanting to believe his words, but never really doing so.

"You're not so bad yourself." I smile. His hands move up my back, pulling me down to him for a deep kiss. Our tongues explore each other's mouths and my hips slide and rock against the smooth, taut skin of his cock. The feeling on my clitoris is spectacular so I continue sliding myself up and down against his shaft, still keeping it outside of my body. I feel myself getting more excited by each movement so I slide my hips further up so that the tip of his penis touches the opening of my peach. I repeat this motion, increasing the desire between us. Jack pulls my hair while our kisses grow deeper and stronger. I try to control myself but the feeling is too intense. Jack pulls his mouth from mine, watching me pant and moan as I slide up and down him. Part of me wants him inside of me, but this sensation is too strong to stop. *Holy shit, I'm going to explode and he's not even inside of me.* "It's ok, baby, just let yourself go," he encourages me. Those words are all I need to hear to send the shockwaves through my body. My mouth falls open, moaning as my body releases.

"Jess, are you ok?" Jack asks, half laughing and clearly pleased with himself for doing this to me.

"Uhhh, um yes, I'm great," I manage to moan.

"Can you handle any more? We've got to do something about this." Jack laughs, nodding down toward his engorged muscle.

"Well we certainly wouldn't want you feeling neglected. What kind of girlfriend would I be if I left you high and dry?"

"Good, because I'm not done with you yet either." With that, Jack takes my hips and slides me forward, and suddenly his throbbing cock fills me for the third time today. I am in awe of its perfect shape, so thick that it's a very tight fit inside me. And it's the perfect length, repeatedly hitting my internal bullseye. His hips control our speed, and this time I feel something even deeper. My last orgasm is still fresh and I quickly feel that tingling inside of me starting to build. My arms push against the bed beneath me, supporting my upper body. As I ride this beautiful man I feel his mouth move onto my nipples, sucking and teasing. I feel my body start to ache for release and I move faster, up and down his perfect penis. The sucking on my breasts is bringing me closer and closer, and suddenly my body explodes around him, even more intensely than the last time. Jack's body quickly responds to this sensation and we find ourselves coming in unison.

Once the aftershocks have passed I lie panting on top of Jack. The intensity has drained me completely. His arms secure me against him and I feel so close to him. We lie like this for a few moments until I get the energy to pull myself off of him.

"What we need is a shower and some lunch. I'll hop in first, you can lie here and recover," Jack says sweetly, leaving with a soft kiss on the forehead.

"Mmm sounds good to me!" I watch my beautiful man, my boyfriend, walk away in his birthday suit from the bed to the shower. I hear the water start, and my mind starts to drift. Before I know it I fall into a dream, picturing myself in a wedding gown, staring back at dapper-looking Jack in a tuxedo. *Sex is not love, Jess. Don't confuse the two.* I remind myself of this reality, but I can't help but think about him. *What's not to love?*

CHAPTER THREE

"Come on, baby, let's go!" Jack calls to me as I finish the final touches of my makeup before we begin our Paris exploration.

"Ok, almost done. *Someone* didn't let me get much sleep this morning, so I have some dark circles to cover up."

"Really?" Jack feigns surprise, his reflection nearing mine in the mirror. "That's odd, I remember being in bed since we arrived." He plants a juicy kiss on my neck, sending shivers down my spine. His hand trails down the curve of my waist, and arousal drips through my veins. "Maybe I should take you back to bed," he seductively suggests.

"Rain check?" I say innocently, tugging on his growing erection. "I did drag you all the way to Paris after all, we should probably see more than the four walls of this room!"

"Huhm," Jack mumbles, shaking his head at my ability to tease. I watch him pout as I dig through my suitcase, deciding what to wear. I settle on my black velvet pencil leg pants and a tight black

Lost

sweater. I add a pop of color with my scarlet red scarf and throw on my tan walking boots.

The falling snow has suspended, and we walk down the Champs-Élysées to the metro station. We decide to spend our first afternoon checking out all of the amazing historical delights in le Louvre. As we approach the world-famous museum it doesn't seem all that spectacular. Typical historic European buildings frame the streets, and we walk past them for a few blocks before stumbling upon a stunning glass-constructed pyramid, signaling we've found the museum.

Nearly an hour into our cultural exploration, I peer at Jack, intrigued by the great works of art. He looks so refined today, his dark jeans, fitted black sweater, and dark rimmed glasses create an artsy air about him, which he wears quite well. His dark blond hair shines underneath the faint museum lighting, preserving the centuries-old masterpieces. I stride up next to him, and he places his arm around my waist as we both gaze at the Mona Lisa. I slide my arm around his back too, feeling the soft wool sweater, and give him a squeeze. I allow myself to enjoy this moment. My feelings for him grow exponentially with each glance, smile, and touch from him. And, now that I've sampled his goods, I've validated his beautiful man muscle isn't just for show. *It's for showing me what sex is supposed to be!* I freeze my thoughts for another realization—I've never, ever felt this way about someone before. *Oh my God.* I swallow hard. *Is it possible? Could I really be falling for him, uhm, falling in love with him already?* My heart radiates with the idea as my brain fills with fear. *Be real, Jess, everything seems too perfect. Do you really think that suddenly you can have a perfect boyfriend, with a perfect relationship, and fall in love? In Paris of all places?* Damn it! I pull my hand away from Jack, frustration filling me from my own self-doubt. *Come on, Jess, you haven't felt love for all twenty-five years of your existence, why would it fall into your lap now?* I want to bitch-slap my hideous inner thoughts, but I can't help but know it's true. Even if my unloved self is right, I can't help but want to finally feel this for someone, and have it returned. But could Jack really be the one to do that?

"What's wrong, babe?" Jack questions me, reaching his arm toward me.

"Nothing," I lie, not wanting to share my unfounded insecurity of our relationship. "What time is it? I want to be sure we have time to see the last wing before it closes."

"4:30," Jack advises, reading from his phone. I watch a slight furrow form on his brow as his finger swipes across the screen.

"Everything ok?" I question him. The phone distraction continues, and I watch him shake his head as his eyes dart back and forth, reading something on the screen. I stare at him, awaiting a response, and realize that he's too lost in this to have heard my question. I slide my arm into his and lean in to get a glimpse of his phone.

Remember V day last year? Vail. Hot tub. Falling snow. Skinny dipping. Champagne. <3 Miss you.

My eyes try to quickly read the sender's name: Lela. Jack senses that I can see the screen, and shuts it off. *What the fuck?*

"Everything ok?" I ask, feeling my heart beat through my chest, trying to recall who this Lela might be.

"Yeah, it's nothing important." Jack gives me a weak smile, which I don't return. "Really, babe, it's nothing even worth discussing. Nothing I even care about, just a stupid distraction." This time his smile is sincere, and he wraps his arms around me and pulls me close.

"What?" I ask, his stare making me feel uncomfortable.

"Nothing. Can't I look at my beautiful girlfriend?" I smile and try to push doubts of his insincerity aside, remembering that love requires a bit of faith and even the risk of a broken heart. I move in and elevate myself on my toes so I can lean in and kiss him. His lips are soft, supple, and draped with reassurance of his feelings toward me, which is exactly what I need right now.

CHAPTER FOUR

The hotel room is warm and a very welcome reprieve to the cold outdoors. The sun has gone down and the temperature has dropped right along with it.

"You ready for a night on the Paris town?" Jack's warm, sexy smile and his relaxed expression allow me to momentarily forget the museum texting situation.

"I can't wait," I say honestly before excusing myself to the bathroom to doll myself up for our first evening out in Paris.

My red lace dress flatters my figure perfectly. The V-neck cut allows for a tasteful, yet adequately sexy, display of my décolletage. The dress hugs my waist, showcasing my curves. My eyes are decorated with a light brown shimmery eyeshadow and lined with a darker brown to draw out the gold and brown tones within them. Curling my lashes gives them an extra flirty lift. The last step is applying my bright red lipstick. I smile back at myself with approval, knowing this is as good as I get! *This vixen is ready to take on the Paris nightlife. And get whoever Lela is out of Jack's mind.*

I strut from the bathroom, hoping to immediately garner Jack's attention. "Wow. Babe. I mean wow, you look amazing," he says, looking up from his computer. *Success!*

I nonchalantly answer, "Thanks. Would you be a doll and zip me up?" I motion toward my dress's zipper, which runs up the side of me, hoping to lure Jack with a peek of my lingerie.

"Sure. Come." Those simple words make me think of doing just that on top of him. I walk slowly toward him and pause at the edge of the bed. He pulls up my zipper and pauses after he gets a glance of my black lacy bra and matching panties. I glance at him through my long, curled lashes and see his pants get tighter as he grows with excitement.

"How about I unzip you instead?" he states, his tone informative rather than inquisitive. He smoothly pulls my zipper all the way down and slides his hand inside of my dress. Strong fingers gently push my hair aside and he begins kissing my neck. His lips move across my collarbone and I feel myself warming between my legs. I grab his head and pull him toward me, anticipating his smooth plump lips. The ringing of Jack's phone abruptly disrupts my erotic plans.

Jack grabs his cell from the nightstand beside him, pausing my forthcoming rant. "Hold that thought. It could be work, and they would only call if it's really important." My eyes roll in my head with annoyance, but Jack fails to notice, and I try to let it go. I see the words "unknown number" on the screen as he pulls it to his ear, and assume it must be his office. This wouldn't be the first time he's been bothered by work when with me. I shouldn't complain though. He's a hard-working and driven man, which means he could provide for our family. *Stop it, Jess! Slow down with the fairytale ending nonsense, it's been six weeks.* My thoughts pause as he answers the call.

"Hello?" Jack greets the caller.

"Jack. Hi. It's Lela." I faintly hear the female caller's voice and my heart races with fear and fury. *Oh God.* I begin racking my brain for all mentions of Lela. We haven't had many conversations about past relationships, but the few we've had haven't yielded that name. I do a mental inventory of anything related to a Lela in Jack's house—and then it hits me like a ton of bricks. Just a few weeks into our courtship, I found myself alone in Jack's home, and used my time wisely to further study some things in his office, namely a photograph of him with another girl: a cute brunette nonetheless. On the back of one of the photos was a written note in female handwriting:

Thanksgiving 2016
Can't wait to visit you in Atlanta.
All my love, Leland

I was so enamored with Jack at the time that I didn't dwell on his past, but allowed myself to enjoy the furiously fast affair that we'd begun. But now, here I sit, the beginning feelings of love being gutted from me. I pause my breath and listen intently, needing to hear every word from the other end of the phone.

"Hi. This isn't a good time. I'm in Paris right now."

"For work?" I hear her question him.

"Um, yeah. Just a sec," he responds, walking further away from me, apparently not realizing I can hear her question. *You knew it was too good to be true. He just lied about being with you in Paris. You're such a sucker, Jess. You really thought you could find love this easily?*

His growing distance prevents me from hearing her next words. "Can this wait?" he asks her. He stands on the other side of the room, too far away now for me to hear her response. His expression is flustered and frustrated as he turns to me.

"Baby, I'm so sorry, I need to take this call for a minute. Why don't you grab a drink at the bar and I'll meet you there in a minute?" I blink as I process this hideous request. *You've got to be fucking kidding me.* I begin to wince as the pain splits my heart into two, and simultaneous rage flashes through me, furious that he would lie about being here with me. I allow my standard defense mechanism to kick in, my subconscious knowing it's less painful to be angry than heartbroken. *He's going to kick me out of our hotel room to talk to his ex-girlfriend while he's here on vacation with me?* My blood boils too much to manage a coherent response.

"Fuck you" are the only words I can muster. I grab my clutch and storm out of our room, desperate for an escape from the fantasy I'd allowed my naïve heart to create for us.

CHAPTER FIVE

The Sofitel bar has an old worldly feel about it. I glance around at the traditional interior, giving my blazing cheeks a moment to cool. There isn't much seating space, but with only a few patrons inside it's not an issue. A few sofas decorated by rich, deep-colored fabrics in shades of plum and maroon line the main seating area. The walls are natural walnut wood, furthering the feeling of a classically sophisticated speakeasy.

I slide onto the wooden barstool and ponder a drink choice, my brain blurred and my heart hardened. Here I sit, twenty-five years old, alone and rejected in Paris on Valentine's Day weekend. *This is what you deserve, Jess. The unloved don't have poetic fairy-tale endings.* All I can do now is deal with this situation. *There's no point in feeling sad. It's a waste of energy.* That's what mother taught me after all. Love, if that's even what I was starting to feel, is too complicated anyway. What good would that have done? Just set me up for a heartbreak down the road if not now?

The bartender delivers a cold, refreshing glass of bubbles, and I drink it rather quickly, cleansing my emotional palate of what

I always knew was inevitable heartbreak. I contemplate my next move. *What do I do now? Disappear for the night? Fly home without him? Confront him head on about this?* I gulp down my delicious sedative, willing it to fend off any incoming tears, or other signs that I'm just a simple, love-yearning human somewhere deep within.

I quickly polish off a half glass of bubbles, and feel my hardened exterior rebuilding around me. There's no point in feeling sad. It's a waste of energy. I recall mother's words again and decide I'll need more to drink if I'm really to believe them.

"Bon soir." The soft purr of an Italian-coated accent floats into my ears. I whip my head around and blink rapidly as my eyes absorb the beautiful man before me. "Is this seat yours?"

"No, it's all yours," I say with a smile, gesturing toward the open seat next to me. I catch the sparkling hazel eyes set inside his chiseled facial features and tall frame. His eyes return my stare for a moment before I force mine to release his intensely radiant gaze.

"No," he shakes his head. I mean, this was my seat. And I think that was my drink." He nods to the near-empty glass of champagne I've downed, and I quickly realize that I never actually ordered a drink.

"Oh, God. I'm so sorry," I blurt out, instantly mortified. I must look like a complete asshole. I storm into this bar and steal the drink of an obscenely hot man, too fiery to even notice I never ordered it for myself.

"It's ok. You must need it more than me."

"I'm so sorry," I say, feeling my cheeks become blisteringly hot. "I will pay for this, of course," I near-mumble. "Can I buy you a drink as an apology?"

"No, thank you." He slides onto the barstool next to me, seemingly done with our conversation. I stare at him, well, as hard as one can through indirect peripheral viewing, to get a better look at his hotness. His wavy black hair is combed back, not like a greaseball, but in a purely sophisticated sense. His navy suit encases a crisp white shirt, unbuttoned on top to allow a slight peek of his olive skin. The suit fits him perfectly, showing off his built but slender frame. And the material is a smooth, vibrant wool, and clearly bespoke.

He picks up the drink menu, but stares right at me. "I'll have a Grey Goose martini, please," he instructs the waiter, all while staring into me.

"Oh, his drink is on me," I instruct the bartender, assuming he's taking me up on my offer. "Oh, and this one too," I indicate raising my own glass.

"Pardon?" the bartender asks, a bit of surprise in his eyes.

The hot stranger spouts something off in French, and both men have a good laugh. I feel my defenses rise when I hear him say the word "champagne," knowing he's talking about me and my stupid mistake. I'm in no way mentally capable of being dissed by another man, particularly one this hot and capable of ego-crushing right now.

"What's so funny?" I snap, ready to have it out with this French-speaking Italian asshat. I can feel myself ready to redirect some of my Jack anger toward this unsuspecting, but likely worthy, jerk.

"You speak French?" he asks, his tone questioning if he's been caught.

"I remember enough. Enough to know you're an asshole." I blurt the words out more loudly than I anticipate, and I see a few patrons pause to look at me. My accusation does nothing but elicit laughter from the sexy victim of my drink theft.

"Maybe you don't remember as well as you think," he says coolly. As he finishes his thought, the bartender sets two new glasses next to us, and begins opening a bottle of Dom. The stranger turns his body toward me, and his eyes burn into me until I raise my defeated gaze. "I said you are beautiful, and that I never let a lady pay for my drinks. And then I ordered us a bottle of Dom." He gestures to the bottle in front of us, affirming his story. *Oops.*

I didn't think I could be more mortified than when I stole his seat and drink, until now.

"Oh," I mumble, wanting to die for the second time in less than five minutes.

"Salute," he says, raising his glass.

"Salute," I respond, clinking my glass against his. I take a sip and sit quietly, unsure of what to make of this situation, or what to do next to keep from embarrassing myself for a third time.

"So what are you running from?" he questions me after a minute of silence.

"Nothing." I shake my head, noting it's an odd question, but realizing my actions likely provoked it.

"Ok." To my surprise he doesn't question me further.

"And you?"

"What about me?"

"What are you running from?" I ask, and he quickly laughs at my question.

"Probably the same thing you are," he says simply, yet metaphorically. "If we aren't running from something, are we running toward something?" I ponder this question, enjoying his mysteriousness for the first time.

"Hmm. Maybe so? Cheers to…running?" I propose a toast, feeling myself relax a little for the first time tonight. He laughs and clinks my glass, and I feel the hatred begin to leave my body, and allow his darkness to pique my interest.

"Do you like running?" he asks, changing the direction of our conversation and keeping it light.

"No. I really hate it actually. I prefer the metaphorical running," I say with my best flirtatious smile.

"Like running away with someone?"

I laugh nervously. "Depends on the person, I guess."

He nods his beautiful head in understanding, then flips his gaze back at me.

"With me?"

I laugh at his question, assuming it's a joke. His slutty stare reveals his truth. *Oh. My.*

"Excuse me, I need to run to the bathroom," I say, giving myself a momentary out to analyze the quickly thrilling and incredibly tempting situation I've found myself in.

"Of course." He stands in a traditional gentlemanly fashion, grabbing my hand to help me from my seat. I touch his skin and feel the connection pulsing in my veins. We both pause, and his wicked smile confirms he's felt it too. My cheeks blaze, so I grab my clutch, flash him a smile, then turn around the corner leading to the bathroom.

I stare at my reflection in the mirror, trying to re-center my mind. *Jess, you just stormed out on your boyfriend, who you just handed your second v-card to. Are you really going to pass out card number 3 to some insanely hot, probably incredibly rich, and equally as slutty Italian on a whim?* I sigh at the thought, knowing that's not who I am. *It's just a flirtation. Nothing more. I'm not the girl who has one night stands, especially not hours after screwing my boyfriend. Ex-boyfriend?*

I re-touch my makeup, adding more strawberry stain to my lips. I wince a little at my reflection, wishing I had skipped those fries last week instead of two morning workouts, noticing every imperfection and of course those unwanted five pounds. I shake it off, deciding I've earned a free night of flirting, and simply need the confidence it provides. I give myself a final touch-up before returning to Mr. Lust.

"Scuzi." My already anxious heart nearly leaps from my chest at the sound of his voice.

"Scuzi," I respond, already feeling myself panting as he inches toward me in the small corridor between the bathrooms.

"You should apologize for bumping into me," he playfully scolds me, standing just a few inches from me.

"I didn't bump into you. I *almost* bumped into you," I correct him.

"Almost," he affirms, slowly closing the remaining gap between us. He grabs my hands and holds them gently, but pushes me forcefully backward into the wall. My fingers are intertwined with his, and our bodies are fully connected, everywhere except our mouths. I feel overtaken with desire for him, craving more of his touch.

"Almost," I mimic his words again as his lips finally reach mine. The burning heat ripples through me, and I squeeze his hands while his strong, soft lips part to taste mine. I want to touch him, his body, his shiny hair, his five o'clock shadow, anything and everything about him—but I can't. He continues this exploration of my mouth and I feel my loins dripping, begging to feel more of him, but his hands remain locked in mine, my body pinned against his. I don't question if this is right or wrong, because nothing has ever felt so good, so right, so mysterious, and so unbelievably hot.

He pulls his lips from mine, allowing us both a moment to catch our breath. He smiles with a wicked, mischievous, "I want to fuck you" grin, and I know my expression matches his. The question is, could I really do that? Could I really fuck a stranger? The thought's never crossed my mind before now. Before him. Before passion like this.

"I don't even know your name," I blurt out the words as they pass through my brain.

He laughs and smiles wider. "It's Max. And yours?"

I open my mouth to respond but can't get the words out fast enough.

"Jess," I hear Jack's voice call to me, and I spin my head to see him walking toward me. *Fuck.* I'm close enough to hear him, but he's not close enough to see the stranger's hands in mine. "Baby, I'm sorry I had to take that call. Let's go to dinner and I'll explain everything."

Max's knowing grin tells me he understands everything. That this is my semi-boyfriend, and that this adventure of ours is now over.

"Nice to meet you, *Jess*." His stinging words hiss into my ear as he drops my hands, leaving me to pick up the pieces of what remains with Jack.

CHAPTER SIX

"So, what will it be, Jess?" Jack lowers his menu to glance at me, forcing conversation with me for the first time since we left the hotel. "Wine or something else?" I glance around La Monde, our restaurant ce soir, filled with modern décor and gourmet dishes, as judged by the cascading smells from the kitchen. Jack's blue eyes are sparkling at me and I start to feel my body pulling me toward him. *Stop it! He's a conniving asshole. What am I doing here anyway?*

"I could go for a martini," I dictate, still filled with hurt and anger despite my best efforts. *I should be having angry hate sex with the lusty stranger right now. Thanks for fucking that up too, Jack.*

"You hate martinis. What do you really want?" I quickly pout and take offense, watching a waiter approach us. Jack is right, I detest the salty hardness of martinis, but it seems to match my mood, as does my obstinance.

"Bonjour, Madame et Monsieur, les specials ce soir sont—"

I cut the waiter off before he can finish reading the specials. "Bonjour, deux martinis s'il vous plaît." I rudely interrupt his spiel to make a point to Jack. The waiter looks surprised by my disruptive request, but politely dismisses himself and says he will return with them immediately. I feel Jack's eyes burning into me without even facing him. I pretend to glance at my menu and ignore his stare, forcing him to break the silence.

"May I ask what the hell that was?"

"I told you I wanted a martini, so I fucking ordered one," I hiss, then promptly resume his silent treatment while I peruse the menu.

"Ok, Jess. What's wrong?" Jack asks me, finally acknowledging my blatant frustration. I let out a long sigh, trying to formulate my thoughts and the true source of my frustration. *Am I more upset that he spoke to Lela or that he interrupted my lust fest?*

"Seriously? You want to know what's wrong? Well, how about you kicking me out of our hotel room so that you could have a little chat with your ex-girlfriend? Never mind that you're on fucking vacation with your current one." I watch Jack's expression fade. Is he upset that he was caught?

"Babe, I'm sorry. But it's not what you think." He shakes his head with frustration.

"Ok. Please. Do tell me how I'm mistaken here," I let my sarcasm rip through the air.

"Jess, look, you're right, that was my ex-girlfriend. She's been calling me lately, trying to rekindle the flame or something. I've been ignoring her, but she hasn't let up."

"Right. So let me guess, you just *had* to talk to her *right* then to tell her how madly in love you are with me, and that you've moved on?" My sarcastic words snap at him.

"Well, yeah. Something like that. I did tell her about you. I told her that things are serious, and that she needs to back off."

"Bullshit!" I shout practically loudly enough for the entire restaurant to hear. "And regardless. I don't fucking care." I feel my defense mechanism taking over again. My high IQ does nothing to help me apply logic to matters of the heart. *Don't be so desperate for love that you put up with an asshole. You're not built for this, Jess. Remember your childhood?* I push the thoughts of my parents, and their fucked-up sense of family and love, from my mind. Now's not the time for unweaving that web of chaos.

"Jess, it's not bullshit. Babe, please." His eyes plead with me to believe him.

I quickly snap back at him. "Um, except for the fact that she asked you if you were in Paris for *work*. And you said yes."

"What?" Jack looks confused at the accusation.

"I heard her. Through the phone. Before you kicked me out. And you lied. You are a fucking liar, Jack. You just needed your current girlfriend out of the room so that you could continue whatever bullshit charade you're conducting with us." I pause to catch my breath. "Well, guess what, Jack? The charade is over. You and Lela can live happily ever after, and you won't have me to get in the way of that!" I jump to my feet and speed toward the door.

"Babe!" Jack's voice follows me, and I hear him keeping pace behind me. "Slow down, Jess. Please."

"Why?" I practically scream at him, turning a few heads at nearby tables.

"Because," he pauses, running his hands through his hair with frustration. "Because I'm falling in love with you." He stops, searching my eyes for a glimmer of hope. My ignorant, yearning heart skips a beat at the thought, but the pain knocks my optimism down.

"Nice try. You're a womanizing asshole. I can't believe I was dumb enough to bring you here. For fucking Valentine's Day of all holidays." I choke back the tears. *Shut it down, Jess. He isn't worth your tears! Not even one.*

"Oh, God," he pauses, his face illustrating the depth of his distress. "Jess. Come on. Please. Just sit back down and hear me out. Nothing is what it seems right now. Just give me two minutes to explain. Please?" I look away, feeling the fury and heartache run through me. *If I leave now, where will I go? Back to the hotel room? The next flight isn't until tomorrow morning anyway.* "Please, Jess." He grabs my hand, and his eyes catch mine. His normally beautiful blue sparkling eyes look a little more gray now. And his stare tugs at the pieces of my heart that still have such strong feelings for him.

"Fine." I nod, pulling my hand away from him, begrudgingly walking back to our table, but subconsciously wanting to find truth in his words.

"Jess, baby, I'm so sorry..." He pauses, waiting to see if I'll let him finish this time. I remain silent as I sip my salty drink and listen to his side of things. "I swear to you, I told Lela the truth about us. I was trying to get her to back off. The only reason I said I was in Paris for work is because I didn't want you to have to listen to my explanation. I didn't even want you to concern yourself with the conversation because she means absolutely nothing to me." I can see the sincerity in his eyes, but remain silent, forcing him to keep talking. Jack's face turns even more serious now, and he reaches for my hand again. My daggered heart leaks naïve hope into me, and this time I let his hand take mine. He looks down for a moment and shakes his head before locking his eyes with mine. "I'm so sorry, babe, I really would never do anything to hurt you. You have no idea how much I care about you." His reassuring words tug at my heart, and my familiar feelings for him flood through me. I want to believe him. I want to be loved. I want him to be mine. *Fuck.*

"Ok, so tell me about her."

"What?" Jack's expression turns inquisitive.

"Tell me about Lela."

He shakes his head at my request. "Babe, she means nothing. There's no reason to discuss her."

"If you want me to believe you, then tell me about her. About your relationship, why you guys broke up."

"You really want to hear about that?"

"Yes. Really."

"Ok." Jack lets out a loud exhale followed by a long drink of his martini. "Well, where should I start?"

"At the beginning. How'd you meet?" I ask coolly, trying to force myself to listen like the mature twenty-five-year-old woman I should be.

"Actually I've known her for a long time. Our dads grew up together, and our families have been friends for as long as I can remember."

"So when did you start dating her?"

"Not until college. We had seen each other plenty of times at family and holiday get-togethers and stuff, but it started when we were in the same city. She was at BC when I was at Harvard."

"You dated throughout college? All four years?"

"No. I was two years ahead of her. Started dating when I was a senior and stayed together while I worked in New York City after school, and then while I was in business school at Stern."

"So, five years?" I ask with surprise, finally realizing how long and serious their relationship must've been.

"Yeah, something like that."

"So why did you break up?"

"Well, because I was moving to Atlanta."

"Jack," I scold him. "You don't break up with someone just because you're moving. Not if you're in love with them."

"Oh, babe," he sighs. "I thought that was obvious. I mean I wouldn't have left New York if I had still been in love with her. I had plenty of job offers there after B school."

"Well why didn't you love her anymore?"

"I don't think it was one particular thing. It was just time. Time for a change. I guess I just fell out of love with her over time. It was too comfortable. It wasn't exciting anymore."

"Ok. How did she deal with the breakup?"

"Seemingly well. She thought I was just bored, and needed the excitement of a move or something new. That eventually we'd end up together."

"Do you think she's right? That maybe you do still love her, but just needed something new or exciting for a while?" I fill with fear at the idea.

"No." He blinks, and I can't help but wonder if he really believes his own words. "She was the easy choice. I don't ever take the easy choice. That's not who I am. Not in love, not in my career."

"What do you mean?" I shake my head, feeling confusion mix with my outstanding frustration toward him.

"I could have had a good life with Lela. We could've stayed together, gotten married, and lived in a big house where I made good money as an attorney in Grandfather's law firm. Hell, I could've run the place someday with my brother. But I saw that path. It's the same path my father had, and now Wells. But not me. I'm not going to spend the next fifty years fumbling through contracts and paperwork, in a quiet town, slowly succumbing to the life that was painted for me. I need excitement. I need passion. I need to live!"

"Jack—" I pause his thoughts, for the first time realizing what drives this man. "You wouldn't be the first person to need something new, just as a test to be sure what you had was what you really wanted. Maybe I'm that distraction for you," I volunteer with a heavy heart.

"No!" he scolds me. "Jess. You're not a distraction. You're everything that I want. Smart. Sexy. Intriguing. Complicated. Headstrong." He begins laughing as his compliments digress to my least favorite, but accurate, attributes of myself.

"Gee. Thanks."

"Baby," he says with a half laughing, half pained expression. "Seriously, you're perfect. Perfect for me." He reaches his hand across the table and I let him take mine, feeling his sincerity through his touch. "I mean it, Jess. I know our relationship has been, well, fast, but I've loved every second. And you need to know how seriously I take it. I'm falling for you Jess—hell, who am I kidding? I'm not falling. I've already fallen." His eyes search mine for acceptance of his words. Those wonderful words, and assurances that I'm the one he wants. *Fuck.* Maybe it's the booze, maybe it's Paris. Maybe it's my desperate heart, but some combination of them allow me to believe him. I slide across our circular booth to be next to him. He slips his hand around my waist and I feel the emotions crashing between us, and my body drawing me to him. Our faces are just a few inches apart now, and I move my hand onto his leg, giving him a reassuring squeeze. I can't help but want this to work. This unplanned, nonsensical, but all-consuming relationship.

He learns forward, nuzzling into my neck, moving his lips closer to my ear. "I'm so sorry, baby," he whispers, bringing goosebumps to my skin. His lips linger momentarily on my earlobe. "Forgive me?" He nuzzles further into my neck. I grab his chin and our lips meet, pulling on my heart with each long kiss. Our tongues intertwine and it's all I can do to control myself and not jump in his lap, undo his zipper, and take him right here and now. Even though it's just been a few hours, it feels as though I haven't kissed him in ages. I put my hand to the side of his freshly shaven face, run my thumb across the curves of his cheeks and down to his chin, then pull him closer toward me, for the first of many lip-locked moments of the evening.

CHAPTER SEVEN

As the daylight of our second day in Paris fades into dusk, we navigate from the metro back to our hotel. The day was spent in the Marais district on the right bank of the Seine, where our eyes delighted from the colorful artwork from local artists, and the eclectic boutiques tucked between architectural gems. For lunch we enjoyed the most delicious falafel I've ever had at L'As du Fallafel, then spent the remainder of the afternoon strolling and kissing along the river.

My falling in love and love-making induced euphoria have only grown since our "discussion" yesterday evening. I peer across the room at my sexy boyfriend, opening his computer to check in on work. I feel so alive. So lucky. So in love? *Ugh!* The image of Max and his divine mouth pop into my head yet again, and I feel a twinge of guilt. I kissed a complete stranger after jumping to conclusions about Jack. It was wrong. *Even if it felt so right?*

"Hey, babe," I call over to Jack. "I just wanted to say I'm sorry for last night. I should've had more faith in you. I know I overreacted a bit." I gloat to myself at my mature handling of the Lela situation, and take slight comfort in my apology, mentally noting it also counts for my kiss. *It was a forgivable mistake, made under the guise that our relationship was over. We've earned ourselves a clean slate, right? We are falling in love after all.*

Jack peers up from his laptop, his adorable, frameless glasses resting on his perfect, sloped nose. He says nothing, but rises from his chair and walks toward me, distracting me from my unavoidable self-doubt that this thing we have between us is real.

"Well then, it seems we're both sorry. Do you think we need to make up some more?" The twinkle in his eyes reappears along with his naughty tone.

"Hmm, you might be right," I giggle. "I guess I will allow *you* to make it up to *me*," I proclaim. I feel myself start to pant as I toy with him. He grabs my head, kissing me on the edge of my lips, then he quickly works his way across to my neck. I'm still bundled up from our chilly day of sightseeing, so he begins slowly taking off my clothes.

"It's like unwrapping a present," he murmurs as he lifts off each piece. He works quickly, leaving me completely naked, save my scarf. My mind flirts with wonder about this sole piece of clothing and why he left it on me.

I watch Jack remove his black puffy jacket, followed by his blue-checkered button-up and navy sweater, and finally his undershirt and pants. I see the throbbing muscle beneath his boxer briefs and the arousal starts seeping through my bones. He slowly shimmies off his underwear, and stands naked before me, his body upright in a full salute. The few inches of space between us feel like an infinite distance, and I want to feel his warm skin on mine. *Now.*

The shower is warm and steamy, just like my hot and unbelievably talented boyfriend's mouth. I let my mind wander while I run the soap across my body, feeling a tingle as the suds fall onto my breasts, which are still sensitive from our incessant and incredible lovemaking. My body recovers in the warmth, and I think of the events this weekend. I've loved being here with Jack. Paris is such a beautiful city, and even though we've fought, I feel closer to him than ever. In fact, the fighting just makes it seem more real. Real relationships have fights, and we're just getting more comfortable with each other. *Real relationships also require fidelity.* I think of the complexities of Lela, and I frown and try to shake away the thought of her. As I do, the image of the lusty Max flashes into my mind again. *Seriously, what is it with me?*

After my shower, I dig through my suitcase and decide on a black and red dress, feeling the need to don some red given it's Valentine's Day. The slinky material is fitted on the front with a straight neckline, and the back of the dress dips down just far enough that I can't wear a bra. I eye myself in the mirror for a moment, and notice how well it clutches my curves, but know I'm threads away from a wardrobe malfunction. *More calorie-burning sex, fewer fries.*

I catch Jack's smile in the mirror, staring back at me from where he's propped up on the bed. I blush, realizing he's caught me in a rare act of self-admiration.

"What are you looking at?" I ask, spinning toward him.

"How beautiful you are." He raises himself from the bed and walks toward me. "Need help with that?" He motions toward the zipper on my dress.

"Please!" He pulls up close to me and I breathe in his fresh scent, a mix of fresh aftershave and refreshing soap. He pulls up the last few inches of the zipper and smooths my hair around my ear.

"No earrings tonight? You're always wearing some, which is why I can't ever do this." He nips my earlobe with his teeth, tugging it gently, then kisses my bare neck, and that familiar rush starts moving through me.

"Well actually, I just need to decide which ones to wear. Tell me what you think?" I walk back to my suitcase and retrieve two pairs. One is a large dangling pearl, the other my standard gold Tiffany knots.

He turns around toward me, with a freshly filled glass of champagne and a happy smile. "For you, my beautiful date," he says as he hands me the glass.

"Thanks, babe. So which ones, the knots? Or should I stick with pearls?"

Jack eyes my options, then in one swift move removes something from his pocket. "Actually, I think this is what you need." I look down at his right hand that extends toward me. My mind races as I see that he's holding a dark velvet jewelry box. *What?* It takes me a few blinks to wrap my head around this.

"What's this?" I ask, as a nervous but excited tone creeps into my voice. My heart beats faster as I anticipate the contents. *Is this a ring? Holy shit. Is he proposing? What would I say?*

"It's your Valentine's gift. Open it." I look up and see him grinning, ear to ear. I pause, trying to take in the moment. *He's not down on one knee, so it can't be a ring. Right?*

I set my champagne glass down on the coffee table, and pry open the box. I instantly see the glimmer of diamonds as soon as light hits inside. The most beautiful, sparkling, heart-shaped diamond earrings I've ever seen are placed perfectly inside, each facet radiating against the dark backdrop. Fifteen round brilliant diamonds set in platinum create these brightly sparkling earrings. The box is embellished with the Tiffany & Co. logo, and my jaw literally drops open. *This must have cost him a fortune!*

I try to reel in my shock and stammer out some words. "Jack, these are stunning! But they're too much, really." I recall the

Valentine's gift I brought for him. A greeting card and a picture frame: both from Target. I considered it a thoughtful gift, something to put a photo in from our trip. I shudder at my naivety and make a note to bury his gift in my suitcase. No gift is far less embarrassing than the cheap frame.

"No, babe, I want you to have them. I know you love hearts, and with Valentine's Day, well, I just thought they'd be perfect for you. Try them on!"

I happily oblige and walk toward the mirror again to place them in my ears. The earrings are big and beautiful. Not too overbearing, just big enough to show off the perfect stones. I admire myself in the mirror for a moment. Hearts are a little cliché, but he remembered how much I loved them as a kid. A few weeks ago I shared this tidbit with him, and this gesture proves he was actually listening! *And he remembered.* My heart melts with emotion toward him. Jack walks up behind me and slides his arms around my waist.

I make eye contact with him via the mirror, our eyes locking in our reflection. "I really love them. Thank you, Jack. It's such a thoughtful gift."

"Well, you're welcome. And Happy Valentine's Day."

"Happy Valentine's Day!" I turn and kiss him. A sweet, love-filled kiss. He breaks away for a moment, but keeps me close and turns me to face him. "And Jess, I know we've had a few"—he pauses, searching for the right word—"disagreements on this trip. But fighting or not, I've loved every minute with you since I met you." My heart returns this notion and my body wants me to show him how I feel. I grab his smooth, freshly shaven face, and kiss him with every ounce of love that floods within me.

CHAPTER EIGHT

The hotel bar is busier tonight. Most of the couches are filled with couples and groups of friends chatting and enjoying their Saturday evening. A light jazz plays in the background, but the sound of it is rather faint amidst the patrons' loud voices. This time I visit the bar happily, giving my darling Jack a few minutes alone to finish up some work in our room before the romantic dinner ahead of us.

I observe the same bartender working this evening. He smiles as I approach the bar. "Bon soir, Mademoiselle. Est-ce-que vous voulez du champagne ce soir?" I flash back to twenty-four hours earlier, when I sat at this same bar with the mysterious Italian. I feel my cheeks redden as I think of him, and how ridiculously attracted I was to him. *But God, that kiss.* I shake my head. *Get out of my brain!*

"Oui champagne. Merci." I turn away from the bar toward the main room to enjoy some evening people-watching. My hand reaches for my shiny diamond earrings, and a smile spreads across my face as I allow myself to be grateful for my boyfriend.

"Buongiorno. You've come to steal my seat, or my drink?" *Holy fuckballs.* My ears recognize him before my eyes do. *It's him.* I move my eyes from his perfectly polished shoes to his pressed suit, and inhale his swoon-inducing scent as our eyes connect.

"Both, actually. But you're late, I had to order my own drink rather than stealing yours." I instantly flirt, just as the bartender places it in front of me.

His glowing hazel eyes and matching expression are clearly charmed by our banter. "Yet somehow I don't remember setting another date before you left with your… friend?" The Italian-tuned English rolls off his tongue easily, the intonation and his judgment of my 'friend' notably intentional.

"Drinking can affect your memory. That must be it." I flirt back, but my thoughts trail off to Jack. Knowing he sits just floors above me finishing up some work gives me extreme guilt, particularly as I sit here literally dripping from the intense pleasure he just bestowed upon me. And yet for some reason I can't help but feel drawn to this stranger. *You should just excuse yourself, Jess. Think about Jack. Right. Jack. My boyfriend. Who I'm totally falling in love with, and who just gave me these ridiculously amazing and expensive earrings.*

I look up at Mr. Lust again and give him my best smile. "I was actually just on my way out," I lie. I quickly search for a few Euros from my purse.

"Jess." Jack's voice startles me, and I instantly feel the guilt of an adulterer who should don a scarlet "A" rather than these stunning diamonds.

"Hey, babe, that was quick! Should we head out?"

"Yeah, my call was pretty quick. Why leave? You haven't finished your champagne? And this bar looks fantastic. We have plenty of time before dinner." I watch Mr. Lust out of the corner of my eye and see his immense amusement at my discomfort.

"Buongiorno," he greets Jack. *Oh, Jesus.* I instantly fear for where this might be going. "Your lovely girlfriend was just telling me all about you, and your time in Paris." *What?* My heart begins to race, my body filling with anxiety. *Will he say something to Jack about our prior rendezvous? Just when everything was back on track with my Jack! Oh, fuckity fuck fuck fuck. Shit.*

"That's my Jess. She makes friends wherever she goes." Jack smiles, not showing even the slightest hint of jealousy. *God, he's so trusting.* "I'm Jack Clarke, I didn't catch your name."

"Jack, pleasure to meet you, I'm Maximus Ferrari." *I nearly wet my pants. That's a real name? Of course, someone as hot as him would have a fucking sports car name.*

"Really? I think I've been working with your company," Jack responds, and I'm immediately confused.

"Ahh, are you a banker or consultant?" Mr. Lusty Sex Car responds.

"A little of both?" Jack laughs. "I specialize in M&A for Cooper Consulting."

"Yes!" Max responds quickly. "On the Brazilian buy-side deal, I presume."

"Yeah, that's me. Been working on it for months. In fact, that's what kept Jess waiting down here by herself," Jack explains.

"I see. Which office are you in?"

"Atlanta. And where do you live, Mr. Ferrari?"

"Please, call me Max." He reaches out his hand to Jack's for the official introduction. I notice his strong hands, and recall them grabbing me intently, while his lips worked magic on mine just twenty-four hours ago. "Well, I am originally from a small town in Italy, but right now I live in New York City for my work. And you are both in Atlanta?"

"Yeah, we both live in Atlanta. Jess grew up there, but I'm originally from the Northeast," Jack answers for us. Lust's smile fades momentarily as he watches Jack pull me closer to him, resting his hand on my thigh. *What was that? Could he be jealous of me and Jack?*

"Ahh, Atlanta is a lovely city. I've only been there once though. I hope to do more business there in the future."

"Yeah, we're pretty happy there," Jack says, squeezing my hand. I look up and notice Mr. Lust once again overly focused on my reaction when Jack touches me.

"Yeah, Atlanta is great," I chime in.

"So what do you do in Atlanta, Jess?" Mr. Lust looks at me and I feel my knees go weak. Thank God I'm sitting down.

"I work for Global Airlines, our headquarters is in Atlanta."

"Ahh, I'm actually flying Global to JFK tonight," he says with a smile. "It's a great airline. And who doesn't love the southern charm?"

"Thanks, yeah, it's been a fun place to work. It's given me the opportunity to travel to places like this! Are you on the 10 o'clock flight?"

"You know your airline's schedule well." Max gives me a wink. "I should probably be going to the airport soon. And I'm sure you have Saint Valentine's plans ahead of you?"

"Yes, heading to dinner after we get a drink here. It was a pleasure meeting you, Max. Feel free to give me a call directly if you need anything on this acquisition." Jack then retrieves a card from his pocket.

"Thank you. It was a pleasure to meet you both. And if you're ever in New York, give me a call—we can even skip business and just have a drink." Jack nods and extends his hand to meet Max's.

"Have a safe trip home, it was great to meet you," I say, nervously extending my hand to Mr. Lust, in a polite farewell handshake. As his skin meets mine, I feel my breath shorten, feeling that familiar surge from his contact.

"The pleasure was all mine." He stares straight into my eyes and moves his finger gently across my hand. I feel his touch move through me, as far down as my panties. He somehow makes me feel so alive, just from a simple touch.

"Arrivederci." Max breaks hold of my hand and walks away, leaving me and Jack to our uninterrupted weekend of love.

CHAPTER NINE

After spending hours navigating the tortuous Charles de Gaulle airport and its unhelpful employees, who are all seemingly on strike, I'm relieved to board the Global Airlines flight filled with smiling, southern flight attendants. The business class service greets us with chilled champagne and large, comfy seats for the ride home.

"Cheers, Jess." Jack leans toward me holding his glass.

"What are we toasting to?" I ask, smiling happily at my handsome boyfriend. I notice how natural he looks sitting up here, amongst the successful business travelers and globe trotters, important enough to blow thousands of dollars on one flight. His blue eyes are drawn out by his navy blue pullover sweater. The fabric stops just below his chin, and the open zipper runs to his sternum, showing just a hint of his dark gray T-shirt. He wears his favorite William Rast jeans, covered with a dark wash and tasteful distressing on the top half. His always-polished appearance makes me pay more attention to my own look as well. As someone who has often flown on transatlantic flights in sweats, I decided to class it up a little today, with an amazingly comfortable, yet classy, cotton sweater dress. With the addition of black riding boots, I almost look as though I belong here.

"To a wonderfully amazing trip, and the best Valentine's Day I've ever had," Jack toasts me.

"I'll drink to that!" I respond cheerily, before leaning over and giving him a slow, sweet kiss.

I glance up from my book and see him walking toward me. My eyes meet the object of my lust and he nods, wanting me to follow him. *But should I follow him? What does he want with me?* I sit in my seat, undecided for a moment. Curiosity wins. I walk toward the galley, expecting him to be in there. I peer around the corner and see no sign of him. *Is this some kind of game?* A forceful hand on my shoulder startles me. I whip around to see Mr. Lust discreetly holding open the door to the lavatory. *Seriously?* He extends his hand and my intrigue forces me to follow him inside.

He shuts the door and I shift uncomfortably. "What are you doing here?" I question him, both scared and excited by the situation.

He lets out a sigh. "Bella, I'm just"—he pauses—"fuck, I'm finishing this." He pulls me toward him and our arms immediately wrap around each other. He grabs my head, pulling my chin toward him. Our lips meet and I feel a burning throughout my body. I never thought we'd share another kiss, especially not trapped in the confines of this tiny bathroom, just feet away from my boyfriend.

"I need you now," Mr. Lust commands, both telling me and asking me at once. I nod my head with approval, desperate to feel him inside of me. He slides my panties to the side with his finger, and without removing them, he pushes forward and I feel him inside of me. We groan in unison, and our bodies start moving in synchronous rhythm. He slides in and out of me, quickly but fully, teasing me with each movement, bringing me closer and closer to the edge. I reach around and grab his ass, feeling how taut it is as it flexes over and over again. My climax begins to build inside of me, and he instantly starts moving faster and faster, somehow sensing that I'm near the edge. I feel my body reaching the point of no return and I grab his neck and deepen my kiss just as my climax explodes through my body. His body responds to my vibrations and I feel him tense, then watch his eyes close as he finds his release with me. I sit with him still inside of me, lost in his eyes. I study his face, trying to tell what this practical stranger is thinking.

Then, my own thoughts return, and I realize what I've just done.

"Do you think she wants something to eat?" I hear a strange voice hovering above me. My eyes are closed, and I hear the clanking of dishes and the smell of fresh cookies swirling above. My body feels tired and my brain sloshy as I try to peel my eyes apart.

"I'm not sure. Let me see if I can wake her." I hear Jack's voice and feel his gentle touch on my shoulder.

"Baby, are you awake? Are you ready for some lunch?"

I force one eye to peep open and see Jack smiling over me. "Morning, sunshine, you ready to eat?"

I blink a few times, trying to make sense of what's in my brain. *I was just in the bathroom having a fuckfest with the handsome Italian stranger. Right?* As I process Jack's question, reality begins to set in. I'm still on the airplane, and I must've fallen asleep. *It was just a dream.* Mr. Lust never got on this plane, and we never had sex. And, I never cheated on Jack. *Thank God.*

"So, you want lunch then?" Jack asks me again, and I realize I ignored his question.

I nod my head and gurgle the words, "Yes please." I adjust my seat to sit upright and take the warm towel from the flight attendant to refresh myself. As I wipe my hands with the fresh linen towel I discover an odd feeling inside of me. *What is that? Disappointment? Am I somehow disappointed that this fantasy wasn't real?*

CHAPTER TEN

I parade into the Corner Café in Buckhead, the usual gathering place for Sunday brunch with my best friends from childhood. I'm grateful for the chance to catch up. I've been so busy the past few weeks, traveling to Paris with Jack and working long hours, that I've barely seen the girls. I haven't even had the chance to share with them my Valentine's trip and the beautiful earrings that Jack got me, which I wear proudly today.

"Jess!" I whirl around at the sound of Emma's familiar tone. After nearly two decades of friendship, I would recognize her voice anywhere.

"Emma! Hey!" She walks over and gives me a squeeze

"So you're back! How was Paris? I want to hear all about it!"

"Oh, it was great! Jack and I had a fantastic time." *And I met a ridiculously hot Italian man who I can't stop fantasizing about.* "How was yours?"

"Um actually pretty amazing! Had a third date with the lawyer." My blonde hair, blue-eyed friend since grade school glances past me. "I'm starved, I did a double spin class this morning. Where is she?" Emma asks, her expression revealing irritation.

"Who?" I ask, as we walk toward our nearby table, seeing Callie already seated in the round booth.

"Meredith. Texted me a few minutes ago. She was on her way," I respond.

"So realistically she's probably at least fifteen minutes away," Emma continues with an eye roll.

"Oh simmer down and eat a mini muffin," Callie, the ultimate peacekeeper of the group suggests, sliding the warm basket of treats toward her. Her always-optimistic attitude made her a perfect fit for her career as a caregiver and perpetual cheerleader of moms-to-be as a labor and delivery nurse. She needs little makeup to accompany her dark eyes and never-blemished porcelain skin. Her wavy dark hair is pulled in a ponytail, an indication of working a long night bringing new life into this world.

"Well I'm starved too. Should we at least order some mimosas?"

"Already done," Callie informs us.

"Thank God. But if she's not here soon we're ordering anyway. I swear, that girl will be late to her own wedding," I joke.

"Ahh hem." We all look up to see Meredith standing at the table before us, grinning ear to ear. Her tiny frame is covered in fitted white corduroy pants with a dark navy blouse. Her long, chestnut-brown hair lays straight down her back, and her gray eyes sparkle with excitement. "I can assure you I will not be late to my own wedding," she announces with a snicker. "Which, by the way, will be happening very soon!" She flashes her left hand before us, displaying a sparkling princess cut diamond decorating her ring finger. We all shriek in excitement and jump from the table to hug our dear friend.

"Oh my God, it's gorgeous!" Emma exclaims.

"So when did this happen? We need details, stat!"

Meredith removes her coat and settles in at the table with us. "Ok, so Cale and I were celebrating a belated Valentine's Day since he had to be out of town that weekend. We went up to his family's mountain house in Jasper, spent Friday night nuzzled up in the cabin, and he made me the most amazing dinner. And then we sat by the fire, drinking red wine, watching the snow fall outside and talking about life. We were curled up on the couch and he turned to me and said, 'You know, Meredith, when I think about my life there's one thing that I know I want to have. And I've known this for a while now, I've just been waiting for the perfect time.' And then he slid off the couch onto one knee and said, 'And the perfect time is any time we're together, because everything's perfect when I'm with you.'" Meredith happily reflects with a tear in her eye. "And then he asked me to marry him! And I basically forgot anything else he said after I saw the ring!" She giggles, wiping away a reminiscent tear.

"Congratulations, Mere, we're so excited for you!"

We all clink glasses and Mere continues. "So there's more news too. You all know I've always wanted to get married in the spring at the Botanical Gardens..." she pauses. "So we talked about it...and we don't want a super long engagement, so, we're getting married in less than two months!"

"Ahh!" We all manage to shriek again, finally quieting down after getting a few stares from across the restaurant.

"Are you sure you're not pregnant?" I ask, half joking.

"Umm, yes. Very sure!" Mere responds with an eye roll and a long drink of her mimosa to validate the point.

"Mere, how are you going to get everything planned so quickly?" Callie questions.

"Oh, you know my mom. She's always up for a challenge!"

"But what about your dress? And bridesmaid dresses? Those normally take months to order," Emma says.

"So yeah, that's part of the other thing I wanted to ask you girls about. Since it's a short engagement, I'm going to need lots of help, and I'm hoping you'll all agree to be my bridesmaids!" We let out a final shriek of excitement, eager for the first of our friends to get married.

"Oh my gosh, yes!"

"Of course we will!"

"We would love to, Mere."

"Wait, so if you're getting married in two months, we need to plan a bachelorette party, like, now!" I exclaim excitedly. The ideas start running through my head of where to go and what to do. And then it comes to me.

"What about New York City?" I suggest. "We could even go dress shopping up there. You could easily fit into a sample size which I'm sure we'll find plenty of!" Meredith's tiny, boyish frame will definitely make finding a dress this quickly possible.

"That's a perfect idea!" she exclaims. "Do you think we could really make it work, and plan something that quickly?"

I laugh. "I think you all know my travel connections and planning skills can make that happen!" I pull out my phone to look at my calendar, and after some discussion we decide to have the bachelorette party two weekends from now.

※

After the whirlwind wedding news, we finally settle down enough to order some food and hear about everyone else's life updates. I dive into my veggie omelet, enjoying the slight buzz that the mimosas have provided.

"So, Jess, tell us about Paris!" Callie exclaims. For some reason, despite the great memories I made with Jack, Master Hotmouth Ferrari pops into my mind at the mention of Paris. I feel my face redden just at the thought of him, and the resounding guilt washes over me. I decide not to tell the girls about him; it would just sound too stupid and slutty, especially since I'll never see him again.

"Jess, you're blushing! Share!" Emma chimes in.

"Hah," I laugh, giving myself a minute to refocus on Jack. "It was a great trip. We saw all the sights and it was such a beautiful city. And, he gave me these." I flip my hair back so they no longer hide my big sparkling diamond earrings.

"Wow! Let me see!" Meredith leans over from across the table.

"Jess, they're gorgeous! And they look flawless," Callie says, with a tinge of jealousy in her voice.

"Thanks! I love them. He did such a great job! He knew how much I loved hearts, and Tiffany, so I ended up with these." I pull my eyes away, a bit uncomfortable with the attention.

"You barely know him! Damn, you must be amazing in bed." Callie snorts.

I nearly spit out the mimosa I've just sipped. "Callie!" I scold her, laughing. "For the record, I am amazing in bed."

CHAPTER ELEVEN

I open the door to Jack's house and immediately hear his voice in the distance, and I gather that he must be on the phone. *Geeze, is he working again? It's Sunday afternoon.* I walk closer, knowingly spying so I can hear what he's saying.

"Yeah, my flight leaves after work that night, so I'll get in around 9:30. What time do you land?" Jack pauses, listening to the other side of the conversation, and I gather that he's talking about his upcoming ski trip. "Ok cool. Have you heard from everyone else? Who all has confirmed?" Another pause. "Right. Ok. Yeah that's what I expected." Silence. "Seriously? Barrett, why would you invite her, knowing that I was coming?"

My ears suddenly perk up at the mention of a "her". *What the hell? Could they be talking about Lela? Is she going on the trip too?* I inch closer to the hallway to get a better listen, and hear the floorboards squeak below me. *Shit, Jack must've heard that.*

"Ok, fine. Yeah, I've got to go, we'll talk later." His voice becomes louder as he speaks, and I glean that he's coming toward to me. I jump onto the couch and grab a magazine off the table, pretending that I wasn't eavesdropping.

"Hey, babe, how was brunch?" He props himself up against the doorway and I can't help but eye him up and down. He's wearing a dark gray T-shirt and his dark wash William Rast jeans, with no belt. His pants fall just below the top of his red boxer briefs, allowing them to peek out of the top. *Mmmm.*

"It was fun! Oh, and Meredith and Cale got engaged!"

"That's great! I'm guessing it's too early for them to think about a wedding date?"

"Actually, quite the opposite. They're getting married in about two months!"

"Wow, that was quick. But I guess when you know it's right, there's no reason to wait." He winks coyly at me. *What does that mean?* It's amazing how hot my boyfriend can look without even trying.

I try to refocus myself. "I know, it is fast, in fact we're going to have her bachelorette party in New York City weekend after next."

"Oh great, I'll be skiing in Vail then anyway."

"Oh that's right." I lie as curiosity of who *she* is pops back into my mind. "When do you leave again?"

"I fly out that Thursday after work, and I'll be back the following Sunday."

"Have you figured out how you're getting to the airport?"

"No, not yet. Maybe my sexy girlfriend will be willing to help me out?"

"I think I can work something out. Speaking of favors, though, will you be my date for Mere's wedding?" I plead with my best smile.

"Whoa, a date to a wedding? That sounds serious." Jack raises an eyebrow playfully. "I think you're going to have to earn that privilege."

"Oh yeah? And how might I do that?"

Jack starts walking toward me and I feel my heart beat faster with excitement. "I have a few ideas."

I wiggle with wonder, unable to sit still. *I hate how unnerving he can be!* "Such as...?"

"Such as this." Jack leans over and places a gentle kiss on my lips. It's soft and sweet, but still enough to send the river of desire rushing through me.

"So...what are you hiding under there?" Jack pulls playfully at my oversized sweater.

I try to find my most sensual, teasing tone. "Nothing, darling. Whatever are you looking for?" I turn my sass up as he reaches toward me.

"You know what I want. You." *Mmm.* I try to push the jealous thoughts of Lela from my mind and embrace the moment with him. *Remember, he was honest before, I have no reason not to mistrust him now. Right?*

I pull up my car to the drop-off area at the ever-busy Atlanta airport. Jack hops out and retrieves his suitcase from the back of the car, then wheels it around to face me for our goodbye. Jack encircles me with his arms and gives me his most loving look. "Miss me while I'm gone?" he pleads.

"How could I not? I'll certainly have something to remember you by." I tug playfully at his belt, remembering how close we've been lately. *Ask him about Lela! If she's going on the trip!* The incessant worrying in my mind again attempts to verbalize itself.

"Have fun in New York, babe. Don't do anything I wouldn't do." Jack winks at me and lifts my hand, planting a soft kiss on there. *Last chance! Ask him now!*

"Hey, Jack," I call to him just as he steps away. He whirls around and plants a hard, slow kiss on my lips, sending tingles through my legs.

"Bye, baby," he says simply, leaving me for the second time. I'm too love-struck to move, embracing his feelings toward me from his kiss. So I simply let him go, deciding to have faith in my faithful boyfriend and our surprisingly happy relationship.

CHAPTER TWELVE

The Atlanta airport is bustling with business travelers this Friday morning, all ready to head home to their families for the weekend. I make my way to Global's airport lounge to kill time before my flight. I walk inside the bright, clean, and modern club and am greeted warmly by the receptionist. "Good afternoon. Welcome to the World Lounge."

"Thank you." I pass her my phone so that she can scan it and retrieve my flight information.

"Thank you, Ms. Bauer. What's bringing you to New York City this weekend?" The agent peers up at me through her red frame glasses, and they begin sliding down her nose as she types my information into the computer. She wears the traditional Global navy blue uniform, with a white collared shirt and blue vest. Her wrinkles give away her age, probably mid-fifties.

"I'm heading up for a bachelorette party. My girlfriends left earlier today, but I had to work this morning so I'm on my way to meet them now."

"Oh how lovely! You will have a such a wonderful time. I remember my own bachelorette party, it was 30 years ago, but it feels like yesterday." She smiles, as if recalling the memory. "Enjoy these moments with your friends, dear. You'll cherish the memories when you're older." I smile back at her, excited for the weekend with my friends, and glad to have the distraction from Jack's absence. I know I should trust him, and I do, but I still feel unsettled by the thought of Lela and Jack together somewhere.

"You have some time until boarding, so please make yourself comfortable. And you're scheduled to leave out of gate T1, just around the corner."

"Great, thank you!" I turn and head toward the bar for a drink. *Who cares if it's barely noon, I've earned it this week!*

I order one of my favorite Atlanta beers, Sweetwater 420, and find an open seat in the lounge. I pick a red club chair, seated adjacent to a coffee table and loveseat. The bar is to my left, and directly in front of me is a line of comfy chairs, small coffee tables, and work areas, all leading out to the windows that face the tarmac. I take a swig of my icy, delicious beer and exhale. I pull out my phone, hoping to have heard from Jack. I know he just left last night, but I'm disappointed that I didn't at least get a text from him letting me know that he arrived safely.

My iPhone screen shows a missed call and my heart warms, hoping it's from him. I slide open the screen to see that my missed call is from Emma. Disappointment once again fills my heart as I dial my friend.

"Jessssssss!" Emma shrieks upon answering the call. "What's up, girl? Are you on your way?"

"Hey! Yes, at the airport waiting for my flight. I should get in around 3:30. What are y'all doing?" I inquire, hearing clanking dishes and laughter in the background.

"We're just brunching right now. Aannnnd we're drinking." Her voice becomes muffled. "Yes, another pitcher of sangria please."

"Jess? Hi! Sorry the waiter came by. And he's hot by the way. I'm totes getting his number for tonight." I can't help but laugh out loud. She's such a lightweight. "You do that, Emma! Can't wait to see you girls soon. I'm ready for a night out."

"Yay! Well we can't wait to see you." I hear more shuffling through the phone, and then I hear the other girls yelling in the background. "Emma, get off the phone! It's time for a shot. Marco just brought tequila for us!"

I hear more muffled chatter as she moves the phone around. "Jess? Hi! Ok, sorry I've got to run, but we'll see you soon?"

"Ok, you girls have fun! Yes, be there soon. Will call you when I get in."

"Great! Have a safe flight!"

"Will do. And don't drink too much, I don't want to arrive to all of you passed out!"

"Ha ha. Ok, Jess, we'll try our best. See you soon. Muah!"

I hang up the phone and can't help but laugh to myself at the sound of my overly drunk friends. The laughter gives me a mental reprieve from the torturous self-doubt about my boyfriend. *Dammit, why can't I get him out of my head? Should I call him? Or text him? No, I need to trust him. Just give him more time.*

"Are you finished with this, miss?" I look up from my magazine to see a young waiter before me.

"Oh, yes. Thank you." I hand him my empty beer glass and debate whether or not I want another one. I watch the waiter walk away, and clear a glass from a well-dressed business man a few rows up. He's facing the window so I can't see his face, but purely judging by the cut of his suit I can tell he's well-to-do. The man lifts his arm to set his empty glass on the waiter's tray, and on his wrist rests a shiny yellow gold watch peeking out beneath his cuff. I laugh to myself. *Definitely rich, it's probably a Rolex.* It's funny, his build actually reminds me of Mr. Lust. I recall the memory of that beautiful, sexy man. *I wonder what he's doing now? And why does that man still enter my mind?*

I still have a few minutes to kill, so I decide to get another drink. I approach the bar and try to get a glimpse of the man with the gold watch reading his iPad. As I walk closer, I catch the side of his face. His jawline, it's uncannily similar to Max's. *But it can't be him. Can it?* My heart races with wonder as I propel myself forward. I stare at his familiar profile, forcing my legs to keep walking so that I don't stop and stare.

"Hi, I'd like another Sweetwater please," I squeak to the bartender, my mind racing with possibilities, desperate to get a confirmation glimpse of this man. Finally, as I wait with baited breath, the man looks up from his iPad as someone sits next to him, and he turns just enough for me to see those same lips that I enjoyed in Paris. *Oh my God.*

What do I do? Do I go say hello? Hi, it's me, Jess, the girl who has wet dreams about you. For all I know he meets girls all the time and won't even remember me. I nervously watch the bartender pour my second draft. *What would I even say? Ask if he's still working with Jack's company?*

I do a quick mental inventory of my appearance. I'm in my dark skinny jeans, cognac brown boots, and a tight black sweater. I did put on a red necklace to add some color to my outfit. It's certainly not the fancy red dress he met me in, but it will have to do.

The bartender returns with my drink. I take a deep breath, move my tongue across my teeth to make sure I remove any rogue lipstick, and give my hair a quick smoothing.

"Here you go, gorgeous." The bartender pushes my drink toward me and surprises me with his compliment.

"Oh, thank you!" I respond, thanking him both for the drink and the kind words. His unsolicited and timely compliment gives me the confidence to move forward. *Ok, here I go!* I whirl around, ready to make my move, and my breath instantly escapes me.

Standing directly in front of me is the beaming white smile of Mr. Maximus Ferrari, posed with his arms crossed across his body. "Hello, Jessica." *Oh. My. God.* I've never really been fond of my name before now. The way it rolls off his delicious tongue, with his beautiful accent, leaves me dripping with desire. "Did you think you could get out of here without saying hello to me?" He raises his eyebrow disapprovingly and my mouth falls open. *How does he do this to me?*

"Oh, hi! I didn't see you in here." I lie and pray he can't see how red my face is from the heat that literally floods my body. He simply smiles as I squirm in front of him, failing to fill our silence with words. "So where are you heading today?" I ask him, hoping I've hidden the quiver in my voice.

"New York. Going back home. You?"

"I'm actually going to New York as well."

"Ahh, with Jack? I didn't see him with you?"

Oh, Jack. The mention of him stings, despite the tempting view in front of me. *Wait, Max is going to New York too? Guess that figures, he did tell us he lives there.* I find my words again. "No, with friends. For a bachelorette party."

"Yours?" He grabs my left hand, turning it over playfully in search of a ring, and I enjoy the slight glimpse into his rarely visible playful side. His smile grows wider and I know we both feel the instant connection beyond our skin.

"No," I laugh. "I wouldn't consider such a thing without an oversized piece of carbon to truly represent my commitment," I joke.

"May I buy you another drink before your flight?"

"You know the drinks are free in here, right?" I laugh.

"Stealing someone's drink doesn't make it free," he quips back at me, and I blush at the memory of the night we met.

I release my biggest smile. "Actually I quit drinking champagne with strange men. It seems to have a bad effect on me."

"Something to remember." His words continue to confuse yet intrigue me. *What does that mean? He will remember that I make poor decisions when I drink champagne? Or I should remember to avoid it as to not embarrass myself?* "Are you on the 1:30 flight?"

"No, the 12:30 actually, so I need to get going." I solicit the clock as regret swirls between my ears.

Mr. Lust's face twists and I can see a slight furrow in his brow. It's as though he wants to say more, but he won't let himself be that transparent. "It was nice to see you, Jess."

"It was nice to see you again. I hope you have a good flight home."

It's an awkward goodbye. I don't know him well enough to give him a hug, and shaking hands would be too business-like, so I simply turn and walk away.

I take a deep breath and will myself to leave him. Right foot, left foot. I walk to the chair where I previously sat, grab my luggage and head toward the door. I feel his eyes burning into me, and I desperately want to turn around for one more look, but I don't. I'll leave him wanting more. *Right, for what? Our next spontaneous encounter?*

CHAPTER THIRTEEN

The brisk, windy New York City air slaps my hair back and forth. I've never seen the taxi line this long before, and it's not the welcome I was hoping for on top of my delayed flight. My standard go-to Uber is quoting me a 3x fare surge, so I'll be planted here, freezing my ass off as I wait my turn for a yellow vehicle to get me into Manhattan.

"Jessica?" My ears perk up at the sound of my name from afar. I glance up from my phone and see lusty Max approaching the side of the taxi line.

"You're still here?" I stand there for a moment, heart racing and befuddled, but ecstatic to see him again.

"Oh, well, our flight was delayed. They didn't have a gate for us when we landed. And this line"—I gesture to the horrendous queue of people around me—"I guess it's just not my lucky day."

"Come on. Let's turn your day around. I'll take you to your hotel."

"You left your car at the airport?"

He snickers at the idea. "No, I do not drive in New York City. My driver is picking me up." *DUH. Of course he would have a driver.*

"Oh, no, I couldn't ask you to go out of your way. Really, a taxi is just fine."

"I won't take no for an answer." His brown eyes furrow with a hint of care and concern that melts me as he awaits my response.

"Well, thank you. If it's really no trouble I accept." I give him a sweet smile and feel the shameful thoughts flood my mind. *Simmer down, Jess. You're spoken for.*

"I insist. Now come on, you're freezing." He reaches his hand out for mine, and I gratefully accept, instantly feeling the warmth from his skin and his spark-inducing touch. I wiggle between the metal stanchions, excitedly swapping my boring yellow car for a short adventure with the one and only Mr. Lust.

I climb into his beautiful, black Maybach in complete awe. I've never seen a car this expensive, let alone ridden in one! He really must have a ton of money—I make a mental note to google him later. The driver puts our luggage into the trunk and quickly climbs back inside.

"Enzo, can you please head to the W Hotel on Lexington? We need to drop Ms. Bauer off there." Enzo turns around, and I can see his gray hair peeking through his driver's hat. He smiles a crooked, toothy, but charming grin back at me.

"Pleased to meet you, Ms. Bauer. It's my pleasure." Enzo's soft wrinkles tighten around his eyes and mouth when he smiles. He's older, maybe mid-fifties, and clearly Italian, based on that accent.

"Thank you, I really appreciate the ride. And please, you can call me Jessica." Enzo nods, acknowledging my directive, and shifts the car into drive. Enzo lifts an earbud into his ear and quietly hums along with some music while he drives. He must be used to tuning our Mr. Lust and his lady friends' conversations.

"Jess. Suh. Cuh," Max purrs the three syllables off his tongue, then turns toward me. "Why would you go by Jess?" I stare at him, a bit dumbfounded by the seemingly obvious question.

"It's a nickname. I'm sure people call you Max, short for Maximus?" He laughs at my simple answer, and I feel my cheeks flush, wondering what I've missed.

"Yes, I know the concept of nicknames. I'm wondering why you're called Jess. Why not Jessa?"

"Oh." I ponder the idea. "I really don't know. I guess Jess is the typical way of shortening it."

"Well there is nothing typical about you, *Jessa*." For a man of few words, these manage to unnerve me completely. I half swoon at the compliment, half ponder his true intent.

"To answer your question, yes, sometimes people call me Max. But you should call me Mister Ferrari." *What?* My face twists into unintended confusion, and I'm left silent. His face turns serious while awaiting my response. "That was a joke!" He laughs, giving my hand a quick squeeze. His innocuously-intended touch radiates every nerve on me, feeling more like a hand fucking if such a thing existed. *Remember your boyfriend, Jack. Yeah, the one that still hasn't called you.* My conscience fights itself for the affections of my boyfriend.

Screw it. Exchanging words doesn't qualify as cheating, right? I push any guilt about Jack aside. "Well, Master Ferrari. You're just a knight in shining armor today, coming to rescue me from the big, bad, taxi cabs. I guess one visit today wasn't enough for you?"

His face becomes more serious. "No. Because I haven't had you yet." *What?* He quickly shakes his head. "I mean, I haven't had enough of you yet." He turns a tinge red at what I can only assume was a Freudian slip, and I instantly imagine having my way with him, over and over again.

"So how is our friend Jack doing?" *Friend.* His words seem so… intentional. He knows Jack wasn't just my friend. So why call him that?

"Ok I guess. He's out of town and I haven't spoken to him." As the words leave my lips, I realize how that could be interpreted. I decide not to clarify the misconception. "Have you been traveling much lately?"

"Yes. I've been back and forth between Europe and New York a lot the past few months. It will be nice to get home for a weekend."

"So you consider New York to be your home?"

"Well, not exactly. Italy will always be my home, but New York is where I live."

"Do you imagine living in Italy again one day?"

"I don't know. I haven't been back since my mother died." His instantly sullen eyes gaze out his window, and I feel my tongue taste my foot that's now jammed into my mouth.

"Oh, I'm sorry." I quickly change the subject, and Max excuses himself to take a phone call. I can't help but wonder if I overstepped, clearly stumbling on a sensitive topic. I grab my own phone, using the opportunity to google him.

We turn onto Lexington and I know the hotel is just a few minutes away. Enzo must realize this as well. "Excuse me, sir," Enzo says politely to Max. He looks up, pausing his now five-minute-long phone conversation in Italian. "We will be at Ms. Bauer's hotel shortly." Lust nods in acknowledgement, and I quickly shut down my open internet search for Mr. Maximus Ferrari, which did everything to confirm that he's obscenely rich, and decidedly unattached. My Google Image review affirmed he's never been seen with the same woman more than a few times.

"I apologize. That call took longer than I expected. Are your friends at the hotel?"

"I'm sure they're nearby. I will track them down as soon as I get to our room."

"We will wait with you until they arrive." I see Max's eyes connect with Enzo in the rear-view mirror, and Enzo nods, acknowledging his boss.

"No, thank you. It's very kind, but completely unnecessary. I've been in many hotels alone before." My words make me recall our first meeting. *Alone, in a hotel. Now here we are. Our fourth rendezvous. What are the odds of that happening on two different continents?*

"Enzo would be happy to drive you and your friends anywhere you need this weekend." Before I can consider this offer, he continues, "We have a bigger car, so it's not a problem."

"I think we'll be ok, but thank you for offering." I immediately reject the very generous offer, without really considering it.

"Just in case, take my phone number, and Enzo's." Mr. Lust grabs my phone from me and begins programming numbers into it. He enters the information and hands the phone back to me. He opens his mouth, as if to speak, but then shuts it, seemingly contemplating his words. "If you need anything this weekend, you can reach me at any time."

I nod my head and simply say, "Thank you. For everything." The Maybach rolls to a stop in front of the hotel, and Enzo quickly jumps out to get my door before I can open it myself.

"Thank you, Enzo. You've both been so helpful to me today. It was lovely to meet you."

"My pleasure. I'm available all weekend, so call me if I can be of service. You have my number."

"Yes, I do. Thank you again." I smile at him. He nods and I watch him move swiftly around the car to retrieve my bags and hand them to the bellman.

Max is now outside of the car, holding my purse for me. "Have fun this weekend."

"Thanks, I intend to," I say with a laugh. I stand there awkwardly, not sure of how to part, given this unexpected afternoon together. Mr. Lust leans forward, giving me a slight embrace and a slow gentle kiss on each of my cheeks. I close my eyes as the want for him radiates through me, willing it to leave but craving that it stay.

"Until we meet again?"

"Until then," I respond, wondering what he really means. *Until our fifth spontaneous encounter? Unlikely.*

"Ms. Bauer, right this way." A bellman appears to escort me inside.

"Oh, ok," I mutter, finding it hard to leave this beautiful, intriguing man, but knowing I need to. I *have* to. "Bye." I leave him with my sweetest smile and follow the bellman inside.

CHAPTER FOURTEEN

"Who wants another round?" Callie shouts across the table. Her brown curls whip around her shoulder as she turns back to the waiter. "Four more shots, puhleeze!" she announces to him, without consulting us.

"What's next on the list?" Emma leans over to show me and I have to squint to help my eyes focus on the words in front of me. "Ohh, this one!" she exclaims loudly enough for the other girls to hear.

"What is it?" Meredith questions.

"Oh, nothing," we respond in unison, trying to contain our laughter.

"Come on, guys, tell me! I'm the bride, you're supposed to be showering me, not torturing me!" Meredith slurs her words.

"This one isn't too bad. We're saving the really embarrassing stuff for later!" I say, glancing down again at the bachelorette party to-do list we came up with.

"Well then, lay it on me!"

"Ok, you have to go up to the bar and get a guy to buy you a drink," I instruct.

Meredith rolls her eyes back at us. "Come on, Jess, I thought this would at least be a slight challenge. I can do that in my sleep." She retrieves her powder and lip gloss from her clutch and begins her touch-up routine.

"Not so fast! We get to pick the guy," Callie proclaims.

"Yeah, whatever. Any of these guys would be damn lucky to buy me a drink." Meredith gestures her wobbly hands toward the bar that sits twenty feet behind us. The restaurant is pretty crowded, no surprise on a Friday evening in New York. I have just enough self-awareness not to start drunk texting yet, and I keep reminding myself not to do something I'll regret. But Jack's complete lack of communication, and having Max's number stored in my phone, is nearly killing me. My fingers are desperate to text both of them, especially considering Max doesn't have my number, so any communication would have to be initiated by me.

Meredith stands up and adjusts her dress, pulling it down to further reveal her petite but perky breasts.

"Well, looks like someone is ready for her challenge!" Callie laughs.

"Challenge? I think not. Who's the lucky guy going to be?" She turns around and waves her pointed finger toward the bar, eyeing the patrons.

"Give us a minute." We all lean in to discuss.

"Oh, what about that guy?" Callie points to a large, balding man and tries to control her laughter.

"No, way too easy! Let's make this a challenge," I yell.

"Oh, how about him?" Emma motions toward a super cute man with dark hair who appears to be in his late twenties.

"Why him? He's cute and all, but we don't need drunk Meredith getting overly handsy and flirty with someone during her bachelorette party. If she does anything stupid, she'll never forgive us!" I respond.

"Trust me, nothing will happen with them," Emma retorts.

"How can you be so sure?" Callie asks.

"Because his girlfriend just went to the bathroom. We've probably got five minutes, tops!" We all shriek excitedly about the setup.

"Ladies, I'm waiting!" Meredith stares back at us, arms crossed and tapping her foot.

"Ok, decision made. Your challenge is to get the guy with the dark hair to buy you a drink." Emma announces.

"The hottie in the plaid blazer?"

"Yes."

"Done and done. And by done, I mean watch how it's done." Meredith flips her hair over her shoulder as she walks away seductively toward her victim. She parades up to the bar and takes a seat next to him. From our table we can't hear their conversation, but based on their body language she's having some success. She tosses her hair a few more times then reaches out and playfully pushes him.

"What the hell is he doing? Is he seriously hitting on her? His girlfriend is in the bathroom. What a sleeze!"

"Actually, how do we know it was his girlfriend? Maybe it was his sister or cousin or something," Callie explains.

"Shit, you're right! Of course I would pick the one seemingly taken guy who will still fall for flirty Mere." Emma laughs back at us.

"Oh, he bought her a drink!" Meredith turns and waves back at us as she takes a sip from the martini glass that just appeared in her hand.

"Oh, time to see if it's his sister. Here she comes!" Emma says excitedly.

"Where?"

"Black dress. At 9 o'clock." Emma mutters the words as a tall brunette in a dark dress passes by our table. We look back at

Meredith and she motions toward us again a few times, and then leans over and plants a kiss on his cheek just as the girl approaches.

We all watch anxiously, as the presumed girlfriend becomes overly animated. Hilarity ensues, her arms start flailing, and it's clear that this guy definitely *is* her boyfriend.

Meredith glares toward us, mouth open, unsure of what to do. She stands and starts slowly backing away from the angry girl. Before she can slip away, the girlfriend grabs Meredith's drink from her hand and throws it in the face of the man, who we now definitively presume is her boyfriend.

We all turn to each other. "Oh, shit!"

"Ok, time to go. Everyone is staring at them, and now us!" I exclaim, as Meredith makes her way back to the table.

"You bitches!" she yells out, practically sprinting toward us.

"And I think that's our cue. Check, please!"

We meander from the restaurant through the frigid but bustling streets, still rolling with laughter from the scene we just created. The bouncer stands just inside the door of the Standard Hotel, filtering people through the line to get in. Callie, wearing a black sequin skirt and shimmery white silk blouse, files in first, followed by Meredith in her long sleeve navy blue dress, scooped low to show off her tiny back. "Girls!" Callie shouts. "The VIP line is right there." She points to a much smaller line of fashionably dressed, beautiful women. Emma files into the velvet-roped line in her tight-fitting maroon dress, which sits just off her toned shoulders. I follow behind, wearing a sparkly, long sleeve, gold and black dress, with black tights and heels.

We get our hands stamped with seemingly invisible ink that can only be seen with a black light. Apparently that's what fancy clubs do these days to keep their clientele's hands unblemished.

We then make our way up in the elevator to the top floor club. Our first stop is the overcrowded bar. I take a quick inventory of the room. The large, open space has small tables surrounding the perimeter walls, leaving narrow gaps between them only for accessing the exterior doors. Outside is a rooftop terrace containing only a few club-goers looking to cool off or vape in the brisk air.

The bar sits close to the front entrance of the club, and on the opposite side of the space is a DJ booth blasting the room with the latest dance music. Large speakers standing hip height vibrate the music furiously. A handful of larger lounge areas occupy the middle of the room, filled by slick, young New York men looking to blow their latest paycheck on the insanely priced bottles of liquor. Scantily clad girls lounge across their sofas chatting, drinking, and moving to the music, while the real partiers dance on the table tops, sloshing their drinks on their thousand-dollar mini dresses as they move.

"Ok these prices are insane!" I shout above the crowd, as I split the bill for our bottle of champagne.

"Meredith, go parade around in your bachelorette sash and get us invited to a table! It's time for booze scavenging," Callie instructs, only semi-jokingly.

"Ok! Come with!" Meredith grabs my hand and leads me around the room to further scope out the tables. We stop midway through the room, trying to squeeze through the crowds.

"Hey, ladies, looking good tonight!" a young, cute guy shouts to us over the music. He's wearing a light gray pinstripe suit in a super modern cut, with a tight black T-shirt beneath. He has light brown hair, combed and slicked back; the standard uniform of a New York City banker.

"Hi! Thanks! What's your name?" Meredith dives into conversation and inches closer to him. They begin chatting and one of slick's friends comes up to approach me.

"Can I get you a drink?"

Lost

"Sure, that would be great!" *Free booze? Yes, please!* Now we're talking. I chat for a few minutes with Rocky, a tall, slim, dark-haired lawyer, who is polite enough to invite us to sit at their table.

I check my phone while I wait in the lengthy line for the ladies room. It's 1:17 am, and I'm completely, ridiculously, disgustingly drunk. We've all spent the past two hours flirting with Rocky and his friends, drinking their booze, and literally dancing the night away. The thought of Jack suddenly pops into my head, and I do a quick scan for any sign of communication from him. I have exactly 0 texts, emails, and missed calls from him. My frustration grows with Jack. He has courted me for nearly two months and I've given him amazing sex, way sooner than I ever gave it up for Will. And he thinks it's ok to go out of town like this and just not even contact me? *What a complete ass.* I try to push Jack from my mind, determined not to let his behavior ruin my night. Max quickly enters my thoughts, and I remember I have his phone number. *I should text him!* In my unfiltered drunken state, I immediately decide this is a good idea.

Hi it's Jess

I begin to type, then remember his name for me.

Hi it's Jessa. Thanks again for the ride today! What are you up to tonight?

I hit send right away before I can change my mind, completely oblivious of my poor judgment.

After my pit stop, I wander back into the main part of the club. I walk back to the table and quickly check my phone. No text messages. A frown begins to settle on my face. "Jess, what's wrong? You ok?" Callie questions me. "Yeah, I just need another drink!" I wipe the disappointment away and fill my glass up with more champagne. "Hey, get up here!" Emma shouts down to us. She reaches out her arm and I grab her hand and join her on the table. After all, you only live once! Feeling brazen, I pull Rocky up on the table with me. He pulls me in tightly and I sway back and forth against him. "You're a good dancer, Jess," he shouts into my ear.

"Thanks! You're not so bad yourself. Do you guys come here a lot?"

"Lately, yeah, we're probably here most Friday nights. On Saturdays we usually go to Ware."

"Oh really, where's that?"

"It's over on 42nd Street, right off of Madison. They have this huge space, and it's a crazy good time. Just lots of people that know how to party hard!"

"That sounds fun!"

"You girls should join us at Ware tomorrow night. It'd be a good time."

"Yeah, I'll definitely mention it to them! Although I don't know if we can just let you guys monopolize our time this weekend. It wouldn't be fair to all of the other guys in New York. They don't get to spend time with fabulous southern girls like us every day!"

Rocky laughs. "This is true, but you should know you won't have this much fun with anyone else."

"Oh is that so?" I flirt back. "You seem pretty confident of that fact!"

"Oh, I am." Rocky leans in closer to me, and I return his big smile with one of my own. He leans in to plant his lips on mine, but I quickly flash to Jack and force his lips to land on my cheek, avoiding one drunken mistake.

CHAPTER FIFTEEN

"Jess, get up! We need to leave for brunch soon. Get your disheveled ass in the shower, now!" Emma yells at me and plops down on the bed next to me wrapped in a bath towel. I open my eyes just enough to glare at her.

"I'll get up when you make the room stop spinning." I grab a pillow and bury my face beneath it.

"You just need another drink and you'll be fine. Best hangover cure ever!"

"No, can't do it. Just leave me here in my misery," I grumble from beneath the pillow.

"Not happening. Get your ass up! Look, it's already 11:45." She grabs my phone and tosses it at my head.

"Ugh, seriously?" I lift the pillow and click on my phone to check the time myself. The screen shows the time is 11:46, and the icon on the bottom tells me that I have five new texts. I blearily begin to scan them. *Oh shit.* I snap from semi-awake to fully sober when I realize that four of them are from Mr. Lust, and the faint memory of drunk texting him fills my mind. I quickly shut off the screen, fearful of what I may have said to him. "Hey, get me some water, please?" I say to Emma.

"Fine. But you better get your ass in the shower after that. You look like hell."

"Yeah, yeah. Just water me, biotch." I flip my phone back on and my heart starts racing again. *Should I read it? Or just delete his messages and pretend it never happened?* I debate momentarily and decide I have to know what he, and even I, said.

I scan through them quickly while my heart beats faster.

8:07 am I was already asleep.
8:15 am Where did you go last night?
9:58 am Jessica, please let me know that you got home ok.
11:42 am Are you ok? Please let me know that you got home last night. You have me worried.

Ok, not as bad as I expected. I let out a small sigh of relief, and a smile appears on my lips. *He was worried about me! Wait, what about Jack?* I quickly check my other texts and see nothing from him.

"What's got you all smiley?" Emma questions me.

"Oh, nothing. I should get in the shower." I toss my phone down.

"So you're just magically cured?"

"Something like that." I smirk back at her and turn off my phone.

"What, is Jack sending you dirty texts this morning?"

"Emma, no!" I retort, again wincing that I haven't heard from him.

"Hmm, Rocky then? He must be ready for some more lip action."

"What? I didn't kiss him last night…did I?" I rack my foggy brain, and have a faint memory of his lips nearing mine.

Emma practically snorts. "Well he certainly tried! You're such a tease. Using him for free drinks all night and then holding out on him."

Lost

"Whatever. Somebody's gotta pay the bills! And better him than us!" I laugh, forcing myself out of the bed. I know I wasn't cheating on Jack, but guilt still settles over me, knowing he wouldn't appreciate my hours of flirting and dance grinding on a stranger, or my texting his lustalicious pseudo boss.

My restorative shower serves to remove all signs of the previous evening's partying, and cleanses my soul. I decide to be the bigger person and text Jack. What do I have to lose?

Hi! How's skiing? Miss you.

I send my vulnerable thoughts out into the world and quickly see that he's typing a response.

Miss you, baby. About to hit the slopes, call you this afternoon? Xo.

I smile at his response, feeling for the moment that things are back in order for us. *Although why did it take him two days to send me a message?* I can't quite get the sinking feeling out of my brain.

The four of us pile into an Uber SUV and head toward Ware, the final stop of our Saturday evening bachelorette fun. I may have had a teensy bit too much champagne from our last bottle, so I sit quietly trying to focus while the other girls sing loudly to Britney's new song blasting through the radio. I can't get Jack and Max out of my mind. Jack is quickly transitioning from my boyfriend to becoming Mr. JackAss. He said he would call me earlier this afternoon, but nothing. *Is it really that hard to take five minutes to call your girlfriend and say hi? Fuck it.* I pick up my phone and dial Jack, feeling a bit feisty at his overly tardy communication. His phone rings and rings, finally yielding his voicemail. I slap his name again, fuming as I try dialing him again. Five rings and nothing. I hastily hang up and try one final time, this time prepared to leave a semi-hateful voicemail. I clear my throat, expecting to leave a message after the fourth ring.

"Hello?" I hear a voice on the other end.

"Hey, turn that down for a sec," I yell at Callie, unsure of who's answered.

"Hello? Jack?"

"Hi, this is Jack's phone, but he's currently unavailable," I hear a female purr in a mock phone sex operator voice. *What the fuck?* "May I ask who's calling?" My mouth gapes open trying to figure out what the hell is happening here.

"Hey, give me my phone!" I hear Jack's muffled voice in the background.

"You have to catch me first," the female shrieks, and I hear laughter ensue from the female and *my* boyfriend Jack.

"Lela, give me my phone."

"Only if you ask nicely."

"Ok, Leland, please give me my phone."

"No, you're not ignoring me for another work call! You have to earn your phone. Give me a kiss first." *What?* I nearly die at these words. *Am I really hearing their giggle-filled charade right now? This can't be happening.* My heart starts aching while my mind processes what I've heard.

"Don't be ridiculous. Give me my phone." I listen, holding my breath, needing to hear what happens next while fighting the will to scream through the phone.

"Just on the cheek. Come on, Jackie, you're no fun." *Jackie? She calls him Jackie?*

"You're such a pain in my ass," he laughs. "There. Happy now?"

"For now," she teases. I hear a muffled exchange as the phone changes hands. *Oh God.* My brain floods with disgust and pain as I piece this together.

"Hello?" I hear Jack's voice ring through the phone this time. "Hello?" I stay silent for a few seconds, gasping for breath and sucked dry of words.

"Seriously? Fuck you, *Jackie*. I'm done!" I simultaneously disconnect our call and throw my phone across the Uber.

"Jess? What happened?" Meredith questions me while the girls exchange a look.

"Well, I guess Jack is spending his ski trip making out with his ex-girlfriend Lela."

"Are you sure? That doesn't make any sense," Meredith says, concern on her face.

"Yeah, and didn't he just buy you those amazing earrings? I mean you guys were just in Paris together," Emma chimes in.

"Could it just be a misunderstanding?" Callie questions.

"I really don't think so." I pause, caught between the verge of tears and screaming.

"I'm so sorry," Meredith says as she gives me a quick squeeze, and I fight the urge to let a tear leak from my eye. *He's not deserving of my tears. He's just another asshole shitbag. I knew it was too good to be true. I knew it couldn't be that simple. That great of a relationship, that quickly.* I feel my world start to cave in around me when I remember all of the hope I had for us. A real future. And now it's nothing.

"Really, I'm fine!" I lie. "This is your weekend to live it up because you've found the perfect man. So we're going to celebrate that, not pity me!"

"Jess, he didn't deserve you anyway. You're such a great catch. I know millions of guys who would line up for the chance to date you!" I respond to Callie's compliment with a weak smile.

"See, they're lining up already!" Emma hands me my phone, and I see a new text from Rocky on the screen, hoping to meet up with us at Ware.

CHAPTER SIXTEEN

Ware is undoubtedly the coolest club I've ever been to. The former warehouse was converted into an event space, and is now a full-time club. Three long hallways, maybe fifty feet wide, extend the length of the building, each one only lit by the random pattern of flashing strobe lights above.

"This place is so amazing!" Meredith shouts over her shoulder. Her long dark hair falls into big curls across her black leather mini dress. Only she could pull off something that trendy, and tiny.

"Girls, keep your phone on you and stay together, or we'll never find each other again in this place!" Callie warns us in her motherly fashion.

"Drinks!" I shout back to them, needing something to numb the pain of my shitbag boyfriend Jack. *Ex-boyfriend Jack?* The thought is too much to process right now.

"Over here!" We follow Emma's tall silhouette in the crowds to a massive circular bar in the middle of the room. There are two other bars in this first dance hall, one at each end of the building.

The bar is staffed with beautiful and very toned bartenders, both male and female. The ladies have on skin-tight black dresses, the men with equally tight black T-shirts. We order a round of "houses," Ware's specialty martini, which carries a slight purple haze when the strobing laser lights flash onto it.

After draining an obscenely strong house, followed by a mind-numbing shot of God knows what, my brain's good judgment is as incapacitated as I am. I fumble for my cell phone from my clutch and take a quick breath before I slap my fingers across the screen, thinking only of how hot Lusty Max is, and how much I need some attention.

Hi. Where are you?

I get right to the point and hit send. Within seconds I see a response.

Dinner. You?

Hot dinner date?

Business dinner, almost done.

I'm at Ware. Have you heard of it? You should come.

Yes. A bit young for me.

Oh, I forgot he's older than me, 35 maybe? What's a decade age difference really matter when all I need is a hot mouth to kiss and warm body to grind?

Don't be old and boring. Come. We'll have fun.

I feel myself smile at the idea and give little thought to the potential consequences of him joining us, further failing to thoroughly consider what I will do if he actually shows up.

"Jess, behind you." Emma gestures with her martini glass, a wide, giggly smile on her face. I whirl around and see Rocky and his clan of boys behind me, and I welcome the opportunity for some confidence-boosting male attention.

"Hey, babe, looking good!" He grabs my arm and twirls me in toward him, focusing his eyes on the sweetheart neckline of my red dress, which perfectly accentuates my pushed-up chest. I found this dress on sale during Christmas and it was too good to pass up. The ruching throughout the clingy material helps hide my insecurities.

Rocky slides his arm around me and plants a big kiss on my cheek. I let his minty mouth linger for a moment, then I pull away, not wanting to actually swap spit. *At least not just yet.* I quickly slip from his arms and say hello to his friends.

"Jess, come on, we're all taking shots!" Rocky pulls me toward him again. I certainly don't need another shot, but in the spirit of living in the moment, I happily oblige. Rocky and his well-to-do friends once again went all out, getting a big table in the middle of the club with table service.

"Look over there!" Emma shouts toward me as soon as I swallow my liquid poison. My bleary eyes move toward the far corner of the room to a platform with a few girls dancing on top. It sits up above the crowd, almost like a mini balcony, hidden until they put the lights on it.

"Ladies and gentlemen, tonight we're celebrating a very special birthday for Miss Karen Cruze! Give it up for Karen!!!!" The DJ's voice overlays the music for his upbeat introduction. The lights flash over and fully illuminate a skinny red head dancing around with a few of her friends. "Happy Birthday, Karen, now come on y'all give her some loooooveeee!!!"

The crowd responds with resounding woos and cheers for the birthday girl. She looks very young, probably just turning 21, and her body moves effortlessly with the encouragement from the crowd. It's clear she's having the time of her life.

"We HAVE to do that for Mere!" Emma shouts to me. I nod my head, and continue swaying to the music, forgetting once and for all about my possible forthcoming rendezvous.

Emma works her magic, and before long it's our turn to climb atop the VIP balcony. "Ladies and gentlemen, we've got another big celebration in the house tonight! Let's all give it up for Miss Meredith Andrews! Meredith is spending her last night out as a single woman. That's right, boys, she's going to be officially off the market soon, so buy her a drink while you still can!"

"Ahh!" Meredith shrieks and waves her hands to the crowd like she's just won the Miss America pageant.

"There she is!" the DJ announces, and a spotlight above finds her in the crowd. "Everybody make some noise while we witness this single lady's final dance!" The crowd starts cheering her on as she makes her way up to the VIP balcony, all of us toting along behind. We excitedly climb up onto the balcony platform, trying not to wobble off the steep steps. Clearly this was not designed for drunk party girls wearing high heels.

The DJ quickly flows the beat into a remix of Beyoncé's best, beginning with "Single Ladies." Meredith excitedly dances around with us and flashes her ring on cue while we boisterously shout, "If you like it then you should have put a ring on it."

"Oh, he liked it!" Our adorable Meredith adds her own words, shouting and flashing her left hand and engagement ring around. The music seamlessly transitions to "Bootylicious" and we all can't help but shriek again. I embrace the words and shake it like I don't have a care in the world. And for a moment, I don't. I simply enjoy the beauty of decades-old friendship, now old enough to dance and drink our asses off.

"Bathroom break? I think we could really use a touch-up now!" I suggest as we disembark from the dancing platform. The girls oblige, and we all duck into the bathroom just a few feet behind us.

God I'm drunk. I stand in front of the mirror and try for a moment to focus on my blurry reflection. I reach into Callie's bag, which sits on the beautiful granite counters in the impeccably designed bathrooms. I use a paper towel to dab off the glow my face has acquired from dancing oh so bootyliciously. I do a quick touch-up with her powder, curl my eyelashes, and put on some red-tinted lip gloss. I give my hair a quick tousle and try to make myself look a bit more presentable.

"Hey, where did Emma and Callie go?" I ask Meredith, who is blotting her face at the vanity.

"They went back to the table, you can go ahead, I'm going to call Cale for a minute so he doesn't have a shitfit and worry too much."

"Ok, sure, I think I need to get myself a water and sit down for a minute," I inform her.

"You ok?"

"Yeah, I'll be fine. Just probably need to slow down for a bit."

"Ok, see you back at the table?"

I nod back to Mere and grab a mint from the attendant on my way out. I exit the bathroom and try to focus on the mass of people dancing and partying in front of me. *The table is that way, right?* I take a few steps when I feel the force of someone's arm around my wrist. *Must be Rocky again.* I swallow down a wave of nausea and turn to him with a full smile. "Hey, you."

It takes my sloshy brain a moment to realize that it's not Rocky, and my heart races with the realization that the one and only Mr. Lust is standing before me. Holy shit. *How could I forget?* Maybe the four unnecessary shots I took had something to do with it.

"Hello, Jesssuh." Max stands in front of me, his right arm holding my left, our bodies about eighteen inches apart. I swallow hard, completely flabbergasted by his presence. I was way too drunk to premeditate what I would do or say to him if he actually showed up.

"Are you having fun?" I manage to shout at him above the music.

He shakes his head, and his eyes peer down to me. He looks more delicious than ever. This is the first time I've seen him without a fresh shave. The flashing lights cast a glow on his slight yet swoon-worthy stubble. He's dressed in a white button-up shirt accented with navy and light blue stripes, and a dark blazer. I've never seen him in jeans before either. "I've been looking for you," he says, meeting my eyes with his. His brow furrows a little. "I've been here for over an hour," he says with a tinge of annoyance in his voice.

Oh, shit. "I…" I look around for a moment, trying to piece this together. "I don't have my phone. I'm sorry." *Wow.* I can't believe he's been looking for me for that long. My normal nerves are completely crushed by my buzz. "Please forgive me?" I bite my lip and look into his eyes and I can see him swallow hard.

"I can barely hear you," he yells at me. "Come on." His delicious accent cuts through the air, and I feel that magnetic draw that I've felt since the second our eyes first met. He slides his fingers in mine and leads me through the crowd, deeper into the building. Every second that our skin is connected sends new surges and naughty thoughts throughout me.

He leads me from the first room through the second, dodging the crowds of late night partiers. We circle around the central bar in the second room, which looks nearly identical to the first but has more of a techno music vibe. We wind around the lines of people waiting at the bar before finally entering the third room. He's said nothing since taking my hand and leading me away, instead only giving me brief but serious glances over his shoulder as we walk.

A dark curtain pools around the elevated DJ booth, certainly there to cover the electronics and wiring beneath it. The placement of the speakers makes this spot quieter than anywhere else in the club, and I welcome the slight reprieve of blaring music into my ears. Lusty Max walks up to the curtain and pushes it aside, gesturing for me to walk through it.

Filled with confusion and intrigue I follow his lead, walking inside the curtain. "Come." *Yes, please.* He guides my hand to the subwoofer, and I feel smooth, long vibrations pulse through me. He places his hand atop mine, and this simple touch makes me feel the want and need for him from deep inside. This man that I've had too many chance meetings with is finally here. Right in front of me. *And I'm single?* I quickly force Jack and my hurt heart from my mind and replace it with the thrill of the desire that stands before me. *It's now or never, Jess. Makes your move!*

"I didn't think you were coming," I finally say, leaning in close to his ear, desperately wanting to move my teeth in for a nibble.

He shakes his head again. "I told you, I have been looking for you. And I don't like to be kept waiting," he says with a teasing yet semi-serious tone, and a playful twist of his succulent mouth.

"I know, I'm sorry. I don't know where my phone is. I must've left it over with my purse at a table."

"So you said."

"Yes. I just meant, I didn't think you would actually show up. I'm happy to see you," I whisper the words into his ear, and his body lets off a slight quiver before his hand slides around my waist. He leans in to my ear now, and I feel his warm breath tingling on my earlobe before he even speaks.

"Why?" He searches my eyes for a response. "Why do you want to see me?" His expression is flat, and I can't read his thoughts. I glance down for a moment, deciding on my next move. He came here to see me, looked for me for an hour, and has lured me away from the crowd. *Don't be daft. Go for it, Jess!* My inner vixen coaches me in my ear. I lean back into him, this time pressing my body fully against his. I take my index finger and thumb, and gently tug at his earlobe before rising on my toes and placing my lips so they graze the edge of his ear.

"Because I wanted…well…you," I whisper with my best seductress tone. He says nothing with his words but everything with his body. He tightens his hold around my waist, pressing me against him. I expect him to kiss me, but instead he pulls me closer and says, "Dance with me." I happily oblige.

Our bodies begin to move as "You Can Be the One" by Late Night Alumni fills our ears. I feel his erection bulging from his pants as my hips move slowly from side to side in rhythm with his. He's certainly not trying to hide how turned on he is. *Maybe he wants me to feel it. Maybe I should do something with it.* My lustful thoughts continue and I mindlessly sway, mesmerized by the fantasy of what could happen with this man. *Why did we meet? Why did we run into each other at the airport? Twice? And why did he really come here tonight? Are we destined to be lovers? Screw it. I can't wait any longer wondering what this might or might not be.*

I pull my head from his shoulder and plant a soft kiss directly on his lips. As our lips meet the fire instantly ignites. His fingers latch onto my hair, pulling me in with his desperate need and desire. My hands grab his skin, wanting more and more of him inside my mouth. He moves his left hand down to my leg and his index and middle finger lightly trace my skin as he works his way to the edge of my dress's fabric. Our tongues still tangle and grope each other, but his hand pauses momentarily, as if asking for permission, before going underneath my dress. All I can think about are his strong hands touching me down there, exploring my body even more. Never mind the hundreds of people in the room with us, the many who sit less than ten feet away from us. I need *this* now. I need *him* now.

I reach my right hand on top of his and lace my fingers in his. My body quivers with anticipation as I guide his hand beneath the fabric of my dress, feeling his light touch as he nears my cavern. As his fingers reach the edge of my lace panties I release his hand, allowing him to begin his own guided exploration down below. He slides his index finger just barely underneath the edge of the lace, and I let out a slight groan into his mouth.

He spends a moment researching my panty lines with his fingers, understanding the territory that lies below. He pulls his lips from mine for a moment, hikes my dress up and silently guides me to turn around. We shift back further into our secret territory, so we now stand just behind the velvet curtains to give us a bit more privacy. There is a three-inch gap between the curtains which allows me to see the crowds passing by. Knowing that an audience could catch us at any moment further fuels the naughtiness of this already forbidden act.

Mr. Lust pulls me back toward his body, but this time I'm left facing the opening of the curtain, my back now pressing against the front of his body. "Shh, don't say anything or we'll be caught." His words drift into my ear while he nibbles his way down my neck. My weight rests against him, and I lay my arms to the sides of his body then against the wall to steady my balance. His right hand slides down the front of my body, and it's as though a shock has moved through me. His hand moves slowly in teasing fashion while I ache for it to return to my panties.

Finally his hand returns there, and my pelvis shifts upward to facilitate his exploration. I lift my right hand from the wall and eagerly touch the right side of his body. I feel his strength through his shirt: strong, hard muscles sit beneath the smooth cotton fabric. I loop my fingers in between two buttons near his lower abs and stroke his smooth skin. For a moment I let them meander across his stomach, finding his solid V muscles, the ones that sit just where the abs meet the hips. He now groans into my ear as my fingers slide into the waist of his pants. Finally, he shifts my panties over to the side, allowing room for him to work his magic. His index finger moves across the smooth skin now freed from my panties, and lands between the slight strip of womanhood that remains below. He wiggles his hand toward the right, finding my erect clitoris, and begins circling it with his hand. I wiggle my hips to align with the movement of his hand. The pleasure is building and I feel my panties becoming more and more wet as he goes. He keeps his index finger on my magic spot, and slides his middle finger just below it, tiptoeing around the opening that desperately waits for him to enter it. I crave a taste of his Italian sausage trapped inside his pants and continue moving my hand further inside. I fumble for his belt and begin tugging at the cool leather, trying to release his waiting prize. He encircles me with his finger one last time and places his lips on my neck, giving a slight sucking motion as his fingers finally reach inside of me.

His first finger slips in easily thanks to my arousal. He slides it in and out a few times and then adds another finger, and another, until three of his strong fingers pull me closer and closer to my climax. I return to my own exploration of him, momentarily distracted by the overwhelming pleasure he's giving me. I tug furiously at this belt and manage to undo it in spite of my clumsy drunk fingers. I continue working at his pants, and upon realizing they're buttons I simply tug harder to expand the opening. Finally, they pop open and I can caress the exterior of his manhood, only separated by the thin layer of his boxer briefs. I move quickly, desperate to feel what lies beneath, so I gently slide my hand below the final barrier. Lust groans more loudly into my ear as my hand feels the rigid prize that I've been lusting over.

His length is excessive, longer than anything I've ever felt before, but the girth is almost more impressive. I circle my fingers around his shaft in an open, u-shaped circle, unable to close the loop of my fingers as his delicious throbbing manhood is too thick to allow it. I move my hand up and down his tremendous length, slowly at first and then more and more quickly. He continues to play inside of me, pushing his fingers further into me while using his thumb to simultaneously delight the top of my peach. He inches deeper and deeper and finally the edge of his overly expensive watch rests against me. The cool steel of the watch band slides just across my clitoris and I feel the start of ecstasy. *I have to have him. All of him. Now.* I've dreamt about it, lusted over it, and now the opportunity has finally presented itself. And I'll be damned if I don't take advantage.

I peer over my right shoulder to meet his smiling gaze. His normally muted expression is replaced by a twinkle in his eye and the devilish grin of a child who's about to knowingly be naughty. I kiss his lips, letting mine linger, and then pull on his sweet, supple bottom lip as I release him. "I want you," I say simply, connecting deep within his stare.

His face completely relaxes, his head falling back against the wall, relishing in my request. He nods back at me and removes his fingers from inside of me, then guides me over to the tall, buzzing subwoofer.

"I have an idea." He kisses me with eager excitement and then places his hands just below my butt, hoisting me up. My legs wrap around him and I feel completely safe, sexy, and ready to succumb to this beautiful man. He turns around and places me atop the subwoofer, which puts me at a perfect height to meet his hips. The plastic is cool on my bare bottom, but my anticipation overshadows this sensation. He grabs my hips and pulls me to the edge of the woofer so that my legs spread around him. He kisses me again and I reach down to fully release him from his boxers, preparing our bodies to meet. The vibrations from the loud music shoot through my body, exhilarating me. The beat of the song speeds up, and I find my body vibrating more and more. *Oh, God.* The sensation hits me suddenly, and hard.

The nausea races through me, and my skin turns cold. *Oh my God. This can't be happening.* I pull my face away from his and take in a deep breath of air.

"Jessa, are you ok? What's wrong?" Lust's aroused expression immediately tenses with concern.

Lost

"We don't have to do this," he reminds me, inching away. I shake my head, fighting another wave of nausea. *Why did I have to drink this much? Please go away. Please go away.* I beg the feelings to subside and suddenly they overtake me. I push Mr. Lust to the side and quickly jump from the subwoofer to the floor, trying to catch my balance as I yank down my dress. "Jessa, what's wrong?" He grabs his forehead, expressing frustration with himself.

"No, it's nothing," I release the only words I can manage and then a full force wave of nausea hits me. My body convulses while cold sweat slaps me in the face. I look for an escape but it's too late. I lean over the subwoofer and release the buildup of alcohol that's been sitting inside of me. *Please kill me now. Please.* I can't even make eye contact with him, so I stand myself up and yell, "I'm sorry," as I pull open the curtain, trying to run away.

My wobbling drunk legs only make it a few steps before he grabs me again. "Jessa, are you ok?" I try to respond but the only reaction my body can manage is a full flood of tears down my face.

"Come here. It's ok." He pulls me, disgusting, vomity me, into him again. He kisses my sweaty forehead and holds me tight, reassuring me. "It's ok. Take my coat, we're getting you out of here." I finally nod, unable to speak, and pull his impeccable designer blazer over my shoulders to cover the residual vomit on my dress. I try to wipe my tears while he leads me through the crowd, praying that no one can smell my filth.

We finally reach the front room of Ware to see that much of it has cleared out now.

"Where are your friends?" he questions me.

"I don't know. We were sitting over there." I point toward a few empty tables where we were hanging out with Rocky and his crew earlier. I look around the blurry room in front of me and don't see anyone resembling my girlfriends. They probably went back to the hotel room when they couldn't find me, knowing I would return there on my own if we got separated. We walk toward the tables, covered with stickiness, sludge, and half-empty liquor bottles, signs of the fun we were having earlier. I scan the couches for my purse, phone, or any other signs that the girls are still here. *Nothing.*

"I should really be going," I say, engrossed by my humiliation and unable to look at Mr. Lust. I start to remove his jacket to give back to him. "I—"

He interrupts me. "No. I'm not leaving you. And keep the jacket on, you'll freeze outside."

"No, I'll be ok, I'll just get a taxi."

"And pay them how? You have no purse, no phone here." *Shit, he's right. Stop being a drunk dumbass, Jess.*

"Oh. Um, I can get money at the hotel when I get there."

"How do you know your friends are there? Here, call them from my phone." I stand there dumbfounded for a moment, realizing I don't have anyone's phone numbers memorized. With everything digital and saved in phones these days, I've never bothered to learn them. And I've never regretted it until now.

"I don't know any of them," I say, letting out an inadvertent sob. "But I'm sure they are there looking for me. I should go." I try to move my feet quickly from him, desperately hoping that my mortification and embarrassment will dissipate with growing distance between us. I move my wobbling legs as quickly as I can away from my near sexcapade turned nightmare.

"I said I'm not leaving you. Here, find your phone. If it's at the hotel then your friends are too." He hands me his phone, having already pulled up the "Find My iPhone app" for me to use. I finally get the login correct after a few fat fingering typos. Within a few seconds the map of New York City pulls up and it begins locating my phone. I quickly see my battery is dead, and the last known location is here, at Ware. *Fuck.* I lift my teary eyes to Lust and realize he's been watching the screen as well.

"I think my phone died in here. But I'm sure my friends went back to the hotel. I'll be fine." I barely finish the words when another wave of nausea hits me. I gag momentarily and manage to sit down on the sofa before getting weak in the knees.

"Jessa? Are you ok? Talk to me." My head falls back on the sofa and my eyes start to close.

"I'm ok," I mumble and nod to him, head and eyes still backward.

"No. You are not ok. I will not leave you here." I can hear the rising concern in his voice, but my eyes remain closed.

"Please, just leave me alone! I'm fine!" I nearly scream the words at him.

"Dammit, Jessa," his serious tone returns. "Stop being so…stubborn!" He struggles for the word in English to describe my obstinate behavior.

"No. Just leave me alone!" I sob again, overtaken by the embarrassment of letting him see me like this. I shake for a moment, sinking my head deeper and deeper into the sofa.

I feel like a child being carried away. It is a nice feeling. Strong, secure, taken care of. Like when you would fall asleep on the sofa as a child and your dad would carry you up to bed. You would be so tired you could barely comprehend what was happening, but you didn't really care because you felt so safe and secure. I hear some muffled chatter in the background, like an old movie playing, but I can't understand the words. But I'm so tired I don't really want to hear them, and I just let the voices lull me back to sleep.

CHAPTER SEVENTEEN

Stop spinning. Stop spinning. STOP SPINNING.
I manage to pry my eyes open, feeling the resistance of my contact lenses that are now glued to them. My eyes attempt a few weak blinks as I try to get my bearings. I know that I'm in a bed, but this is not my apartment. Or Jack's. *Wait, you're still in New York City, Jess.* The sight of yellow cabs out the window quickly validates my hypothesis. But this isn't our hotel room either. *Where the hell am I?*

I look down to see I'm wearing a plush white robe, something that does not belong to me. I'm plopped right in the middle of the bed, and judging by the arrangement of the pillow and sheets, I was sleeping alone. *Phew.* Maybe there's one less thing I can regret today. My bar tar-covered shoes have been placed in a perfect line next to a comfy gray and white chair that occupies the far corner of the room. On each side of the bed sits a mirrored nightstand, a perfect complement to the gray and white theme of the room. Wherever I am, it's impeccably decorated. A bottle of Fiji water and an upside-down glass sit atop a silver tray on the nightstand. The other side of the bed has a clock, telling me it's 5:30 am. *SHIT.* My only chance of getting home today, given I'm flying standby, is on the 7 am flight. *I've got to get out of here. Wherever I am.*

On the chair sits a bright red pillow, as well as a perfectly folded set of white towels. I stumble out of bed and peer out the flowing, red, semi-sheer curtains against a set of French doors. I see bits of snow on the ground and a few yellow taxis filling the streets below. I'm only about two stories from the ground, and I assume I must be in an apartment of some sort, or maybe a townhouse.

I walk into the bathroom, similarly styled but in a black, gray and white theme. The floors and tiles and countertop are all beautiful Italian marble. I glance at myself in the mirror and gasp at what I see. A blur of dried, sweaty makeup and tears. And better yet, dried puke remains on the tips of my hair. I'm a walking ad for the dangers of overindulgence.

I anxiously climb into the shower to cleanse myself of my remaining war paint. The water warms up quickly and I let it wash over my dirty skin. I start trying to piece together the night before. The last thing I remember is taking shots with Rocky and his friends. *Is this Rocky's apartment?* I open my eyes and see some toiletries tucked neatly into a built-in marble shelf opposite the shower head. I reach forward, grateful to have something to clean off with. There are three bottles: soap, shampoo, and conditioner, I assume. I grab one of the clear bottles to see if it's body wash or shampoo. I blink a few times and as my eyes begin to focus, I realize I just can't comprehend what the writing says. It looks like Italian. *Italian!* Mr. Lust. Holy fuck, I must be in his apartment. I begin scrubbing my scalp and try to recall how I got here. *Oh, God.* A flash of me and him together at Ware enters my mind. And I can remember feeling his hand between my legs. *Did I sleep with him? Did he bring me back here? We couldn't have had sex here, right? No, even if he is a complete man-whore, he wouldn't have slept with me, not the way I looked.*

I finish scrubbing the filth off of me, but the humiliation still remains. I swing open the glass shower door and set my feet against a plush bath mat. I spy a brand new toothbrush and some toothpaste inside of a white porcelain container on the vanity. *Yes!* I gratefully rip open the plastic and begin brushing my teeth. *No wonder it looks like a hotel, he probably has a new guest every time he's in town. Probably because he has plenty of female friends stay over.* The thought of another woman staying here wrenches my stomach. *Be real though, Jess. Someone as rich and beautiful as him probably has girls lined up to stay here.*

I refocus my efforts to catching the flight and avoiding further embarrassment. I find a comb and hair tie, and quickly work through my wet locks and tie them back in a loose pile at the nape of my neck. I towel myself off then walk into the bedroom. Laying on the bed in a neat little stack is my clean dress, bra, and panties. *Someone must've come in here. Was it Mr. Lust?* I shudder with embarrassment, realizing someone washed my foul vomit clothes. I quickly get dressed, knowing I have to run out of here. I tiptoe through the dimly lit hallway, walking toward a living room area. Large white sofas fill the room, along with a dark gray patterned area rug and black-and-white checkered chairs. A light peers from beyond the living room, illuminating this space just enough for me to see the entry door. I tiptoe behind the sofas and near the front door.

"Good morning, miss. Did you sleep ok?" I nearly jump out of my skin at the sound of the Italian-accented voice. It takes me a minute to place the familiar voice. *Lust's driver. Butler? Man servant?*

"Hi, Enzo. I'm sorry if I disturbed you. I just wanted to get a quick shower before heading out."

"You did not wake me at all. When you get to be my age, sleep is hard to come by. I'm just catching up on the news." He wiggles the newspaper in his hands. "Can I get you some coffee? Espresso? Anything to eat?" *Wow. Wonder if he's this nice to all of Max's guests. It's his job, Jess.*

"No, thank you. I need to run, but please tell your boss thank you for letting me stay."

"Let me get him for you. I know he'd like to see you." He rises to his feet.

"No, really no need to wake him. I do appreciate your hospitality. But, please, don't get him."

He nods back to me. "Ok. Where would you like to go? I'll have the car ready in two minutes."

"Thank you, but I can just get a taxi. I'll just be on my way." I start walking toward the door but he leaps up.

"Please, Miss Jessica, let me drive you. I have strict instructions to ensure you get home safely."

"But it's really—"

"No buts. I drive you where you need to go. Come. Put this on to keep warm." He hands me a Burberry scarf and starts out the door with keys in hand.

I climb into the back of the Maybach, my neck wrapped in a Lust-scented scarf. It smells divine and immediately reminds me of his presence. "Where to, Miss Jessica?"

"Just back to the W Hotel, please. I just need to get my stuff and then I'm off to the airport."

He glances back at me from his rear-view mirror. "Airport? You fly home today?"

"Yes, I'm hoping to get on a flight this morning. Well, in an hour actually."

"At seven? You don't have much time. I will take you to the airport too." I open my mouth to argue with him, but decide to embrace his generous offer. He's right, if I'm going to make the flight, I'll need to take all the charity I can get.

Twenty minutes later we're on the bridge en route to LaGuardia. I was able to get a room key from the front desk, and sneak into our hotel room without waking the girls. Thankfully my clutch, phone and wallet were all present, so I threw everything in my bag and left them a note to tell them I've headed home. I sit quietly in the back seat, slowly sobering up as I take in the early morning city views, until he interrupts my thoughts. "You will visit us again soon?"

Oh. I hadn't thought about that. Will I ever see Lust again? Hell, he saw me throw up, does he even want to see me again? I'm just a young, drunk party girl. And he's, well, Mr. Sophisticated Mysterious Lust.

"I don't think so," I respond honestly.

CHAPTER EIGHTEEN

Can we please talk?

I roll my eyes at Jack's most recent text. It's been over a week since the Lela phone call incident. My logical side tells me not to respond, to force him out of my life. I already extended him the courtesy of trust. In Paris. After he talked to her! And then she was answering his phone on the ski trip, when he hadn't even told me she would be there. I try to get my heart to agree. It's black and white. He's a shitbag. He cheated. Well, may have cheated. So it's over. *But what if it was a misunderstanding? Shouldn't you hear him out?* I still want to believe him. *Just see him once. Get closure so you can move on.* My fingers hover above my phone as I decide how to respond.

"Jess!" The peppy voice of my dear friend and work bestie Sarah interrupts my thoughts.

"Hi," I respond with unmatched enthusiasm.

"Geez, you look like shit."

"Thanks?" I respond with my heavy heart. I can even feel that my normal smile and occasional optimism have been erased. I let out a deep sigh and smile at my friend. Her blonde hair and green eyes look perfect against the deep jade green of her spring-colored dress. "You look super cute. Way to make me feel even worse," I say, laughing. "New dress?"

"Yeah, just came last night. Do you think it fits ok? I think it's a bit tight?" She steps back giving me full view of her uber petite yet curvy frame. Her five foot eight frame couldn't look any more model-like in the vibrant colors.

"Ok, if you think that's too tight, then I'm horrified of what you think of my outfit!" I laugh, reflecting on how my hormone-induced bloat gives me the look of a fresh pregnancy.

"Stop it! You're crazy. But seriously, how are you? You just look, well, sad."

"Is it that obvious?"

"Well, in our three years of working together I think I know Jess's typical Monday face. And that's more than just the 'I fucking hate Monday because it's Monday' face. Have you talked to him?"

"No. Well, not in person anyway. He sent me another text." I hold up my phone for her to read along.

She nods her head as her eyes dart through our text conversation. "How long has it been since you've seen him?"

"About ten days. It's getting worse each day. I thought"—I pause, fighting the swelling tears because I'm not *that* girl who cries at work—"I thought I was done with him. I mean, he cheated! And I know I shouldn't care about him. But it's not getting any easier." My sweet friend wraps her arms around me for a reassuring hug.

"I know. I can see it in you, you had fallen for him. Whether you want to believe it or not you were falling in love."

I swallow hard at the reality of her words.

"It's not fair. Everything was so great. Why do people have to cheat? It ruins everything."

Sarah instantly picks up on the double meaning in my words. Sharing a cube wall and hundreds of lunches together over the past few years has given her a glimpse inside my far-from-perfect love life. Both the fucked-upness of my own parents, and my own ups and downs of dating.

"Are you sure he cheated? I mean, I know what you heard. But is it confirmed? What if it was just a drunk kiss that he wholeheartedly regrets?"

I ponder the idea for a moment.

"And furthermore, what you did in New York City wasn't exactly *kosher*," Sarah emphasizes the word a bit too loudly.

"Hey, are you talking about me again?" Ben stands up from his cube, which shares a wall on the front side of mine.

"Yes, Ben. We have nothing more exciting to talk about than your Jewishness." Sarah rolls her eyes at him. His apparent crush on her over the years continues to be of great annoyance to her. "Could you stop eavesdropping? We're having a very important conversation."

"Ok, ok. I promise to put one ear bud in so I can only listen to half of what you're saying." His gray eye winks at us, and we watch his ashy hair fade below the cube wall.

"Ugh, where were we?" Sarah asks rhetorically. "Oh, yeah. Jess, you weren't exactly angelic *that* night, so maybe Jack's sins are forgivable? All I'm saying is talk to him. At least see him to get back your favorite shirt. That has to be worth it."

"Maybe you're right"—I laugh—"100% Egyptian cotton with five years of wear and a rip in the seam is surely a reason to forgive cheating."

"Just give him a chance. I know misery may love company, but this company does not love your misery."

―――✥―――

My heart seems to have moved into my throat on the drive over to Jack's house. Damn Sarah for talking me into this. *Worst case you get your shirt, and some closure.* I remind myself of the reasons I'm doing this. I loathe these types of conversations. They're so adult. So painful. Why can't we all just shut down our feelings and go drink our sorrows away in a dark apartment? I recall my tried and true method of managing my emotions.

I still have to fight my excitement to see him. My fantasies want it to all be a misunderstanding. For us to get back to where we were before. To pick up the on-the-verge-of-love relationship we had in spite of this. *But how could I trust him anyway? Be realistic, Jess.* My brain prepares me for the worst. *It's over. Just get your stuff and get out. He's probably officially back with Lela anyway.* What if he just wants the earrings back? He must've spent a fortune on them.

My wobbly finger rings the bell and I try not to faint and/or shit my pants as I hear the approaching footsteps get louder. *Here goes nothing.*

Wait, how do I greet him? Normally he would give me a hug and kiss hello, but that's when we were dating. And I was his girlfriend. What about now?

"Hey there!" Jack greets me with a kind voice. He's still dressed in his work clothes, dark gray pants with a blue and white patterned button-up, covered with a navy blue wool sweater. He always looks so handsome when he's dressed up this way. *Damn good-looking, cheating asshole.* "It's pretty cold outside, come on in," Jack instructs me. I walk inside his familiar home, normally warm and inviting, but much more intimidating today. I step inside the foyer and Jack closes the door behind me.

"I know, it was in the sixties on Sunday, and now they're saying there's a chance of snow tonight."

"Do you think it will actually snow? Or is everyone just worrying about nothing?" he asks me.

"In my many years of living here, it's very rare for us to get snow in late March. But the weathermen usually like to give us a scare every year or so. I think they're in cahoots with the grocery stores to help clear out the stale bread inventory every once in a while."

Jack laughs. "You're probably right. Well, I won't keep you here too late in case there is any truth to the inclement weather." My heart sinks as his words settle in. *I guess he has a short agenda in mind then.*

We settle into the sofa, red wine in hand, with a blazing fire a few feet in front of us. I decide to let Jack lead the conversation; after all, he's the one that has explaining to do. *So you're not going to explain your "adventure" with Mr. Lust?* I shake the embarrassing, yet memorable, mistake from my mind, and focus on the man in front of me.

"How's the wine?" Jack asks me as I finish my first sip. He sits a few feet away from me on the couch, his body turned toward me in a relaxed position. *Is this how adults handle breakups? Red wine and fireside conversation?*

"It's great," I say with a forced, nervous smile. I sit in the awkward silence, waiting for Jack to lead the conversation *there*, or at least somewhere else. I nervously bite my lip and gaze at the fire to avoid his eyes.

"Well, I guess we should talk about what you came here to talk about," Jack finally says.

I glance back at him with a nervous smile. "Ok."

Jack takes a deep breath before he dives in to the conversation. "The truth is, Jess, I've had a great time with you since we met. I've never met anyone like you, and I haven't fallen for someone as quickly as I fell for you. In some ways, it really caught me off guard." I watch him intently as he shifts his wine glass between hands, seemingly preparing for the uncomfortable "but" that inevitably follows. I hold my breath as he continues. "When I went out to Colorado I had a chance to see my friends, and really think about things for a few days. And in my soul-searching I realized two things: one, that I really care for you, and two, that idea scares me." His words settle me momentarily. They don't include the "but" that I was expecting, but now I'm at a loss for what comes next. What about Lela?

"Ok," I say, prompting him to continue.

"And then two more things happened. My ex-girlfriend, Leland, was also on the skiing trip." *Oh, fuck. Here we go.* I swallow hard. "I didn't want her to be there, but she's still friends with these people too, and I didn't think it was my place to say she couldn't come." He lets out a deep exhale and I can barely breathe. *I knew it. They're back together. Get to the point. Please. Now.* Every second that he waits I create the worst possible scenario in my head, and by now they've undressed each other and she's licking his balls in my brain.

"I feel like such an ass even telling you this, but I don't want to lie to you about anything." Jack looks deep in my eyes and I see the concern and pain that he's harboring inside.

"It's ok." *Must. Remain. Calm. And get his balls out of your mouth, you slut!* I slap the wench in my vision.

Jack's eyes move down to his wine glass. *Oh, God, he can't even look at me when he says this part.* "Well she was really flirty with me and I brushed her off most of the time, but we were both very drunk one night and, well, we kissed." Jack looks back up at me with his brow furrowed and shame dripping off of him. He watches for my response, but I don't even know what to say to that. Is he telling me it's over?

"So that's what I heard." I pause. "On the phone that night. That's why she answered the phone. You rekindled things." I squeak out the words, unable to fully verbalize their reconnection.

He shakes his head slowly. "No. Not exactly. I'm really sorry that happened. It didn't mean anything to me. Really." He goes silent and looks away again, taking a sip of his wine as his expression appears remorseful.

So there it is. He did make out with his ex-girlfriend. Asshole. The idea of them together punches me in the gut, even though it simply confirms what I already knew.

"You're being really quiet."

"I didn't think you had finished your thought," I prompt him, unsure of where to take this.

"Jess, I know this isn't how you wanted to hear this, but kissing her—well, it made me realize something." He pauses, locking his eyes in mine, and letting out a sigh. "That I love you." My heart stops to contemplate this revelation, and I feel myself wanting to believe him. The words repeat again and again in my brain, and my paused heartbeat begins to flutter rapidly. *He loves me?*

"Baby, I care about you. So much. And I'm sorry for the stupid mistake I made, and for making you feel like you were an afterthought to me. That was never the case." Jack's hand reaches over and grabs mine. That same pull between us hasn't changed at all, and now feels even stronger than ever. I pull my fingers around his, letting him know that I feel the same way.

Does this mean he's thinking of us having a future together? What about my own transgression? Do I come clean about Max? He was honest with me after all. But would that really do me any good? Or would that ruin any chance we have of working things out? I know that it was a stupid circumstantial mistake, so is it really worth the trouble it could cause? I find myself so lost in thought, staring at the fire, that I don't realize Jack is staring into me, awaiting a reaction.

"Jess, I missed you so much."

"Me, too," I respond honestly, without filtering my emotions. Jack moves toward me in a quick, swift movement. He reaches his hand behind my head, his fingers sliding through my hair. His grip tightens, pulling me, needing me, wanting me. I lift my hand to his cheek and stroke his smooth skin gently. I take in his familiar scent and feel the pull of him deep, deep inside of me. Our eyes are locked and we speak without words. Somehow we both know that all is forgiven, and that we both need each other.

Jack leans into me, breaking the gaze, and plants his sweet lips onto mine. My body tightens, unable to control the feelings from deep inside of me. My tongue meets his and I begin to melt away. The lustful pulses shoot like lightning bolts throughout me, and I reach my hands to his face and begin stroking his smooth skin. He moves his arms around me, and I feel his strength as his arms tighten and pull me closer into him. His succulent lips pull at mine, with gentle but passionate nips and nibbles.

My body sits close to him now and I shift my arms around his neck. *God, I want him.* I force myself to pull my lips away from his magnetic draw, giving us both a chance to catch our breath. I rest my head on his shoulder and hold him tightly, relishing in his strong, loving arms that hold me. We sit there quietly for a moment, unable to see each other, tied up closely in our embrace. After a minute or so goes by, Jack releases me just enough so that I can pull my body from his. He takes my hands and gives them a squeeze while looking me straight in the eye. His face turns into a saddened smile before he finally speaks. "I missed you, Jess." He pauses with a serious face. "I'm not usually one to admit this, but I was crushed this past week. You've cast some kind of spell on me."

I squeeze his hands back, grateful for the reassurance. "I missed you." As I mutter these words I think back to all of the mistakes I've made. Those that Jack doesn't even know about but that do still fill me with guilt.

"I need you, Jess. Don't leave me." He pulls my arm, forcing me to get closer to him, and his sweet vulnerability draws me in.

"I'm here. I'm yours," I whisper into his ear and then lean over his horizontal body and place my lips on his. He pulls my hair, wrenching my body and my desires. He quickly unbuttons my pants, and I tear at his. I lower my hovering body and he slides right into me. We let out a simultaneous groan into each other's mouths as he fills me completely. I pull my chest upright so I can see his face and the pleasure plastered across it while I move my body. My arousal continues to grow with each slow churn of my hips, and my eyes focus on his. Our gaze connects us further, elevating this sexual act to a sensual connection.

My sweet, vulnerable Jack, finally exposing his soul, and now revealing his raw sexiness with each thrust of his body. His hands slide easily underneath my shirt and his fingers climb their way up to my waist. He guides my hips, controlling the movement and speed. Faster. And faster. And even faster I grind against him, causing the sensation deep inside me to build with each movement. Jack lifts my blouse over my head, leaving me exposed, save my bra.

He slides his finger inside the lacy fabric, scooping out my breast for his viewing pleasure. I lean my chest down to kiss him again, hungrily nibbling on his plump lips. I pull back up to resume my speed and Jack swiftly unhooks my bra, fully exposing my ample upper curves. He gently guides my chest forward so that I lean into him, but this time I bend straighter so that his sweet lips have direct access to my perched nipples. His tongue is the first sensation that I feel. He gently sucks on my nipple, pulling it harder and forcing a moan to slip out of my mouth. I slowly move my hips back and forth, causing him to slide in and out. And in. And out. Nice and slow, allowing my orgasm to build with each slow stroke invigorating my clitoris. He switches to my other breast, and I groan again at the sensation on this neglected part. I continue sliding back and forth against him until my explosion rises against my control. My body clenches in preparation and I pull Jack's face to mine, finding my release as my tongue slides into his mouth. His arms clench around me, pulling me in tighter to him, and as we kiss sweetly I feel him let go into me.

CHAPTER NINETEEN

"You ready?" Jack asks me, giving my hand a reassuring squeeze as we walk outside of the small, but clean, Portland airport. Maine's fresh air and sunshine greet us as we wait outside for Jack's brother.

"Yeah, a little nervous I guess," I say honestly, while smoothing the wrinkles in my navy and white cotton dress.

"You have nothing to be nervous about. My family will love you as much as I do." Jack leans in and gives me a sweet kiss, weakening my knees as his soft lips meet mine. I kiss him back with an equally love-filled kiss. My feelings for him have grown even stronger since our misadventures, his kiss with Lela, and my sloppy semi-whoreness with Mr. Lust. In just three weeks we've gone from almost never speaking again to me joining him on his trip home to meet his family and celebrate his brother's engagement. It feels a bit fast, but for once it feels so right.

"Hey, get a room!" Jack pulls his lips from mine and turns toward the approaching car. A preppy, almost twin-like version of Jack jumps from an open-air jeep to greet us. My face reddens from our overt PDA, not exactly the first impression I was looking to make with Jack's family.

"Wells!" Jack calls to his near Irish twin, the two separated in age by only fourteen months. Their identical builds, similar broad features, and sparkling blue eyes easily confirm they share DNA. The only visible difference is the shaggier, blonder, and wavier hair that Wells sports, compared to Jack's shorter, ashier blond locks.

"Hey, man." Jack gives an excited hug to his big brother.

"This must be the one and only Jess!" Wells wraps me in a warm embrace, helping me to instantly feel welcome.

"Great to meet you! And congratulations. I've heard only great things about Gabby," I say.

"Thanks, yeah we're excited. Come on. Mom and Dad are eager to meet the girl that's got our Jack so smitten. And so quickly!" Wells's comment unsettles me a little. I know things with Jack are moving fast, but are they too fast? Can a love that develops this fast really be the real thing?

The jeep navigates the picturesque streets of South Portland, and the fresh ocean air rejuvenates me for the task at hand: meeting who could become my future in-laws. *Slow down, Jess. Who do you think you are, Mom and Dad?* I shudder away the thought of their six-month courtship turned decades-long tumultuous and adulterous relationship. That's not what I want. Not with Jack, not with anyone. I want love. True, unconditional love. And for once, I'm starting to believe I might not only deserve it, but that I've found it.

We stop in front of a large, stunning, Hamptons-style home. The two-story blue home is covered with cedar shingles, and welcomes guests with a grand, circular, pebble driveway with a perfectly sculpted line of boxwoods. It's no surprise that Jack and his seemingly perfect family have a perfect house, too.

Mrs. Clarke is the first to greet us, and she quickly jumps from her perch on their oversized yet welcoming front porch. Her smile is as infectious as Jack's, wide and happy. She wears little makeup, and her dark hair falls to her chin framing her round face and brilliantly blue eyes. She wears cropped white pants and a warm red linen sweater, looking very beachy chic.

"Oh, such a wonderful sight, my two precious boys together again! It's been too long," she gushes as she gets sandwiched in a hug by her loving sons. "And Jess, we are just so thrilled to have you here. We've heard so much about you, dear." She wraps me in a warm hug hello, as a handsome, gray-haired man emerges. He carries a strong build similar to his sons', and his smiling eyes match the shade of his hair.

"It's lovely to be here. Thank you so much for having me, Mrs. Clarke." I return her hug, grateful for the warm, loving welcome.

"Don't be silly, dear, please call me Annie."

"Thank you, Annie."

"And please call me Alan," Jack's father says as he wraps me in a kind hug hello. "It's certainly better than what these knuckleheads call me!" He releases a jolly laugh and escorts me inside their beautiful home.

The serene view of Casco Bay captivates my attention, distracting me for a moment from the engagement party that surrounds me. I rest my champagne on the edge of the balcony, breathing in the salty air. I imagine Jack as a boy, growing up in this beautiful home, with breathtaking scenery and a family that loved him so obviously, so unconditionally. *God, he's so lucky.* I think of my own childhood, spent in an equally beautiful home, surrounded by a lush golf course, but filled with anxiety and self-doubt. It's apparent from watching Jack and Wells interact with their parents the last few days how "normal" their family is. They have fun together, like spending time together, and are even capable of filling time with meaningful conversation.

"There's my beautiful date," Jack's voice sings into my ears as he wraps an arm around me, joining my viewing party.

"Hi," I gush at him. He looks unbelievably preppy cute in his white and blue seersucker pants and complementary blue polo. His tan leather shoes are woven and airy, perfect for this warm spring air.

"Who are you hiding from? Better not be me." Jack smiles, giving me a squeeze.

"No, just my other boyfriend," I tease him.

"Oh yeah? You must work quickly. You've only been in Maine for forty-eight hours. Is he here? Let's give him a show!" Jack grabs me and dips me backward into a full-on kiss. I can't help but feel that pull for him as our lips meet. We haven't had much alone time since arriving here, given his parents' traditional ways and our separate bedrooms. I kiss him back hard, and begin to get lost into him, before remembering where we are. I give his hand a squeeze as it creeps down my cobalt silk dress, not wanting to put on a show, or steal it from the betrothed couple.

"Jackie." I hear the sound of an ageing voice and my eyes pop open as my cheeks fill with scarlet embarrassment.

"Papa!" Jack pulls his arms from me to wrap them around who I assume is his grandfather. His face fills with pride as he introduces me. "Papa, this is my beautiful girlfriend, Jess," he boasts, filling me with even more admiration for him.

"Beautiful indeed. Now, Jess, come give an old man a proper hello." He extends his arms toward me too and places his line-filled lips on each of my cheeks. I can instantly see some of Jack in him, from the sparkling blue eyes, still filled with so much life, to the practically identical seersucker pants and blazer. Preppiness must run in this family!

"Lovely to meet you," I pause, unsure of what to call him, "Mr. Clarke".

"No, no, you call me Papa. Now Jess, come, let's get to know each other, I think you could use a glass of champagne." *Yes, please.* A little more liquid courage always helps to sedate the social anxiety that worms into my brain.

I follow Papa's lead to the bar and join him for another drink. Scotch is his poison, but I stick with the celebratory bubbles. I'm eager to get to know this seemingly sweet old man. Having grown up without grandparents, I've never had much interaction with the greatest generation. I learn that Papa's name is Wellsley, hence the derivation of Jack's older brother's name. Papa is a Vietnam veteran, who spent years flying for the Navy before coming here to complete law school, and eventually retiring in serene Portland, Maine. He spent decades proudly growing his business before fully retiring less than a decade ago and handing the reigns over to Jack's father.

"Papa, you're not trying to steal my girl away from me, are you?" Jack approaches us a half hour into our conversation.

"Watch your back, Jackie," he teases him. "This girl is filled with southern charm. I can see why you like her so much." Papa gives me a wink and playfully wraps his arm around my shoulder to tease Jack.

"He was just catching me up on his life story, and the amazing law firm he built from nothing. And, of course, the family he had and raised in this lovely town," I compliment Papa and watch Jack's broad smile fade into bitterness with my words.

My confusion grows as I hear Jack's tongue sharpen. "Jesus, Papa, are you now shaming my girlfriend into convincing me to come back? I thought we talked about this," Jack snaps at him.

"No, son. I said no such thing, I was respecting our agreement, but now that you've brought it up maybe I should set things straight." I watch Papa rise to his feet and can sense the blood beginning to rage through each man's veins.

"Everything ok?" Wells approaches hand-in-hand with Gabby, his beautiful and exotic-looking fiancée. Her olive skin, dark hair, and chocolate eyes come straight from her Cuban roots. And her tiny but curvy frame makes me beyond envious, but her genuine heart makes her impossible not to adore. After just a day together we've become fast friends, and I can see by the concerned look on her face she knows where this conversation is going before I do.

"Yeah, fine," Jack grumbles, looking away as he takes a long draw of scotch.

"No, it's not fine," Papa barks, and I watch Alan's ears perk up from a nearby conversation. He excuses himself to quickly join us.

"Dad, come on. Now's not the time," Alan cajoles his father.

"Damn it, Alan. It's never the time. Why can't someone explain to me why the business I built with my own two hands isn't good enough for my spoiled grandson?" *Oh.* I swallow hard, beginning to piece this together.

"Papa, come on. This isn't about you. It's about me wanting to have a different life. Why can't you understand that?" Jack questions him.

"Why can't *you* understand? That I laid the path for your father, and then Wells and you. This is our family's legacy and you're turning your back on it. You said it was just college. And then you chose business school instead of law school. All for what? Some extra money and a southern girl? No offense, Jess. I think you're a lovely girl, but so was Lela. It just seems nothing is good enough for this boy. Don't let him lead you on like he did her." My breath escapes me, and I suddenly feel sick and weak. Lela. How the hell did she get into this conversation? And what did he do to her? I watch Papa storm away, and Jack turns and throws his near-empty tumbler over the deck into the dark beachy sky.

"Son, come on." Alan escorts Jack with his arm around his shoulder, pulling him away for a "calm down and don't fuck up your brother's party" chat. Gabby watches me, her face filled with concern, and mouths "are you ok?" *Am I ok? I don't know. Am I? How could I be?*

"Jess, Gabby, why don't we get a drink over here," Annie says, swooping in to quickly diffuse the remains of the situation. I force one foot in front of the other as my head spins about me. Almost instantly Annie gets pulled away by a party guest, so Gabby sweetly grabs my hand and pulls me further away from the crowd. We sit on the steps of the back deck, close enough to the ocean to take in the soft sound of crashing waves.

"So I can tell by your expression that Jack may not have briefed you on the, um, situation with his grandfather."

"You can safely assume that." I shrug, processing all of this new information. "I guess I knew that he had branched out, and wanted to do something different than his family. But I didn't know it had caused such a rift. And then Lela"—I pause, feeling my heart weaken as her name leaves my lips— "what did he do to her? I mean it can't be good if Papa says he did her wrong."

"Well, um, what has Jack told you about her?" Gabby asks, her soft eyes filled with concern, but I can see she's balancing giving me the candor of a friend with her loyalty to her soon-to-be family.

"I know about their relationship. That they dated for a long time. And I presumed it was serious, or at least not insignificant since they were together for so long." *And that he kissed her last month on his ski trip, we basically broke up because of it but I decided to forgive him. Stupidly, now it seems.* I leave out these last details, not wanting to tarnish her opinion of our relationship. "But why would his grandfather care so much about their relationship?"

"Well, Jack may not have let on how serious they were. They were engaged. Well, sort of anyway." These words hit me so hard in the stomach I nearly puke on perfect Gabby in her bridal-looking white eyelet dress. *Oh, God. Why wouldn't he have told me that? Maybe he's not over her. I'm just his attempt to move away from his past. His forced attempt to have roots in the south, prove his family wrong that he can make his own career, and find his own life. And love for that matter.*

"No, I didn't know that. Oh, God, I feel like such an idiot." I choke back a sob, not wanting to become a hysterical basket case in front of Jack's family.

"Jess, no. Gosh, I'm just making things worse. There was never a proposal, or a ring, or anything like that." I sniffle and choke back another tear, now feeling more confused than ever. "It was expected. Assumed. By all of us. Lela's parents practically grew up with Annie and Alan. It was Papa and Grandma Kate that were dear friends with Lela's grandparents. Papa and her grandfather fought together in the war, and both came back here together afterward. It was the closest thing you could have to an arranged marriage these days. And once they had been dating for that long everyone assumed, and I think the parents and grandparents hoped, that they would get married and settle down here."

These words crush me and do nothing except confirm that I'm his rebound girl. The rebellious escape from his predetermined fate.

"I still feel like an idiot." This time I can't stop the sob, and I feel the warm tear roll down my cheek.

"Jess, sweetheart, are you ok?" Annie sneaks up on us, and I'm mortified to be caught crying.

"I'm so sorry, Annie," I apologize, jumping to my feet. "I just need a minute, I'll be fine." I try to attempt a smile, but I know it's not fooling anyone.

"Gabby, honey, do you mind giving us a quick minute?" Annie asks.

"Of course. Jess, I'm here if you need me." Gabby gives me a sweet squeeze as she walks away.

"Well, well, what a mess you've walked into tonight." Annie's eyes are soft and concerned, mirroring her sincere tone. "I'm guessing Jack may not have shared with you everything that he left behind here." I simply shake my head no, knowing that words will only come with more tears. "Alan and I have never forced anything on Jack. Not his choice of college, or career, or even who he should date. But I can't say the same about Alan's father. It's his pride, dear. You can understand how a man that spent decades building a legacy and foundation for his family would want them to honor it and appreciate it. And I know Jack does, but he's always been a bit different. We always knew that he might go a different route, and while we would love if he lived closer to us we truly only want him to be happy." I nod, acknowledging her words.

"And most importantly we want him to have true love. I'm sure you have questions about Lela, and I can say she is a lovely girl. And yes, her parents and grandparents will always be dear friends of ours. But that doesn't mean that Jack should, or would, end up with her. She didn't make him happy, dear. I think he tried for so long because of us. But I think he knew in his heart that they weren't right together. It was that missing sparkle, and it was something that I haven't seen with him until now. He has that with you, Jess. I can see how much you mean to him, how happy you make him. So don't let any of this nonsense disrupt your courtship. I can see a great future for you and Jack."

I want to believe her words, and the hopeful remains of my heart do. But she doesn't know the rest of the story, what happened last month. If he knew they weren't meant to be, and the spark was gone, then why did he risk our relationship for a dumb kiss? *And why did I run into Mr. Lust in New York? And practically sleep with him?*

These thoughts startle me. I've managed to push him far back into my brain, and now here I sit, having a heart to heart with Jack's mother, and Mr. Lust pops into my head.

"Annie, thank you. For your kind words, and your amazing hospitality. I can truly see where Jack gets his good nature from." I force another smile and hug the woman who hours ago I thought

Lost

could be my future mother-in-law. Now I can only wonder, will that day ever come? My heart aches at the thought of losing Jack, his love, and his wonderful family, save his selfish Papa. But where do we go from here?

CHAPTER TWENTY

"Happy wedding day!" I yell cheerfully at Meredith, giving her a hug hello as I walk into the beautiful St. Regis hotel.

"Hiii! So glad you're here. I was afraid everyone would be running behind," she says, already sporting a bridal glow. Her white sleeveless dress has a high cut v, and she wears a pink cardigan over her shoulders.

"I am absolutely starving. This brunch better be delicious," Emma says, still fighting her hangover.

"It's the St. Regis. Has it ever not been delicious?" I retort.

"Ok, true. Let's hope their fancy menu doesn't discriminate against my needs."

"And what exactly are those needs today? It is all about *you* today after all." Emma glares back at me when she hears the sarcasm in my voice.

"French fries, hash browns, or really anything covered in grease and sure to absorb the liquor from last night."

"No wonder you work out so much," I say with a laugh as we make our way up the beautiful dark wood staircase. Just around the corner at the top of the stairs sits a long table, decorated with beautiful light gray tablecloths and light blue flowers. Waiters roam the crowd of women: the mother of the bride, mother of the groom, aunts, grandmothers, and bridesmaids. It's the perfect gathering of family and friends to celebrate our beautiful friend's wedding day.

"Can I offer you a glass of champagne? Or a mimosa?" A friendly waitress approaches us as we make our way into the party area.

"A mimosa would be great, thank you," I order. I too indulged a bit too much last night, thanks to a mix of open bar and relationship anxiety. After last weekend's events in Maine I have more questions than ever for Jack, but bridesmaid duties have sucked up all of my time this week, not allowing the opportunity for a meaningful or productive discussion with Jack.

"Hey, girls!" Meredith's mother comes over and gives us a cheerful hello, followed by hugs.

"Hey, Eleanor! Are you excited for today?"

"Oh, yes. I am so excited! You know we just love Cale, and I think the wedding has come together just perfectly!" she says excitedly with her sweet, southern drawl. "And Meredith just has the most beautiful bridesmaids and wonderful friends. I know she's just overjoyed to have you girls stand up there with her today." Oh, sweet Mrs. Andrews. Meredith was undoubtedly blessed with her mother's optimism and positive attitude. I've always wondered what it would be like to have a mother who was that way. Mother would probably spend my wedding day fat-shaming me, or finding some other way to make the day all about her.

My thoughts turn to the impending arrival of my parents. I haven't seen them in months, despite them living just an hour away, and I feel guilty when I realize how much I'm dreading it. Things with Jack are a bit tenuous, at least in my mind, until we have a chance to talk. Plus, I wouldn't normally want to introduce a boyfriend to my parents this soon, but since they'll be at the wedding tonight and Jack is my date, there's really no way out of it.

The rest of brunch is filled with laughter and fun, and ends just in time for us to head to the ceremony.

"Ok, I'll see you all at the church shortly!" Meredith says excitedly as she and her mom leave the brunch.

"We're right behind you Mere!" Emma says.

"I'm going to run into the bathroom and then I'll meet you downstairs?"

"Ok, see you in a few."

As I approach the top of the stairs and begin my descent, I see Emma in the lobby speaking to someone. As I take a few more stairs, being careful not to let my oversized heels wobble me over, I realize she's talking to my parents. *Oh, fuck me. What are they doing here? I thought I could avoid them until tonight.* I take a deep breath, force a smile to form on my lips, and join them.

"Jessica, don't you look lovely," my sweet daddy says, giving me a squeeze hello.

"Thanks, Dad. What are you doing here?" I question him, assuming I wouldn't see them until the reception later tonight.

"I had some business to handle up here, and your mother is never one to turn down a shopping day in the city. So we decided to get a room for the night, and she's having a spa visit tomorrow before we head home."

"Oh, how nice. So where's Mother now?" The smile fades from my mouth as I say her name, and I peer around the lobby, catching a glimpse of her shiny blonde hair near the concierge. She catches my eye, waving back at me. Great, guess our reunion won't be waiting until tonight. My plan had been to distract her this evening by introducing her to Jack, thus pushing her focus on him rather than allowing her to pick at me.

"Come say hello," Daddy says, seeing Mother gesturing us over.

"We have to be quick, ok? We're on our way to the church."

"Of course," he says leading us over to her.

"Sorry," I say quietly to Emma as we walk over.

She smiles back, knowing all too well of my tenuous relationship with my mother. "Don't worry about it, Jess, we'll be quick," she says reassuringly, giving my arm a squeeze.

I force my posture to straighten and suck in my belly in hopes of minimizing the judgmental looks from her. "Hi, Mom," I say, forcing a smile for the woman who gave me life. "We just wanted to say a quick hello, we're off to the church."

"There's my girl!" She gives me a hug that would seem warm and genuine to anyone on the outside, except me, who knows her all too well.

"Emma, dear, don't you look lovely. And so fit!" She gives my friend a hello, and can't resist the opportunity to slight me. Not that Emma doesn't look great, but Mother only ever notices additions to my weight. Of course, being that I inherited daddy's side of the family's curves, I will only ever be fat in her eyes.

"Thank you. It's nice to see you both," Emma responds politely. "But we do have to run, can't hold up the wedding! We'll see you shortly?"

"Yes, of course. You girls run along, can't keep a bride waiting!"

I start reeling as soon as we step away. Why do I always feel like shit around her? Even after a simple sixty-second conversation I feel slighted by her lack of compliment for me when she finds it so easy to give one to Emma. Is she that calculated? Or just that disappointed in me?

The valet pulls my car up just as we reach the hotel entrance. "Thank you," I say to the young man as I hand him a tip. I glance at the black Mercedes that has just stopped in front of me, waiting for the passenger's exit so I can depart. I pull up Waze while I wait, looking for the quickest route to the church.

As my eyes return to the windshield, my pulse fades. *This can't be happening.* I do a double take. *What is he doing here? Is it really him?*

I blink, processing his arrival and the situation. I can't exactly go talk to him, I'm already running late to my friend's wedding, and I'm sitting here with Emma, who knows nothing of my, um, adventures with Mr. Lust. But God, just seeing him takes me back to that place, and the feelings I had for him. *Have for him?*

He straightens his jacket as he waits for his luggage from the car. He turns toward my car and my heart stops. His stare is blank for a moment, and I watch his dazzling eyes blink before his mouth turns into his lust-worthy smile.

CHAPTER TWENTY-ONE

The angle of the sun through the stunning stained glass windows makes the perfect backdrop for this beautiful spring wedding day. Just like in the movies, the big doors swing open, and the organ begins piping "Canon in D". We all stand silently in the line, peeking into the older but classically styled church, framed with dark wood and tall windows, all softened by the white floral arrangements throughout. We stand in order of height: Emma, Meredith's younger sister Kelly, me, and Callie, waiting our turn to begin the march down the aisle. I watch as Emma's tall, model-like figure flows easily through the crowd, smiling at the photographer as she strides. I glance back at Meredith, her face reflecting her steady but excited demeanor. I catch her eye and give her a big smile before the wedding planner nods me in. I begin my stroll, focused on Kelly's speed to ensure we stay the appropriate distance apart.

The pews are filled with smiling faces, many familiar to me due to our decades of friendship. I spy my parents sitting on the bride's side and daddy gives me a cute nod when our eyes meet. Mother smiles at me too, but her eyes seem to judge more than laud. I immediately adjust my posture, pushing my shoulders back and raising my chin upward. These dresses are not the most forgiving on a curvy figure like mine, especially since I have to stand next to my model-like friends on display. I refocus my eyes ahead and see my wonderful Jack sitting, watching me in the crowd. He smiles brightly to me, and I glow with admiration of him, appreciative of his eagerness to come alone to a wedding ceremony to support me, and his willingness to meet my parents so early in our relationship.

I join my friends on the altar, and within a few seconds Callie makes it safely down the aisle and stands next to me. Meredith steps forward into view, and I whirl my head toward Cale. The best part of a wedding is undoubtedly watching the groom's face when he sees his blushing bride appear before him. His nervous expression softens, and his eyes lock onto her. Meredith flows easily down the aisle, her broad smile gleaming, her hair perfectly shaped into a low bun, accented with large curls pinned into an almost flower shape. Her deep V-neck silk dress hugs her tiny frame from top to bottom, just until it widens into a small train at her feet. Behind her cascades a cathedral-length veil, and in her hands a bouquet of white roses with a hint of greenery. She makes it to the altar and her face is calm, confident, but her broad smile makes her excitement impossible to hide. When she finally takes Cale's hand at the altar, I watch him let out a deep sigh. The love between them is undeniable, and I take the moment into my memory, hoping that one day I too will walk down the aisle as confident as they are, knowing that I want nothing more than to publicly commit my life and love to someone else for all eternity. I imagine Jack as my groom one day, but my heart quickly aches at the idea of him having a happily ever after with Lela.

Stop it, Jess! You know you love Jack. And he says he loves you. Don't poison your relationship without validation. I decide to believe my innermost conscious, at least for the moment. I know my chat with

Jack has to happen, and soon. *Really, even though you were drooling at the vision of Max a few hours ago?*

Following the bride and groom's lead, we once again make our way down the aisle; this time each bridesmaid is escorted by one of Cale's groomsmen. We whirl past the guests before I can get a glimpse of Jack in the crowd, so I wait for him in the hallway just outside the cathedral.

"Hello, sweetheart," Daddy says, giving me a warm squeeze as he and mother approach me outside of the cathedral.

"You girls made for such a beautiful wedding party. And these bridesmaids dresses she picked are so nice. Where are they from?" Mother asks me with feigned innocence, before sliding her finger into the back of my dress, a familiar attempt to check the size of what I'm wearing. I watch as her eyebrows raise, the telltale sign of her seeing the horrific and shameful number 8 on the tag. I almost open my mouth to justify my size. To tell her that everyone orders a size or two up in bridesmaids dresses because they notoriously run small, and that I even had it taken in to fit me better. Before my lips open I see Jack approaching us from behind. *Oh no, here we go. Time to meet the parents.*

"Hey, you made it through the ceremony," I say, smiling to Jack as he approaches. I hesitate for a moment unsure of how to greet him. It's too awkward to lay a big kiss on him in front of my parents, so instead I gently grab his arm and pull him toward me.

"Mom, Dad, this is Jack." Jack reaches his hand out confidently.

"Hi, Jack. Daniel Bauer, pleasure to meet you." Daddy extends his hand outward and I spy mother scanning him, judging everything from the cut of his suit and the polish of his shoes to the blue sparkle in his eye. Her level expression shifts into a slight smile and it seems he's gotten the first impression stamp of approval.

"Hi, Jack, I'm Emily Bauer, nice to see you." She takes her delicate hand and places it into his for a limp looking shake.

"Nice to meet you both." Jack flashes his all-American smile back at them both, and I notice how his dark blue tie brings out the deep blue of his eyes. I allow myself to be proud for a slight moment, happy to have him standing by my side as my cute, well-dressed boyfriend, who I've really fallen for.

"So, Jack, I hear you're new to Atlanta. How long have you been living here?" Mother asks him.

"It's been about six months now, I'm finally starting to learn my way round the city."

"And where are you living, Jack?" *Uh oh, here she goes again.* I hope that Jack is oblivious to her prying, trying to gauge his status from what part of town he lives in.

"I actually bought a house in Buckhead, about ten minutes away from here."

"Oh, lovely. You're in a great part of town," she acknowledges, and I once again see through her pointed questioning.

"Yeah, it's a great location, close to work, and not too far from Jess's place." He slides his arm around me and I watch mother's lip twitch upward, into a nearly approving smile.

"Jess, we've got to go," Emma says, walking toward us.

"Ok, I'll see you guys at the reception, we have to head over for wedding party pictures. See you shortly?" Jack nods and releases his hold on me, sliding his hand down my arm, and pausing to squeeze my hand affectionately before letting me go. I feel bad leaving him there with my parents, defenseless to my mother's questions, but he seems to be handling it well, so we head off on our way.

"Ladies and gentlemen, please come to your feet to help me welcome the new couple, Mr. and Mrs. Caleb Michaels!" Applause rolls through the ballroom, everyone eager to celebrate the happy bride and groom. The wedding party surrounds the dance floor, ensuring they have a cheering section for their first dance. The music begins to play to "It's Your Love," one of Tim McGraw's sweet ballads, a perfect fit for the southern-rooted marriage. Cale whirls Meredith around the dance floor effortlessly, and a happy smile settles on my face. There's nothing better than seeing a dear friend so perfectly happy, except maybe being that happy myself.

After a few minutes the song comes to a close and we all cheer, happy that they made it through without faltering, but even happier because it means bridesmaid duties are done. I secure myself a glass of champagne, and turn back toward the ballroom. Just a few feet away is my handsome boyfriend, making his way toward me. "Hi," he greets me cheerily. "Do I finally get you to myself for a minute?" Jack asks, smiling broadly. "It's been torture watching you but not being able to get my hands on you. And in this dress..." Jack lets out a sound, somewhat of a cross between a sigh and a groan, showcasing his desire for me. I can't help but giggle and be lured in by his reaction. He pulls me in close to him and I slide my arms around his neck, forgetting about the public space we're in. The thought of my parents' presence flashes through my mind and I almost pull myself away, but the closeness to his lips draws me in. I'm desperate to have his feelings affirmed after last week, and his mouth isn't a bad place to start. He plants a hard but sweet kiss firmly on my lips and pulls my body closer into his by grabbing my hips more tightly. I can feel him pressing into me through his pants, and I'm immediately aroused just by knowing that he is.

"There you are!" Mother's voice sharply interrupts us, and I immediately blush at having been caught in our PDA. I awkwardly shift away from him and extract a fake smile from my ass to my face.

"Where are you sitting?" she asks us.

"I was just wondering that myself," Jack says coolly.

"We have a spot at the main table, Meredith wanted us all sitting there with her," I explain, willing the redness to leave my cheeks. I notice Jack sneakily adjust himself in his pants when Mother turns toward me, and I have to trap my giggle so that I don't give him and his excitement away. "Where are you and Daddy sitting?"

"Over there, near the other bar. We're with Emma and Callie's parents. It's lovely to see them all and catch up." She turns back toward Jack. "Speaking of catching up, I need to spend more time with you, my dear, so I can get to know why my Jess is so crazy about you." She winks at me. "Perhaps a dance later?"

"I would love that. Especially if it means I get to hear how crazy she is about me." Jack and mother have a good laugh, and I take a long drink of champagne, enjoying the small victory: escaping an interaction with Mother sans insult or embarrassment.

"Jess! So what's the plan for later tonight? Are we all going out? Grabbing a drink anywhere?" Emma catapults questions at me, her buzzed state helping her to become very chatty very quickly. "We could go to the St. Regis bar, some of the guys mentioned that earlier. Thought it could be fun since we're all dressed up."

"Oh, um, I haven't really thought about it." Or about *him*—until now that is. Truthfully, and amazingly, I haven't. I've been having such a wonderful time with Jack this evening that I even managed to get the surprise of seeing Mr. Lust out of my mind. But now the thought of the St. Regis…would I see him there? I do know his propensity to hang out at hotel bars…his chiseled face and amazing allure slide into my brain. I ponder this more and realize that if we see Max, he and Jack will inevitably chit chat. He wouldn't possibly tell Jack about our little rendezvous in New York. W*ould he?* Better safe than sorry, I decide. "I don't know, Emma, I'm not sure I'm feeling the St. Regis tonight."

"Hey, beautiful," Jack woos me, wiggling up behind me and planting his lips on my cheek. "So what's the plan?"

"Emma and I were just talking about options—"

"How about the St. Regis?" Jack chimes in immediately.

"Yes! See, Jess. It's decided then. Two against one," Emma laughs.

"Is that ok with you, babe? We thought it would be fun, and I know some of the out-of-town groomsmen are staying there tonight so it's convenient for them." I quickly look for a plausible excuse to avoid the swanky bar.

"It's just kind of expensive, I was just trying to be a little more frugal after all of these wedding expenses," I lie, not about the need for frugality, but about the other reason for my hoped aversion.

"Well, luckily I know someone who loves and adores you that will gladly buy you drinks all night. Although I might need something in return." He gives me a naughty glance and I feel myself drawn in. My mind and body do need to be reassured of his feelings for me.

"St. Regis it is!" Emma announces. "That will be convenient in case you two need a room," she teases us, leaving us for a quiet moment together.

"Jack," I start, unsure if this is the right time to bring up the Maine situation. "I'm hoping we can talk about some stuff later."

"Ok," he lets out a half laugh, "that's specific. Everything ok?"

"I hope so. Just want to talk about some stuff from last weekend."

"Sure, babe. But let's just have fun with our friends tonight and we can talk later? I have some things I want to talk about as well."

CHAPTER TWENTY-TWO

The St. Regis bar is crowded, completely packed with a young, attractive crowd who loudly chats, drinks, and parties the night away. The dark leather sofas and tan club chairs can barely be seen through the piles of people sitting on and around them. I spot the mural of a phoenix on the wall up ahead, an indication that the bar isn't too far away. My stomach is wrenched, wondering if Max might be here, and what Jack's chosen topic of discussion will be.

"So do you think they're here?" Emma questions me, looking around the room for our fellow wedding goers.

"Well they left just after we did, so I'm sure they'll come find us," I respond.

"Screw that. I'm going to look for them. Caleb's tallest groomsman is hot. What was his name? Ryan something? Oh, yeah! Ryan WantsAPieceOfEmma." She laughs loudly at herself and I can't help but giggle. She turns and walks away to begin her prowl, and despite my own drunkenness I notice that she's a bit wobbly. High heels and alcohol always seem to fight each other, yet ironically one always makes the other seem like an even better idea.

I turn my focus to my own handsome date. "I'm going to look for an open spot to sit since we've got a few more people coming. You mind grabbing us a drink?" I ask Jack.

"Sure, what do you want?"

"You know what I like. Surprise me."

"Sure, baby." Jack gives me a squeeze, then leans in to give me a swift kiss before walking away. I stand in the back-right corner near the far wall of the bar, inching my way through the crowded room.

"So how was the wedding?" The familiar, salty voice rings into my ears and I know that lusty Max is here. *Surprise, surprise. The international manwhore frequenting a hotel bar.* I'm instantly excited yet flustered by his presence.

"Hi," I stammer. "What are you doing here?" He quickly unnerves me as our eyes connect. He's dressed in a suit sans tie, and is freshly shaved, unlike many men who take the weekend off. His hair seems a bit longer now, his gentle dark waves easily tucked behind his ears. Even in the dark mood lighting he would make any woman swoon.

"Well, I'm staying in the hotel. And this here," he pauses, gesturing around us, "is called a bar, where they serve drinks. I have come for such a drink."

"What a surprise, you, in a hotel bar?" I instantly flirt with him, and guilt follows just as quickly. "How did you know I was at a wedding?"

"I am a detective, didn't you know?" He laughs at his own joke. My blank expression clues him that I missed the joke. "I saw your twins running around here." *Oh, I guess a flock of identically dressed bridesmaids are a dead giveaway.*

"What are you in town for?" I attempt to revert our conversation to a more casual tone.

"Business. Just here until tomorrow night. I didn't realize I would get to see both you and Jack. It's a nice surprise." He raises his eyebrows, and I'm immediately confused. Which of us was he expecting to see? "So you and Jack are still…friends?" It's apparent that Lust quickly did the math, realizing that if we are still together now, then we likely were during our rendezvous in New York.

I choose my words carefully. "We are together now, yes. We had a period when we were"—I pause looking for the right word—"apart." I don't want to relive the details of our semi-breakup, and how I technically was still with Jack when I nearly mounted him in the club.

"I see." His eyebrows raise again and then his expression changes suddenly into a smile. His eyes look past me, and I turn to see what has caught his eye.

"Jack. How are you?" Mr. Lust extends his hand out to my boyfriend, and I want to die caught here between these two men.

"Hey, good to see you made it. How is Atlanta treating you?" *Oh. So Jack was expecting to see him?*

"Atlanta is great. Lots of southern hospitality all around. And lots of beautiful women." Max smiles and gives me a subtle wink, one that only I would notice standing next to him in this dim room.

"I certainly can't complain about that." Jack gives my hand a squeeze. "Jess, I found us a table over there, want to find Emma?"

"Sure, see you there." I'm grateful for the opportunity to escape. Max's normal quiet mystique is notably absent, and his confident and flirty presence have an unbelievable ability to flap me, even in the presence of the man I love. As I leave them to chat, I silently pray that Max keeps his mouth shut about our past.

I find Emma at a corner table, set up with four chairs and a perfect view of the surrounding room, which will make it easy for us to spot our other friends.

"Did you find Ryan?"

"Who?" an overly buzzed Emma responds.

Lost

"The hot groomsman?"

"Oh, no." She immediately pouts. "He and his boyfriend went to Blake's."

I can't help but laugh. "Sorry, but you know that's the world we live in. All the good ones are taken, most of them by men!"

"I know. Maybe I'll get lucky and meet someone—" she pauses, mid-thought. "Umm, who is that?" I turn my head around and see Max and Jack chatting as they head toward our table.

"Oh, that's Max." I try to think of the most appropriate way to describe his relationship to me and Jack. "He and Jack work together." I leave it at the simple answer, knowing this isn't the time to consider opening up my deep, dark, slutty secret.

"Well good God, Jess, be a friend and introduce me. I mean holy shit is he hot."

I instantly fill with jealousy for the man who is not, and never has been, mine. "I will. But Emma, he's not really the boyfriend type. And he lives somewhere between New York and Paris. So just don't do something you'll regret."

"He looks like a mistake I'm more than willing to make." She laughs and I'm instantly en guard of what remains of my fantasy with him. *Why, Jess? You love Jack. Max is nothing more than a fantasy.* She hops from her chair and heads toward my man. *My men?*

"Hi, I'm Emma." She jumps to her feet before I even send a signal to my mouth to speak.

"Max. It's my pleasure." He extends his hand to hers, and I can see the effect he has on her. His not-so-subtle eye-fucking of her doesn't go unnoticed, either. *Slutty, slutty shitbag.*

"I hear this is your first time in Atlanta. Can I buy you a drink to welcome you?" she asks with a sweet, flirty face and an extra ounce of southern drawl in her words.

"No," he says sharply, leaving her expression hurt for a moment. "A lady never pays for a drink. Come." He winks at me and places his hand outward toward Emma, offering an escort to the bar. Her hand in his is enough to send my jealously soaring. *Simmer down, Jess.*

"Come here, beautiful," Jack says, approaching me. "Everything ok?" I realize my distress over the prospect of Emma stealing Max and having what could have once been my mind-blowing sexcapades must have my face twisted about.

"Yeah, it's great," I lie, replacing my jealousy with anxiety about our conversation that's yet to come.

CHAPTER TWENTY-THREE

A blonde waitress in her mid-thirties returns to our table and eyes our beautiful men. I follow her gaze for a moment while she politely waits for a break in the chatter to ask if we'd like another drink. She looks at Jack, and I watch him speaking. The sparkle of his blue eyes is hidden in the dim lighting, but his genuine laugh and smile shine through, making him as handsome as ever. His oversized features, big eyes and lips, fit perfectly into his larger, athletic frame, and his face fits perfectly together with his firm but not overly chiseled jawline. Max on the other hand is equally handsome, but has smaller features, and it's as if his pores just radiate sex appeal. It must be some combination of his liveliness, accent, and dark features, which are perfectly accentuated by his heart-shaped lips to make women swoon. And this waitress is no different.

Jack notices her lingering and pauses the conversation, turning to face her.

"Hey guys, can I grab you one last drink? It's last call, so make it a good one!" The guys look across at each other, gauging the other's interest in another round.

"I say why not enjoy the good company with a final drink?" Jack proposes.

"Well said. What should we have?" Max looks across at us. "Ladies, you decide."

"Champagne!" I blurt out without thinking of my history with said drink and present company.

Jack turns to me quizzically. "We've been drinking bourbon, Jess, not sure that Max will want to switch to bubbles." I catch Max smiling to himself, and I know he's remembering the night that we first met.

"I love champagne. It has many fond memories for me," Max recalls, giving me a glance.

"So one bottle of champagne?" the waitress confirms.

"Sounds good," Jack says, shrugging his shoulders.

The waitress departs, and I'm forced to watch Mr. Lust and Emma flirting across from me. "So you're really Italian?" I hear him ask Emma.

"Yes! Half. I can even speak Italian. Ciao!" she exclaims loudly.

Lust laughs at her unimpressive display. "Well, now I am truly convinced."

"You're a terrible liar!" She pushes him gently on the shoulder. The sight of her touching him makes my blood begin to boil. He's a completely different person with her. His normal mysterious demeanor is gone, he's all smiles and flirting with her. *Could this just be a show to make me jealous? Would he even care about doing so? Jess! Pay attention to your hot, sweet boyfriend and stop being a jealous friend.*

"Bathroom break?" Emma says to me, upon a rare pause in their conversation.

"Sure."

We wander into the beautiful, expansive marble bathroom and the girl talk ensues. "Oh. My. God. Jess, seriously is he not the hottest thing ever?" I try not to hit her, and remind myself that she has no idea about our past indiscretions.

"He is very handsome," I say with a slight smile.

"He's seriously like drop dead gorgeous. And those looks with that accent...wow." She looks back at me in the mirror and I look down to wash my hands, avoiding a response.

"So do you think he'll come home with me? Or ask me to stay? You know I have a three-date rule but he's totally worth breaking it, right?" Her voice gets high-pitched at the end of her thought, another sign of her inebriation.

"I just don't want you to do anything you'll regret, you know?" I say, trying to be a good friend and selfishly hoping that I'll steer her away from a sleepover.

"I know what you mean. But come on, I don't really think I'll regret that one!"

"Then just let it play out, I'm sure he'll make it obvious if he wants to hang out with you more."

"Yeah, you're right. I don't want to come on too strong," she says as we leave the bathroom.

We approach the table and the boys are chatting away while the last few patrons leave the bar. I realize that it's about to shut down and begin to fear what may or may not happen with them.

"We've had a great time with you tonight, Max," Jack says, signaling the close of the evening. "So glad you stopped in town, but it looks like we're going to be kicked out soon," he continues, nodding toward the circling hotel staff.

"I think you're right," Max acknowledges, coming to his feet. "If you're not ready to head home, I have a big suite with a balcony upstairs, you're all welcome to hang out there if you'd like."

"Yeah, that sounds fun!" Emma responds annoyingly quickly. Ugh, the thought of the two of them hanging out together alone is not something I want to deal with tonight. I'm drunk, tired, and have barely had time to process this whole Max and Jack being friends thing.

Jack clearly has plans of his own, though. "We appreciate the invite, but we should get going. You guys go enjoy it." He gives a little smile to Max, insinuating that we don't want to intrude on any alone time for him and Emma. *Fuck.* I can't reasonably argue with him. *Shit, Jack still must want to talk tonight. Is it about Maine? Lela?*

Jack climbs to his feet, indicating our imminent departure. He reaches his hand out to me, helping me to my feet, and Max stands to say goodbye.

"Hope that business brings you back here soon," Jack says, extending his hand.

"As do I. You've all been so kind to let me crash your evening. I'm now starting to understand the charm of the south."

"You have to watch out for these southern girls though. They aren't like any breed I've seen before," Jack says laughing.

Max chuckles and catches my eye. "I have no doubt these girls are full of surprises." He slides in a quick wink and then he and Jack shake hands goodbye. My eyes turn to Emma to see how she's going to play this. I stare at her for a moment but she refuses to catch my eye.

"Emma, did you want to ride back with us? We'll just catch a taxi out front." She pauses for a moment and looks to Max for reassurance.

"I think I might just hang out here for a bit." He smiles at the news. *Slutty, schmucky, fucking asshat.*

"Don't worry, Jess, I'll take good care of her and make sure she gets home safely." He smiles. "Nice to see you again, and thank you for letting me join you tonight." He extends his arms toward me and I realize he's going in for a hug. I lean into him and wrap my arms back around him. I breathe him in for the brief moment while I feel the lovely reminder of his closeness, only to quickly let him go.

CHAPTER TWENTY-FOUR

"What's on your mind, baby?" Jack pulls me close to him in my bed. *Um everything? Maine, Lela, slutty Max probably fucking Emma.* My eyes can barely stay open but my mind races.

"Nothing in particular," I lie. "Just reflecting on the day."

"It was a great day. If you're not too tired," Jack probes, "I did want to talk to you about a few things." Jack's words make my heart rate quicken, and my mind refocuses on the status of our relationship. *Right, say words like that and see if I can fall asleep.*

"Sure, babe. Let's talk."

"I really hate your apartment complex," Jack says to me, matter-of-factly. I let out an audible laugh.

"Gee, thanks?" I respond sarcastically, not sure where his comment is coming from. "Is that really what you wanted to talk about?"

"Well, sort of. I don't think you should live here anymore."

"Um, ok. And where exactly should I live? I can't really afford much else," my response is a bit snippy this time.

"Baby, no it's not that," Jack senses the frustration in my voice. "It's that I love you. So much. And even more every day. And it's days like this where I realize how much fun I have with you, and how I don't want to leave you at the end of the day. I want you to come home with me. To our home together." *What exactly is he saying?*

"I want you to move in with me, Jess." *Oh.* This unexpected proposal of sorts has my head spinning.

"Are you over Lela?" I blurt out the words before I can filter them.

"What? Jess, come on. I just asked if you wanted to move in together? And you think I still care about my ex-girlfriend?"

"Well, I don't know what to think. After what happened in Maine…" My voice trails off, unsure of how to describe that situation.

Jack releases an audible sigh then rolls over, putting his arm beneath mine and pulling me in close to him. Our eyes meet, our gazes only lit by the faint moonlight pouring in through the open shutters. "Jess, I love you. YOU. No one else. I'm sorry about what you witnessed at my parents' house. Lela has nothing to do with my life anymore, or the life that I want. I want to be here with you. I want to keep building my life *here* with *you*."

"Well that's just it, Jack." I break away from his loving gaze. "Are you just trying to throw yourself into this life here to prove your family wrong? To force yourself to get over Lela because you're too prideful to go back home and to her?" My candid words even surprise me. Although after a week of stirring in my head, I'm grateful to release them.

"Jess. No. A thousand times no. I understand why you would think that but it's absolutely not true. When that thing happened with Lela—it meant nothing. I've told you that. I think part of me let it happen because I had the same questions. I wondered if I had given up on her because I was looking for a new life. But kissing her," he stops, closing his eyes as he sees the painful memory enter mine, "validated that I feel nothing toward her. I know you don't want to hear this, but I'm glad it happened. Because I am one thousand percent sure that she and I broke up because we're not right together. Not because I live down here. She offered to move with me, you know. I told her no." *Oh.* I process his words, beginning to feel slightly more assured of his feelings toward me.

"Jess, I've never lived with another girl before. It's something I take very seriously. It's the next step before marriage. And it's a step that I'm ready for. With *you.* And I hope you are too." Holy shit. What is he saying?

"I think we should be pragmatic about such a big decision. We should test things out, make sure we would both know what we're getting into before taking that step." My brain is near-explosion of this revelation. *He really loves me that much? Crazy me? That he wants to live together and test things out before marriage?* My never-truly-loved soul devours his words, and craves their truth. *Could this be real? Could he be the one? The love that I'd always dreamed about?*

"Baby, you're being really quiet. What do you think?"

"Jack, I love you too. Really. That's why I'm so scared about Lela and question why you really left home. I want to believe you. And I do. I guess I'm just scared of a broken heart."

"I won't break your heart, baby. Trust me?"

I nod my head, allowing my brain to record how full my heart feels.

"I do, Jack. I just need to think about it. It's a big decision, so I want to make sure I've thought it through."

"Of course. Take your time. I'm not going anywhere." I smile back at these words, wondering if this could really be as it seems. "I love you, Jess. So fucking much." His eyes stare into me, and I feel my desire for him rush through me.

"I love you, Jack. More every day." I run my fingers across his temples and into his hair, lightly scratching his scalp as they slide into his locks. He lurches forward, pushing his needing body against mine. His lovely loving mouth meets mine, and I feel every ounce of love rush through me.

"God, I love you so much." The intensity of his eyes matches his proclamation, and I wordlessly respond to his request, wanting and needing to feel him just as badly from within. My urges run rampant and I quickly slide off my oversized T-shirt. I lean my bare breasts into his chest, relishing the skin-to-skin contact before planting my lips onto his once again. His hands grab my hair, moving my head forcefully and my hips slide upward, desperate to satisfy my need. I reach one hand below and shift his boxer briefs down as far as I can pull, exposing the throbbing, needing part of him. Without breaking his kiss, my hips grind upward, and my body glides across the tip of his need, and a slight moan escapes my mouth. "Fuck, baby, I love you so much. I want to feel you," Jack urges me again, tired of waiting. I nod back at him and push my hips up a few inches just to slide them back down onto him.

"I love you, too." My response falls from my tongue with ease. It feels so natural with him. He groans at my words and slides into me again. Jack moves his hips slowly and pulls me underneath him for some good old-fashioned lovemaking. The slow but erotic movements quicken at first, but remain steady, stroking me inside. Again. And again. And again. I feel the sensation rising through me, the real love combined with his lovely lovemaking is too much to handle. My heart feels ready to burst, but instead I do, coming over and over around him and collapsing deeper into his embrace. His body mimics mine and we come together, both groaning from the extreme intensity of our physical and emotional connection. Jack kisses me sweetly, and I fall deeper under the spell of the man I love.

CHAPTER TWENTY-FIVE

The screeching sound of rolling packing tape bounds through my nearly empty apartment. It's still hard for me to believe that I'm moving in with my boyfriend. After two weeks of deliberation, soul-searching, and advice-seeking, the overwhelming consensus was to go for it. I know I love Jack and see a future with him, so why not test it out? There are, of course, the naysayers who remind me of the old saying "why would he buy the cow when he gets the milk for free?", implying he'll never propose if he already has what he wants. I never gave that consideration more than a passing thought. I know Jack well enough to know he's not a serial dater who lives with girl after girl. I will be his first live-in girlfriend after all.

Even more surprising was that my parents were all for this step forward. I always assumed that they would be against me living with a guy before marriage. Not that we were ever the religious type, but from a practicality standpoint I figured they would be against it until we knew we were serious. In fact, Mother's response was quite the opposite, I recall. "Jess, if you think this man has potential, then you need to understand what life with him would really be like. You know how quickly your father and I married and I'd like you to take your time and know what you're getting into so you can decide if you see your life with him. Plus, you know your father and I hate you living by yourself, and we'd feel much better if you had someone like Jack there with you." Her words from our phone call two weeks back ring through my ears, and I once again reassure myself that I've made the right decision.

"Knock, knock." I hear Meredith's familiar voice announce her arrival.

"We're here to help finish packing!" Emma chimes in.

"You guys are the best! I didn't expect to see you here, Mere."

"I was in the neighborhood picking up some old things from my place, so I thought I'd stay and help," she says, giving me a hug hello.

"Yeah, you're both leaving me to live with guys! It's already been weird with you gone, Mere, but now I'll be totally alone when Jess moves," Emma says in a melancholy tone.

"Well you know I'm not moving far away, it's like a ten-minute drive from here, if that. And you say that now, but give it a few months and you'll probably be moving in with someone too! This certainly happened faster than I expected," I admit. "So anything new on the dating front? You always seem to have something in the works!"

"Ugh. Definitely nothing exciting right now. The last guy I shacked with was Jack's hot friend. The Italian."

I feel Meredith's eyes glare into me. I revealed my near tryst to her under the heavy cover of darkness and red wine last weekend, and she knows I still have a lingering lust for this man despite being in love with Jack.

"Have you talked to Max since that night?" I try to ask with a nonchalant tone, even though my heart beats faster as I await her response.

"Yeah, we've texted a few times, but he's just rarely in Atlanta. But come on, for someone that hot I'd be willing to do the long-distance thing! Among many other things with him." I swallow hard and look away, not wanting to meet Meredith's knowing glance. My mind immediately wanders back to that night, imagining his lips on someone else's, and I shudder.

"So where can you use our help?" Meredith shatters my thoughts and I happily direct them to wrap some dishes in the kitchen.

Packing up four years of life in this apartment in a matter of days calls for reflection and liquid relaxation. The Saturday afternoon sun peers through the windows, shining light on my near-empty wooden floors. My furniture was picked up this morning and moved to storage, after all, Jack has a fully furnished house so there's nowhere for it to go. But there's no way I'm selling it yet. Because, well, just in case things don't work out quite the way we planned. *Yeah, maybe you'll run away with a hot Italian guy and live happily ever after,* my slutty subconscious says to me. *Or maybe he will realize that you're his rebound.* I force the evil Jess and her hateful thoughts from my mind.

"So where's Jack today? He's not helping you pack?" Meredith asks me, sliding her empty wine glass toward me.

"Working, as usual," I sigh. "Well technically he's flying back from a work trip, he should be landing soon. But he was great this week, even came over and packed some stuff for me when I had to work late," I say gleaming, while I twist the wine cork from the bottle. My phone makes a beeping noise from two feet away on the kitchen counter, and I see a new message from Jack.

"Well speak of the devil," Emma says, catching a glimpse of my illuminated phone.

Just landed. How's the packing going?

Pretty good! Emma and Mere and here helping me, should be wrapped up in a few hours.

Great! Just got an email from Max, said he's in town just for tonight and wanted to see what we're doing.

What? You've got to be kidding me. Way to ruin my perfect, happy moving day with my lovely boyfriend by throwing that distraction into the mix.
"Eee!" Emma shrieks from across the room.
"What is it?" Mere and I question in unison.
"Max just texted me, said he's in town for tonight and wanted to see about a double date tonight!" she exclaims gleefully.
"Well that's very last minute and presumptuous of him," Meredith snaps. "If he wants to spend time with you he really should have given you more notice," she warns.
"Yeah, I know. But beggars can't be choosers and it's not like I'm tied up on a date tonight, so why not?"
"Well you don't want to seem desperate. You should make him work for it." Emma's eyes roll back at Meredith.
"In a perfect world, fine, but he's too hot to pass up so I'll let it slide."
"Or let him slide in and out of you?" Meredith jokes and I punch her with my eyes. I watch her face redden as she silently mouths an apology to me.
"Come on. You know I didn't sleep with him last time," Emma assures us.
"So really, what did happen last time?" I finally ask her the question that's been burning in the back of my mind for weeks.
"We kissed," she glows as she recalls it. "But he was a gentleman. I was quite disappointed in fact that he didn't try a little harder. So, Jess, what do you say? Double date? Puhlease? Be a friend and give me an excuse to see that Lusty man."
Fuck. What can I say? And what the fuck is wrong with me? I love Jack. I love Jack. I love Jack. Max is just a fantasy. Was. Was just a fantasy that simply needs to be replaced by a new one.

I see the curiosity overtake Meredith's face, awaiting my response. "Well, Jack and I were actually just planning a quiet night at home to celebrate the start of our cohabitation"—I pause, seeing Emma's face drop—"but I'm sure Jack won't mind if you join us. I'll ask him now."

"Oh, that would be awesome! Thanks, Jess!"

Meredith catches my eyes as Emma turns around to type away into her phone. I shrug my shoulders at her. After all, what am I supposed to do? Emma isn't the best secret-keeper around, so I don't dare extend my near indiscretions with Max to her.

I quickly type a response to Jack.

Yeah, he texted Emma as well. Double date at your house? I'm sure I can stretch our dinner to feed two more.

I hit send and take another long drink. Seriously, why can't I get away from this man?

The familiar ring of Jack's doorbell chimes into my ears as I stand outside of his house for the final time as a visitor. I hear the sound of Jack's feet shuffling before the dark, stained wood door swings open, revealing my handsome, grinning roommate. "Hey, babe! I missed you," he says, giving me a minty fresh kiss. His hair is damp, and skin soft and moist, the telltale signs that he just showered. He's wearing his dark but perfectly faded William Rast jeans, my favorite on him. His dark blue T-shirt perfectly accentuates his strong chest and arms, without coming across as a guy trying too hard to show off his body.

"No more ringing the doorbell, next time you use your key since you're not a guest!" Jack says to me, helping me with my belongings.

"Ok," I relent. "So I can't ring you to help when my hands are full?" I ask, realizing I'm setting foot into my new home. Or, our home? Such a strange idea. The home of my boyfriend where I now live and pay no rent. You know, just a modern-day, live-in hooker. I will live here and have sex with him, and he's paying me for my services with free rent. *Stop it Jess, he loves you for God's sake!* My subconscious snaps back at me. I know she's right, but it's going to take some getting used to.

After unpacking my clothes, I take a quick shower, and come out to hear soft jazz playing down the hallway. I tiptoe into his study while he focuses on his work. The clicking of the keyboard is rapid, and Jack's face is firmly concentrating on the work on his screen in front of him. I watch him for a moment, noticing how handsome he is, and remembering how lucky I am to have him. A slight layer of scruff has formed on his face, indicating he skipped his morning shave today. His rimless glasses add an air of sophistication, intelligence, and hotness to him. He pauses for a moment and takes the final sip of the dark liquid in his crystal rocks glass.

"Can I get you a refill?" I ask, interrupting his thoughts.

A big smile spreads across his face and the furrow in his brow disappears. "Hey. I'd love one. Is this one of the perks of living together?"

"Well it just might be…if you keep spoiling me I'll be more likely to return the favor." I giggle, walking toward him. I slide my arms around his neck and peer onto his screen, seeing a half-written email staring back at me. "Do you have a lot of work to finish tonight?"

"I'll stop soon, just trying to get down my thoughts from our meetings this week before they evade me."

"I hope I'm not too much of a distraction," I purr into his ear, placing my lips onto his neck, and then nibbling my way up to his earlobe.

"Mmm this type of distraction I'm ok with," he says, spinning his chair around to face me.

"Good. I was hoping you could spare a few minutes for me," I say, climbing onto his lap. I slide my legs to the back of his chair, pulling my body close to his. The scent of scotch rolls from his mouth, and my lips covet his. My tongue pushes into his mouth while Jack's hands slide easily down my satin robe. He traces the curves of my waist and hips through the fabric before finding my skin. The fabric inches upward and he glides his hands across my bare bottom, working his way toward me. My legs are spread against his stomach, and I feel his growing desire push against me. His arms wrap tightly around me and then he stands up, my legs holding tightly while he maneuvers. He spins me around, pushing aside the keyboard and then sets me on his strong wooden desk. *Mmmm.* As I wiggle backwards to balance myself into place, he removes his T-shirt, exposing his toned body before me. I tug at the button on his jeans, desperate to find my prize that hides beneath the denim. While I work to free him, Jack pulls the tie of my robe, and the fabric falls open easily, exposing my naked body. His erection bulges from beneath his boxers and I slide down the remaining barrier between us. My right hand caresses his sexiest muscle, and I can feel the blood rushing through there. Jack slips two of his fingers into my mouth, and I swirl my tongue around them. He draws them out slowly, and then gently parts my body below, inching one finger easily inside of me. My body is wet and wanting, and my hips cradle inward with the movement of his fingers, aching for more. He watches my expression, and my sultry gaze tells him I'm ready for more. Another finger slips inside of me, and my hips move more quickly, responding to his touch. Jack bends forward, and his mouth moves over my breast in expert fashion, sucking and then gently tugging on my nipple with his teeth.

His mouth slips across my chest to the other side, ensuring each breast gets equal attention. I squirm as he teases me, feeling the heat building inside of me, and my patience wanes. I move his hand from inside of me and pull my hips forward to the edge of the desk, then grab Jack's body, moving it into me. He slides right in, and he begins moving slowly in and out, and in and out, until my body can fully accept him. He moves gently at first, and with each thrust I feel him hit my bullseye, and my body heats even more.

Jack pulls himself forward and wraps an arm around me to steady me before he quickens his pace. The speed forces me to shift my arms backward to keep from falling over. I brace myself for each movement, and Jack's pleasuring doesn't relent. His mouth moves to my neck, sending tingles down my body, and then he kisses his way down to my breasts, and I can barely take it. I lift one arm to guide his speed, and I pull him toward me faster and faster, feeling his butt tighten with each push forward. My fingers grab into him tightly as my body begs for release. He senses my urgency and speeds his movements, everywhere. His tongue speeds faster across my breasts, and he pushes into me more quickly with each movement. My body begins to shake, trembling around him, and he looks up as he senses my closeness. I wipe a bead of sweat from his brow and kiss him hard, and the sensation of his lips on mine is enough to send me over the edge. I convulse around him, and feel his body release into mine.

―――

My cheeks are still flushed from my recent tryst, so I barely need any blush as I apply my makeup. I decide to go with a shimmery brown eyeshadow with dark green eyeliner that draws out the sparse flecks of green in my eyes. I add some mascara and coral pink lip gloss while my old-school curlers set my hair.

I slip into my dark fitted skinny jeans, a jade silk blouse, and a tall pair of black heels, set with big leather cross straps across my feet. The shoes are definitely on the edgier side of my style, but tonight I'm feeling extra frisky. Having just spread my legs for my new live-in boyfriend, I force my brain to remove all thoughts of the living, breathing Mr. Lust that I have to watch on a date with my best friend tonight.

I meander into the kitchen and Jack is standing over the counter, expertly slicing bread for our appetizers.

"Need a hand?" I ask, sliding my arms around him with a loving embrace. His head turns over his shoulder and he strains his head backward to give me a kiss. He lays the knife and bread on the counter so he can turn and give me his full attention.

"You look beautiful, babe. Should I expect you to dress up like this for dinner every night?" I laugh at the thought. I'm going to have to ease him in to my habit of coming home and immediately changing into house clothes.

"Maybe if you cook for me like this every night," I offer.

"Hmm, that might be worth the effort," Jack says eyeing my tight outfit. "Can you take care of the meat and cheese plate? I'll grab you a glass of wine."

"Sure." I watch him walk away into the dining room to grab a wine glass from the bar. He strides easily in his dark jeans and light blue button-up. His sleeves are folded to his elbows, and accented with a tan belt and woven leather shoes of the same color. I arrange the prosciutto, along with some brie and manchego, then gather some nuts and fruit to complete the platter.

"Sauvignon blanc?" Jack says, passing me a full glass.

"Yes, please." I gratefully accept it. My earlier wine high has almost completely faded, leaving me fully sober, save my post-sex buzz.

Jack raises his own glass in the air. "I'm thrilled to have you here. Here's to making memories and sharing a home together, for what I hope is many years to come. I love you, Jess." His words are short and to the point, but filled with hope and love, and big enough to tug at my heart.

"Cheers to that. There's nowhere else I'd rather be. I love you too." I look into his eyes as I say the words; our feelings radiate between one another. We clink our glasses together and barely have time to finish a sip before the doorbell chimes through the house.

"I'll get it," Jack says, releasing me. *Deep breaths. Deep breaths.* Why the hell do I care so much? I absentmindedly adjust my hair, smoothing it perfectly in front of my shoulders. My tongue runs across my teeth, checking for any rogue lip gloss while Jack answers the door.

"Hey, Jack, buongiorno!" I hear his beautiful accent sing through the house and I clutch my wine for a long drink. I peer through the dining room and get a glance of my two favorite men shaking hands. Mr. Lust is beautifully dressed in in dark gray linen pants and a crisp white shirt. His normally tan skin looks even darker, revealing time recently spent in the sun.

"Hey, come on in," Jack says, extending the door open for him.

"I brought some wine for us. I know you like scotch, but I thought the women would like this more."

"This is great. Thanks. Come on in."

"This is such a great neighborhood. So many trees, and so close to everything. I can see why you chose it."

"Yeah, I've been pretty happy here," Jack says, escorting him through the house and into the kitchen.

"Can I get you a drink?" I ask, bravely entering the kitchen instead of watching from afar. Lust turns his head toward me, locking his eyes with mine and I feel as though my vagina gasps. I'm like an awe-struck teenager, unable to mask my likeness of him.

Sensing my flushed cheeks, I walk quickly into the dining room to prevent Jack from noticing.

"Hi, Jess. Nice to see you. How are you?"

"Doing well, thank you. I was just finishing up some hors d'oeuvres for us," I explain. "Can I get you guys a drink?"

"Jess, baby, I'll take care of that. You've been on your feet all day. Have a seat with our guest and I'll get the drinks." Jack slides past me, placing his hands on my hips and giving me a squeeze as he walks by. Lust smiles back at me, enjoying my obvious discomfort.

"Please, after you." He gestures his hand out and I take in those long, strong fingers as I walk past him toward the sofa. The memory of them stroking the most delicate parts of my body seems all too real, so I quickly tear my eyes away. I settle into the sofa, facing Mr. Lust in a matching leather chair across from me. The darkness in his eyes has a twinkle and I pull my eyes down to avoid catching his magic stare.

"Are you in town for business again?" I question him.

"Yes. Just until Monday, you know I never get to stay in one place for too long."

"Are you staying at the St. Regis again?" I ask, continuing the questions to prevent my mind from going *there*.

"No, I'm at the Four Seasons this time. Figured I would try somewhere new." He responds matter-of-factly. "So you've been on your feet all day?" he asks me.

"Oh, well I spent the day cleaning out my old apartment and moving stuff out."

"Where is your new place?"

I pause for a moment, realizing he hasn't yet pieced together that I'm now living with Jack.

"She's living here now," Jack says proudly, passing Max his glass of scotch.

"Oh. That's great!" he manages, his response seeming to overcompensate for his true feelings. I see the expression on his face change completely. The cocky, confident Mr. Lust I saw last time now looks somewhat sullen, but he tries to force a smile to hide it. The giveaway is his eyes, the sparkle has faded even when he plasters a grin across his face. "Really, congratulations."

Jack sits down next to me on the sofa and gives me a loving squeeze on the knee, catching my eye and grinning ear to ear. He really is happy to have me here, and I'm happy to be here, but my heart breaks with Max's expression. *What is it about this man that I can't let go of?*

CHAPTER TWENTY-SIX

"Who's ready for dessert?" I ask the attendees of our dinner party.

"I couldn't eat another bite, Jess," Emma responds, her words beyond irritating given she's barely touched her food, seemingly trying to impress Max. It's a phenomenon I've never understood, other than being a cheap date, why would a guy want to date someone who doesn't eat? I mask my irritation with a smile and turn to the men.

"Anyone else?" I say, standing to clear the plates from the table.

"Why don't we give ourselves a break and have it a little later?" Jack suggests.

"Ok. More wine in the meantime?"

"Yes, I'll take some!" Emma immediately chirps, again grating on my nerves. I fight the urge to use the steak knife in my hand to jab her in the eye. *Good idea, don't eat and get really drunk so you can just screw the sexy Italian man.* The bitter thoughts ring through my mind. I want to be happy for my friend, happy that she's having fun on a date, in Jack's – rather, our – house, with a guy she really likes.

"Let me help you, Jess," Max offers, standing with me. I start to say no, but I wouldn't mind getting him away from Emma for a moment.

"Thanks," I say politely.

Max follows me into the kitchen, and for a moment I lament that my own boyfriend didn't offer to help. It is his house after all, he should be playing the host. *Stop with the petty bitterness!* I scold myself, unable to handle the jealousy surrounding a man who isn't and never was mine.

"This dinner was delicious, thank you." Max smiles as I turn around from the kitchen sink.

"Oh, thanks. Glad you liked it." He hands me a plate to rinse and as I reach for it our fingers touch, and the quick connection with his skin electrifies me. We've barely spoken directly to each other since he learned of my new living situation just hours ago. His eyes catch mine and I know he feels it too. I quickly grab the plate and turn back around to the sink to rinse it.

"Where do you keep the wine?"

"Oh, it's back there, in the wine fridge." He glances off to the far end of the kitchen. "Here, I'll show you." I turn off the faucet and face him bravely. We walk into the back of the kitchen, a part not viewable from the dining room. I hear Emma and Jack laughing and chatting away in the other room. "What do you think, another white? Or should we switch to red?" I try to ask calmly.

"Either will be fine. You should pick what you like."

"This is one of my favorites. It's not Italian, but I promise it's delicious!" I whirl around to hand him the bottle of Claret, and turn straight into him. "Oh, I'm sorry!" I say embarrassed, realizing he must've been leaning over me to view the wine selection.

"No, please. My fault." His words are calm, but the emotion runs through his chiseled cheeks, and he makes no attempt to move backward or create space between us. He suddenly pulls the bottle from my arm, setting it atop the wine fridge. He takes my hand and pours his words into me. "Jessa, I still think about you all the time. About that night in New York..." his voice trails off. I pause, dumbfounded and shocked by his proclamation. I freeze, fearing that Jack will see us like this, but then I hear his voice talking to Emma, confirming he's safely out of earshot of this whispered profession. I swallow hard and want to fall deeper into his embrace, but I know I shouldn't. Despite my buzz I have enough clarity to see how wrong it is. I watch his eager eyes and gather my words.

"I'd be lying if I said I didn't think about you. About that night."

"Why did you leave my apartment so quickly? I never got to say goodbye, and then I never heard from you again."

"Because I was completely embarrassed. What I did was wrong."

"Wrong? It feels wrong to see you and not be with you," he says exhaustedly. "I know you just moved in with Jack, and I don't want to ruin that, but I had to tell you. I can't let it go." *Think, Jess. Think.* The logical side of me goes to a sudden death battle with the yearning and desire I feel toward him. I look down, unable to think straight when I look into his dark eyes, only seeing pure lust.

I focus on the here and now. I just moved into this house today. With my boyfriend, who I love. I gaze back up at him. "I think about you sometimes. But *this* would be wrong. We would be wrong. I just moved in here with Jack. I have to be fair to him. I really do love him." My eyes plead for his understanding, and he shakes his head.

"You're right. I'm sorry, Jess. I shouldn't have said anything," he pauses, "but if you change your mind, and if this doesn't work out..." his voice trails off. He leans forward and gives me a gentle kiss on the cheek, and I force myself not to push my lips over onto his. I close my eyes and he pulls away, grabs the bottle of wine, and leaves me breathless and alone.

Less than two steps separate us before he turns around and takes me. We grab each other like animals, pawing at any scrap of clothing we can find. I rip his clothes off, forcefully, desperately, panting with excitement. His freshly shaven face glides against my fingertips as I caress his strong features. His skin smells of divine Italian soaps and my body fades into his when his strong lips pull at mine. I pull away for a moment and hold my breath, wanting to be certain that they can't hear us. Emma laughs loudly as she and Jack continue to share stories over wine in the living room. I know we only have a few minutes before we're notably absent and I intend to make the most of it.

I catch the intensity in his eyes as our bodies separate briefly, allowing him to maneuver up my shirt. There's no time to completely undress, so he simply slides my bra down a few inches, giving himself immediate access to hard, waiting nipples. I feel inside his pants and catch a handful, and a very large one at that, ready for me to take him. I give him a long, wet kiss then drop to my knees to taste him at once. His size is captivating, overwhelming me as my lips and tongue move across his throbbing muscle. I can barely hold myself off from jumping onto him, and having him inside of me. I slide his erection between my lips and massage him with my tongue, but after a few moments he pulls me up to him. "Now," he says through a whisper, "I need you now." His fingers dip into my jeans, inching closer to me and my hips flex toward him, willing me to connect with his.

The top button of my jeans pops open easily, and with one hand he guides my zipper down. He pulls his other arm over to shimmy down my pants and panties just enough to allow him entry. "Come here," he says whirling me around so my back rests against his stomach and chest. His lips find my neck and gently nip down a trail from my earlobe to my shoulders. His mouth moves to my other side, repeating the same cycle and sending shivers down the opposite side of me. His hand cups me and he easily slides two fingers into me, causing my knees to buckle beneath me. Sensing my collapse, his left arm swings around my waist, holding me upright and against him. "Are you ready?" he whispers at me. I nod my head in affirmation, too afraid to speak. He pushes my head and upper half of my body forward, and spreads my legs further apart. Leaning over me he places a kiss on my back, and then guides my hips backward into him. My body awaits him, needy with anticipation. His hips thrust into me and I have to cover my mouth to silence the delighted scream that's trying to escape.

CHAPTER TWENTY-SEVEN

What is that? My body twitches against the soft sheets, and I pause, caught between reality and the sexcapade playing in my head. *Argh, another dream about him.* It's been two months since the night of our double date, yet practically every night my brain creates another fantasy of us being together. It never happened. And it never will. That evening ended with Max leaving our house, and me feeling relieved that Emma didn't go with him.

The 5:45 workout alarm is singing its morning tune, so I force my body to get out of bed. Might as well burn some calories rather than spending the next few minutes fucking his royal lustiness in my mind. I remember the dinner plans I have with Mother and Daddy tonight, giving me the motivation to get up and sweat out some preemptive stress.

"Mother!" I wave my hand and force a smile onto my face. She gives her standard feeble wave back to me. I stand in the bar area of Bistro Niko, one of the tastiest and most fabulous French restaurants in Atlanta. The restaurant's decor pays homage to its cuisine, decorated as an elegant brasserie, filled with happy hour attendees on this warm Thursday evening.

"Hello, Jessica. You look nice, dear. Skinnier in fact?" I hear the surprise in her voice as she verbalizes an accidental almost-compliment.

"Hi, Daddy." A more genuine smile emerges as he approaches. "Did Mom make you coordinate with her?" I joke, noticing the pink and blue stripes in his shirt that complement her pink sundress.

"Anything to keep her happy." Daddy winks at me before giving me a warm embrace.

"Should we grab a drink while we wait for Jack?" I feel the sting of a punch in my gut as soon as I hear his name.

"Actually, he's not coming. He sends his apologies but he got tied up at work. Again." I cringe awaiting the judgment or disappointment in their voices. He's already the reason we moved the location of dinner from "our" house to a restaurant since he wouldn't be home in time to properly host. And now, here I am, stood up by my own live-in boyfriend, feeling the sting of his choosing work over me. *Is that really the only reason I feel resentment toward Jack?*

Ever since we've moved in together things have been good between us. I know he loves me, and I him, but I'm living with someone I barely see. Yes, he's always worked a lot since I met him, but he still made time for me, enough that I still felt like a priority. I still see him every day he's in town, but it's typically dinner alone, and a quick kiss hello just as I'm getting into bed. And tonight is no different. I really thought he would come through when it came to my parents, especially since he knows how tenuous my relationship can be with them. But here I am, alone and embarrassed by his absence.

"I'm sorry, sweetheart. But we're thrilled to have you to ourselves." Daddy says kindly, trying to console me.

"Should we head to our table?"

I nod at Mother's request, grateful she's at least attuned enough to my feelings to change the subject.

"Excuse me, ladies, I need to visit the little boys' room." Daddy politely excuses himself from the table, leaving me alone with Mother for the first time tonight. She watches him depart and turns her attention back to me.

"How's your food, dear?"

"It's good. The beef bourguignon is one of their specialties."

"You've barely touched it, Jess." She pauses, setting the fork down next to her own half-eaten plate of duck. "How are things really going with Jack?" *Damn Mother and her damn nosy questions.* My heart clenches in pain, having been grateful to avoid his name for the last hour of conversation.

"They're good," I lie, never having been one to fully divulge the details of my love life to my mother.

"Are you happy? I can see you're disappointed that he's not here tonight." I glance away and fight the release of the salty water that sits on the edge of my eyelids.

"I do love him, if that's what you mean." I unintentionally reveal, realizing that's not the question she asked. "Are you happy with Daddy?" I tartly change the subject, shutting down her veiled attempt at mother–daughter bonding. I then realize what I've implied. I do know about her slutty past after all.

"Of course I love your father."

"But are you happy with him?" I spew the paralleled question back at mother, unsure of my own happiness with Jack, and why I'm questioning it.

Mother lets out a deep sigh, and *in vino veritas* prevails. "Jess, I know it's not something we ever talk about, but I think you need to hear this." My ears perk up, flabbergasted that she might be going *there*. "You know that I wasn't always faithful to your father." Now it's her turn to look away, and I see a hint of water pooling in her normally impassive eyes. I nod my head, acknowledging her words. "It's something I regret. Every day. But what you probably don't know is why it happened." She pauses, seeking her own composure. "The truth is, Jess, your father put work before me. I barely saw him. You barely saw him, at times. And I was tired, angry, and lonely. And after some time, attention fell upon me and I didn't turn it away. I should've talked to your father more, been more explicit about my needs, and tried harder to work things out with us before this happened. But I didn't. And while I do regret that this happened, I'd be lying if I said it hadn't changed things forever. For the better even. It took that painful experience for all of us to realize how much we meant to each other. And now your father always puts us first."

I drink in her words. I've spent more than a decade assuming mother was just a selfish slut when she cheated on daddy. But in reality, she was just a lonely, vengeful, selfish slut.

"So do you understand what I'm trying to tell you dear?" I consider this for a moment. Is she saying that I should cheat on Jack? "I'm saying you should learn from my mistakes. You should talk to Jack. If you love each other then you'll work through this. He'll make you a priority. And if he doesn't, well, at least you don't have a child and a marriage to untangle."

CHAPTER TWENTY-EIGHT

"So you know how my mom used to be a whore?" I semi-whisper to Sarah, leaning closer to her so our conversation doesn't extend beyond her cube walls.

"Of course. That's our usual topic of conversation," she says with a giggle.

"Well, she kind of came clean to me last night. About why she cheated on my dad." Sarah's green eyes get big and she inches closer to me.

"Oh, do tell."

"She said she wasn't a priority anymore. He was working too much, and she hit a breaking point. She needed attention that he wasn't giving her, and eventually she just found it elsewhere."

"Wow. Ok. So, dare I ask why your usually poignant and clammed-up mother divulged this to you?"

"We were at dinner last night. Jack didn't make it—he had to work—and I guess she saw some of her former loneliness in me. Or maybe it was just the large consumption of wine." I lighten the heavy thought, not ready to fully reflect on this.

"Oh, Jess, I'm sorry."

"Thanks." I manage a feeble smile, as the knowing look of a friend is enough to extract my tears. "So the moral of Mother's story was that I shouldn't be her. She said I should talk to Jack. Give him a chance to fix this. To give us a chance, to get back to the relationship that we had. Otherwise..." I pause, thinking of the alternative, and swallowing back the fearful reality. "Otherwise I need to move out and move on."

"Wow. So, things are really that bad? I thought he was just busy at work?"

I open my mouth to speak, and my brain stops, reflecting on Sarah's question. *Is Jack's work schedule really this inexcusable or am I simply trying to justify the lingering lust for a hot Italian? Maybe he's just working hard because he's young, and trying to secure a great future. For both of us.* This idea begins to play in my mind, and unsettles my subconscious. "I don't know, I guess it's just a lot of things adding up," I say, withholding the full truth, while further realizing my own lustful thoughts might be contributing to my frustration with Jack.

"So is he still joining you in New York this weekend?"

"As far as I know. I still have to be up there to make sure the agency is set for the Global event. He hasn't cancelled on me. At least not yet."

"Jess, I think you're smart to talk to him. You need to get your feelings out there. But can I give you a word of advice?"

"Of course. Please."

"Give the weekend a chance to have fun together. Without his interruption of work, without the stress of the inadequacies of your relationship. Give yourself a chance to feel for him how you have before, and probably still do. You guys haven't even had the time for that in weeks."

"You're right. Maybe this is just the weekend we need. To get away, drink some great wine and enjoy fabulous food, and most importantly each other. If we can do that then I think our conversation will take a completely different tone." *Especially if I can get Max out of my head, and stop sabotaging my relationship with Jack.*

I know I love Jack. Me, the master of loveless relationships finally found love! So why am I so willing to let it go? My heart aches too much at even the thought of leaving Jack, and I weigh why I am even considering the thought. But even still, I can't get *him* out of my mind, and can't help but wonder why.

CHAPTER TWENTY-NINE

The taxi line at the Waldorf is brutal. Not surprising for New York City on a Friday evening during rush hour, but frustrating nonetheless. The temperature hints at the upcoming summer season, with a tinge of salty humidity mixing with the smoggy air.

"You should have let me order a black car," Jack says impatiently.

"The line is moving, it shouldn't take that long," I respond in an irritated tone. For some reason Jack woke up on the wrong side of the bed today, and we've been bickering with each other ever since. We barely spoke on the plane ride, where he was occupied by his work, and I by my thoughts. Now we stand on the busy corner of Park Avenue, impatiently waiting our turn for a car, already late to meet Max for dinner. I'm still wrapping my head around how we've gotten here; just yesterday I was planning to be 100% focused on Jack this weekend, and permanently force Mr. Lust from my mind, up until he dropped the Max news on me this morning...

"So I was emailing with Max, he'll be in New York this weekend, and we talked about grabbing a drink or dinner one night. Does that sound ok to you?" Jack's question prompts a lusty daydream of him and slaps the sultry image of the delicious Italian right into my mind. *Great, seeing him will do wonders for my already Lust-filled dreams,* I think guiltily.

"Sure, that's fine. I didn't realize you guys kept in such close contact," I say curiously, my heart rate quickening with this news. My mind jumps to the clothes I'm throwing in my suitcase, instantly reevaluating if what I have packed is suitable for this unplanned encounter.

"Yeah, I'm still supporting one of his European deals now, so we've been in touch for some of the planning." *Great, just what I want, you to spend even more time with him and work, and less with me.*

"Oh really? Small world. What deal is this for?"

"Something called Pegasus," he says, and I instantly roll my eyes. All of his projects have stupid code names. "Babe, you know I can't tell you that," he reminds me, giving me a kiss on the cheek as if to make up for his secrecy.

"Yeah, yeah, I know. You know I only ask because I'm interested in what you do. I'm not dating you and living with you to steal your trade secrets and play the stock market with the information," I huff back at him.

"Jess, I know that. It's just easier if I don't tell you. Trust me, it's not that interesting anyway. I'd much rather talk about you and interesting things in your life." Jack tries changing the subject to soften me back up. He's gotten to know me well enough that he can tell when I start closing off. I huff back to my closet to look for my sluttiest classy dress. I will my frustration to leave my mind. *Doesn't he trust me? I'm fucking living with him after all. What else does it take?*

My mind mixes with frustration and guilt, thinking about Jack's seeming lack of trust for me, and my shameful thoughts of

Lost

my Italian objet d'affection. *Come on, Jess, you promised yourself. This weekend is about reconnecting with Jack, with or without a Maximum distraction.*

―‖―

Tonight Jack is dressed in his dark jeans, light blue button-up, and cotton navy blazer. His frustration is showing in the form of a bead of sweat on his eyebrow. "Take off your jacket, it's like eighty degrees outside," I suggest.

"No. I'm fine," he snaps back. *What has gotten into him?* I wince a little at his snappiness, enough that he must notice. "Jess, I'm sorry," he says, placing his hand around my waist and attempting to pull me in close. I plant my feet firmly into the ground, not wanting to get any closer to him.

"It's fine," I murmur back at him, looking away.

"No, it's not fine," he says with frustration, running his fingers through his growing golden locks. Even in my frustration I can't help but notice how attractive he looks. Always so polished and well put together, and the longer hair makes him look more like a classy gent than the shorter, more military-esque style he wore previously. My subtle suggestion to grow out his hair was taken seriously, and my hypothesis that he would wear it well was correct. He frowns as I stand reluctant to forgive him.

"Babe, come on. I'm sorry," he pleads into my ear, not wanting the line of people behind us to witness our tiff. "It's been a stressful day, and you know how I hate being late to things." He gives me a soft kiss on my neck. "Did I tell you how beautiful you look?" *Actually, no, you haven't. You were too busy huffing around the hotel room on a conference call to notice.*

Part of me feels guilty, knowing that I put so much effort into looking good tonight when it wasn't just for Jack. My blonde hair is flat-ironed super straight, placing the ends of it just below my breasts. I chose a black cotton dress with vertical sections of fabric, helping to elongate my very average height. The material falls just above my mid-thigh; short for me, but nothing compared to the standard New York City girl. The sides of the dress have open slits, showing a few more inches of skin from the right angle. I finished it off with my diamond heart earrings, a shimmery gold clutch, and gold peep toe shoes. The heels give me an extra four inches or so, necessary for lengthening and thinning my legs in this dress.

 A young bellman whistles a cab over to us, and I notice him giving me an extra glance as I climb inside the taxi. Jack notices too, but says nothing. Not even an ounce of jealousy seems to pass through him when it comes to me. I'm secretly flattered at the stranger's glance; it gives me a boost of confidence that I can pull this dress off, and maybe even garner a seductive glance from Max. *Stop it, Jess.*

We head across town to a restaurant called Quality Meats. The name leaves much to be desired, after all it sounds like a local butcher shop, but knowing Mr. Lust and his expensive tastes, the restaurant will be far from it.

 Jack checks in with the host and we're immediately escorted through the bustling restaurant. The decor is a mix of modern and rustic, half of the walls revealing exposed brick, and the other half covered in rich, deep woods that extend across the ceiling. Small clusters of diners occupy every table and chair, an indication that the food must be fantastic. The host weaves us through the main dining area and up a set of modern stairs to another section of tables. The lighting upstairs is dimmer, but strategically placed candles light the perimeter of the room just enough to enable us

Lost

to view the diners. We finally stop at a booth in the back corner, where the handsome Italian sits chatting casually and sipping a cocktail with a pretty, petite woman.

"Ciao!" Mr. Lust practically shouts at us as we approach the table. He jumps to his feet to shake Jack's hand, and then leans in to give me the standard double cheek kiss, undoubtedly my favorite part of his greeting. But his usual slight lingering on my cheeks is absent tonight, and I can't help but feel disappointed.

"Ciao," I respond back with a forced smile, curious to know who this brunette tart is with him tonight.

"Jack, Jess, please meet Lia," he says, extending his arm out toward her. Her petite frame stands and she greets us with a flat smile back, saying "Ciao." The one word is enough to give away her perfect Italian tongue. She shakes Jack's hand, and then mine, and I'm immediately unimpressed by her flimsy, floppy attempt at a handshake.

"Please, sit." Max gestures for us to sit at the table, already broken-in with a basket of bread, olive oil, a near-empty old fashioned glass, and a drained glass of bubbles. Jack and I each slide into opposite ends of the round booth, him next to Mr. Lust and me next to Lia. The horseshoe shape prevents me and Jack from sitting next to each other. Not the start we need to a rekindling weekend, especially after our bickering. Plus, judging by first impressions, Lia will be far from the world's best conversationalist.

"A drink for my friends," Lust says, raising his hand, and a waiter seems to appear from nowhere.

"Of course sir, what can I get you?"

"Ladies first," he says with a wink, his dark eyes catching a sparkle from the dancing flames on the table. His eye almost catches mine, but I avert them to the drink menu resting on the table before me.

"What are you having Lia?" I ask with feigned interest.

"Prosecco. It was...this one," she says pointing to a name on the menu.

"Would you recommend it"?

"Yes, it's almost as good as something you would find in Italia." *Snobby bitch.* Seeing as though it was imported from *Italia* I'm sure it's exactly the same as what I would have there. *God, why do I instantly hate her? Be nice, Jess.*

"I'll have a glass of the Prosecco, please," I announce to the waiter, holding my tongue and trying to play nice.

"Another for me," Lia snaps at the waiter, pushing her empty glass toward him.

"Right away, ladies. And anything for the gentlemen?"

"Another Negroni, please," Max says, jiggling the last bit of drink in his glass before taking the final sip.

"Grey Goose martini, please," Jack says. The young waiter nods and disappears from the table as quickly as he came.

"How was the trip from Atlanta?" Max asks us. I begin to open my mouth but Jack beats me. "Trip was good, no complaints," he says, and I bite my tongue to allow his lie to continue. I guess it wouldn't be appropriate to describe the true nature of our trip, filled with arguing, anger and frustration. It's not exactly suitable dinner conversation.

"How long are you in town for?" I ask Max.

"Not long enough," Lia says, pouting and grabbing his arm. Seeing her touch him sends rage through my veins. *He's not yours, Jess,* I try to remind myself, but every time I see him my mind goes back to that place. Mr. Lust lets out a laugh, and places his hand gently over hers. *Fuck me.* I die a little inside watching their skin connect.

"Unfortunately just until Monday, then back to Europe."

"Ahh, the life of a road warrior," Jack exclaims.

"So how do you and Lia know each other?" I ask, realizing Max never disclosed the nature of their relationship upon introductions.

"Our mothers were close friends for many years in Italy," he responds, smiling broadly at Lia. I watch her face light up as he looks at her, and it's clear how desperate she is for his attention.

"Yes, Max has been nice enough to help me get acquainted to New York City, I've only been here for a few months."

"Really, so did you just move from Italy recently?" Jack asks.

"Yes, before that I have never been to America, but there are more opportunities here," she says through imperfect English.

"What opportunities are you exploring here?" I ask inquisitively.

"I am a model," she quips proudly. *Fucking whore bitch, of course she is a model.* I try to think of something nice to say back to her, or to pretend I'm interested in furthering the conversation, but I can only think of evil and envious thoughts while I glare at her perfectly tiny and toned legs popping out of her skin-tight maroon dress.

"Do you find it hard to start modeling now? I know many models start when they are still teenagers." My bitterness cuts through in the form of my question, and I can sense Jack staring at me as if to say "don't be rude."

"Not too hard," she says, taking the question in stride. "Most of the models are younger, maybe nineteen is the average age of girls I work with. I feel like a mother to them sometimes," she admits. Max snickers at her comment.

"What do you know about being a mother?" He laughs. "You are barely twenty-one, you are just a baby still!" I swear I puke a little in my mouth. The perfectly tiny and beautiful date of my Lust is a twenty-one-year-old model. *Fuck my life.*

"Maximus!" she shrieks, playfully pushing his arm. He laughs harder, then places his arm around his shoulder, pulling her into a hug. She glows with affection for this older, handsome man, and I can't say that I blame her. The jealousy stings as I watch them playfully interact, briefly wishing that I were the one here with Max, or at least that Jack had the same feeling toward me tonight.

The waiter reappears, and quickly begins distributing drinks to each of us. "Can I get you something to start with? May I recommend the meat and cheese plate for the table?"

"That sounds delicious," Jack says, taking the lead on ordering. We all select some form of meat or fish, and order Brussels sprouts, spinach, gnocchi, and corn crème brûlée for the table to share. Jack and Max select an overpriced bottle of red wine for the table, and I attempt to indulge rather than festering in my jealousy.

I spend the next hour watching Lia pick at her food, probably eating a grand total of two bites of Brussels sprouts, a teaspoon of spinach and an ounce of steak. The only part of the meal she doesn't skimp on is the booze. The guys have turned this double date into a business dinner, talking over intricacies of European laws and how they will impact the negotiation to buy or sell whatever Pegasus is, so I'm stuck making small talk with the anorexic teenage model.

"So you and Max knew each other from Italy?" I ask her the obvious question, tired of half listening to the guys' work discussion.

"Yes, our mothers were good friends. Since he was older I didn't know him that well in Italy. I mainly knew of his reputation." She raises her eyebrows and laughs.

"Oh, really?" My buzzed, frustrated self can't help but run with this one. "What was his reputation back home?"

"How do you say…" she pauses, "he had lots of girlfriends. Or friends who are girls, anyway." This idea shouldn't surprise me, as a known playboy businessman never having been spotted with the same girl more than a few times.

"I think I would have guessed that. So, did you know any of these girlfriends?"

"I met a girl friend once, at a party when he was visiting a few years ago. But he barely knew her. She was probably just his evening entertainment."

I smile and nod, thinking she must now be filling those same shoes. "But you know what they say," her eyes get bigger as she leans closer to me, speaking more softly. "He never says goodbye. Just goes cold chicken, and women never know when it will happen." I giggle at her expression, her English idioms faulty given our Prosecco consumption.

"So what does he do? Just sleep with a girl and then never call again?"

"I wouldn't know," she smiles, and I instantly want to punch her. Wait, what does she mean? They've slept together and he's still calling? Or that they haven't slept together? My wicked brain gets ahead of me. *Be real, Jess, even if they haven't slept together yet, you know he's a manwhore. If he hasn't, he's thinking about it. About her. Not you. And you shouldn't be either! Remember Jack?*

We finish the last drops of our third bottle of wine and I realize I'm sufficiently drunk, and exhausted from the forced small talk with Lia. I've spent three hours watching her drool over Mr. Lust, and three hours watching my boyfriend have a work discussion. Even when he and Max have taken a breather from the shop talk, he's failed to give me more than a glance or he would realize that I'm bored to tears.

"Want me to order us a car?" I ask Jack, hoping that we can finally end the evening of torture.

"Please, you can ride with me," Max quickly offers. "My driver, Enzo, can bring the larger car and we will drop you off at your hotel." *Oh, fuck.* I can't see Enzo around Jack. The sweet old man would probably remember me, and then how would I possibly explain the fact that I've met him before. My fuzzy head is too strained to think up a quick lie.

"No need to do that, Max. We appreciate the offer though. I'll just get us a car." I pull up the Uber app on my phone and hit the request button as quickly as possible.

"Jess, it's no problem," he persists.

"Too late, I've already requested it. I can't cancel and risk my perfect five-star rating. Thanks for the offer though. Enzo can just take Lia home, I'm sure models need their beauty sleep!"

"Oh, it's not problem, I live with Max." *What?* Her words punch me straight in the gut. *Oh, God.* They *must* be sleeping together. That's what she meant—she wouldn't know if he just leaves girls because he's screwed her and is already living with her! My expression must reveal my surprise, as Max looks directly at me while I digest this news.

"I am just giving her a place to stay why she gets settled in the city," he says, almost as though he is trying to explain away her comment.

"Yes, Max and Enzo have been taking care of me for nearly three months! I don't know what I would do without them." Lia squeezes him gratefully. *Three months? But I slept in his apartment less than three months ago.* I quickly deduce that she must have been there that night. What an enormously slutty asshole. A flood of emotions wash over me. Disgust. Anger. Betrayal. Was he sleeping with her the night we were at Ware?

"Really, you've been staying with Max for three months?" I question brazenly.

"Yes, since February, just after Valentine's Day weekend," Lia confirms. I shoot daggers from my eyes into his, ensuring he knows that I've figured him out. *That disgusting shit.* What did he think was going to happen that night? I would just hop into bed with him and Lia? Or did he just have to hide me away to keep her from knowing I was in his apartment too? That's probably why Enzo was so helpful and quick to get me out of his apartment. So his man-whore boss could keep his trysts separate. I want to scream at him and call him out but I can't without revealing to my boyfriend why I was there, and why I would even care.

"Looks like the car is almost here, Jack. We should probably go," I say, heated and desperate to leave this man. For the first time ever, my attraction to him is replaced with disgust and I only want to flee from his presence.

CHAPTER THIRTY

My dry eyes open to the harsh brightness of the sun spilling through the tiny cracks between the floor-to-ceiling maroon drapes. The brilliantly bright line of light manages to land just across my left eyelid, disrupting my sound sleep. The faint sound of honking horns mixed with occasional sirens reminds me that I'm still in New York City, and of the fast-paced world ten floors below me.

I glance up to see Jack sitting at the desk, his glasses on, and typing away at his screen. I toss the covers off of me, realizing the imminent need of a bathroom to relieve my full bladder. The rustling of sheets garners Jack's attention and he turns to greet me. "Morning, sunshine," he says to me. I glance at the clock to see it's already 11:43 am, and that the day is half gone.

"Morning," I say without enthusiasm, still filled with irritation from yesterday's events. The day of fighting and the evening of being ignored did little to help our situation. I shake away my negative thoughts. This weekend is about us. *I have to give it a fair try.* I fight my inner bitchiness and put on a smile. "Glad you're getting some work done, we have a day of fun ahead of us!"

"Remember, we're supposed to meet Barrett and his wife for brunch at 12:30."

My fuddled mine begins to process this. "Where are we meeting them? That's not even forty-five minutes from now." I vaguely remember a conversation about meeting his business school bestie and wife for brunch.

"We're supposed to meet them at Sarabeth's near the park at 12:30. So we should probably leave in about twenty minutes."

I immediately fume at the thought.

"Jack, I know we've only been living together for a few months, but you know it takes me more than twenty minutes to shower and get ready for the day. Why didn't you wake me up earlier?"

"I don't know, Jess. I didn't think you would sleep until noon. And I reminded you before bed. You said you were setting an alarm?" His claim invalidates my victim status. "I mean how much wine did you have last night?" His tone makes no secret of his judgment of me.

"I don't know, Jack," I snip, returning his attitude. "My boyfriend was ignoring me at dinner so maybe I had a little more than I should have."

"Yeah, I think that was clear to everyone there. You seemed to have left your southern charm in Atlanta, you weren't exactly playing nicely with Max's date." I let out a big, frustrated sigh. This is so not the start to the morning that I had expected. I assumed Jack and I would wake up and immediately make up, with some amazing sex and apologies all around to start off a day of gluttony and indulgence. Having only been awake for two minutes, I decide not to further provoke the argument, and instead walk silently into the bathroom.

I brush my teeth and then hop into the shower, scrubbing myself as quickly as I know how. The usual luxuries of sitting down to shave are forgone to expedite the beautification and cleansing process. I pop out of the shower as quickly as I got in and towel myself dry.

I wipe the steam from the mirror and open the bathroom door to let the humidity escape, the only chance I have of successfully blow drying my hair. As the door swings open I get a view of Jack getting dressed. He pulls on his favorite dark jeans and a white button-up, with his sleeves rolled at the elbows. He wears his tan belt and matching woven leather shoes. Jack glances up from his bent over position as he pulls on his shoes. "You about ready?" he asks me.

"Umm, do I look like I'm about ready?" My hair drips water, and my body is wrapped in a bathrobe, clearly displaying how unready I am. I shake my head with frustration and begin combing my wet hair.

"We'll be late if we don't leave now," Jack says, checking his watch.

"Well then maybe you should just go. I can't exactly leave the hotel looking like this."

"Come on babe, just throw something on. We can be a few minutes late," Jack's tone softens.

"No thanks. I saw last night how much fun you are when you're late to something. And I've had enough grumpy Jack for one weekend."

"Jess, please. What will you even do here without me? Sleep off some more hangover?" His snarky tone returns and quickly boils my blood.

"I can entertain myself, Jack. I'm a big girl and I'm fully capable of taking care of myself," I yell back at him, infuriated by his tone. *Just like every day at home.*

"So, what, we'll just meet up later for the festival?"

"Whatever. Just text me later when you've gotten off your high horse. Heaven forbid we spend any time together this weekend. Only *we* could come all the way to New York to spend the weekend apart!"

I turn back into the bathroom and proceed to slam the door behind me. I collapse onto the plush bath mat on the floor and draw my knees into my chest. I pray the noise of the bathroom fan covers my sobs, which begin to flow easily from me. I try to hold back any audible discontent until I finally hear the sound of the hotel room door close, signaling that Jack has finally left.

As he exits the room my pent-up emotions escape. The tears flow easily now, and I try to wrap my head around my feelings. He's an asshole. He's married to his work. Now I'm not even a priority to him. I'm just an accessory in his life, one that he can easily leave home without. I sob loudly at my stupidity, and for the situation I've put myself in. *Or, the situation I've created because I can't let myself be happy.*

And then there's Mr. Lust. Why, on earth do I even care about him? For the first time ever, I've had someone wonderful to love. And I do love Jack. But this slutty stranger from a world away cast some spell on me. A stupid, lust-filled spell. He is with Lia, and he apparently was when I stayed at his house, and when we nearly screwed at Ware.

The sobs escalate and I replay all of the events in my head. The trip to Paris, and my first time with Jack. Meeting Max, the undeniable attraction to him, and our kiss in the bar. My first fight with Jack, and almost super slutty mistake at Ware. Making up and falling in love with Jack, and feeling like a part of his wonderful family.

I focus more on Jack for a moment. Is everything with him my fault? Yes, he's been busy with work. But is that really inexcusable? I haven't really even talked to him about it. To tell him how I feel. That I miss him. And yes, we fought this morning. But I didn't do anything to help settle it. He did offer to wait for me. Why was I so quick to push him away? *Because you've been in lust with someone else.*

This startling thought pauses all others. Is it really possible to be in love with one man and in lust with another? My lust for Max has virtually ruined the first loving, meaningful relationship I've had. Shit, maybe this isn't Jack's fault. It's mine.

After a thorough emotional cleanse, the sobs finally end, my eyes red and body exhausted from the realization that *I've* fucked this up. My head feels clear, and my mind made up. Time to get my life back in order.

CHAPTER THIRTY-ONE

My second shower of the day helps to wash away the anger and frustration of the two men in my life. I throw on a sleeveless dark blue casual dress, adding a belt to give more shape to this flowing frock. I grab my black crossed heels, equipped with platforms to making city walking somewhat realistic. Screw the blisters that are inevitable today, they'll simply match my chapped love life.

I parade into Pier 94, home of this year's Wine and Food Festival, tossing my long blonde waves over my shoulder at a crowd of young men nearby. My side vision, hid stealthily beneath my oversized Prada shades, allows me to enjoy their brief attention. It really is just what I needed. To feel sexier. More in control of the tailspin that has surrounded me.

I walked straight up to the first place I could get a drink. "So how do I know if a Prosecco is good?" I ask the round-faced brunette staffing the La Marca booth.

"Because it has our label on it," she jokes with me as I finish my third tasting-sized glass, drinking in the refreshing bubbles. I giggle too, and feel my body relax a little for the first time after my emotionally exhausting morning.

"There is no bad prosecco from Italia, but the best is D.O.C.G." His pure sexy tone cuts through the air and the blood drains from my face.

"Hi," I stammer, my ears instantly telling me that it's the beautiful Mr. Lust. My normal greeting for him, a smile and heated cheeks, is replaced today by ambivalence with a side of hate. Hate mixed with anger and hurt. Hurt that he almost used me when he was with Lia. Hate that he's such a manwhore. And anger, well, at myself, for falling for it.

"Hi, yourself," he says with a big smile, which quickly fades as he realizes it goes unmatched. Despite my anger toward him, his presence quickens my pulse, and I repeatedly remind myself that I'm done with him.

"Enjoy the festival," the words fall from my mouth, unsure of what to even say. I pull my eyes from his and storm away, quietly enough that I'm the only one around us to realize it.

"Jess." He grabs my arm just as I'm nearly out of reach. The touch of his skin radiates through me, and I feel that pull to him. But my angry feelings quickly boil over and replace the lust I would normally have toward him.

"What?" I snap back, pulling my arm out of his possession.

"What's wrong? What am I missing here?"

"Nothing. I have nothing to say to you. Absolutely nothing." His handsome face falls, wearing the look of a clueless man.

"Ok." He shakes his head, processing my atypical reaction to him. "Is Jack here?"

"Maybe. I don't know," I say, leaving out the truth of why I'm not with him. "Where is Lia?"

"Who knows. Probably off with some friends or something. I don't keep track of her."

"Really? You don't keep up with the whereabouts of your live-in girlfriend?"

"Girlfriend?" He practically snorts at the word. "No, Lia is not my girlfriend. I let her stay with me while she gets settled in New York. She is like"—he pauses—"a little sister to me."

"Of course. I should have known *you* wouldn't use the word girlfriend. But sister? Really? Let me help you with your English. Last I checked *sister* isn't the right word for someone you're currently fucking. And have been fucking for months," I hiss at him, causing my voice to rise and a nearby festival-goer to gape at me.

"What are you talking about, Jess?" His confusion looks genuine draped across his movie-star face.

"I'm on to you, Max. I know that Lia was living with you back when…" I pause, unsure of how to verbalize our New York encounter. "When I stayed at your house. And frankly I have nothing else to say to you. I made a mistake that night, thinking you were something other than your reputation. So, shame on me." I pause to catch my breath before delivering the final blow. "I hope I never see you again."

I thrust my clutch beneath my arm and begin my rapid escape from this man. I feel the tears flooding my rapidly blinking eyes for the second time today. The crowd and my jumbo heels are the only things keeping me from a full-on sprint rather than my more controlled gallop. I look up to keep the tears from falling and simultaneously search for an exit.

Finally, I find one and blast through the door at full force, landing just steps from the edge of the pier. I drop to my knees and the tears instantly run free. I don't dare look up at the two maintenance workers who occupy this space, but keep my head in my arms until I watch their cigarettes fall to the ground and hear the door close behind them. Any last bit of self-control has now vanished, and the tears join forces with body convulsions to absorb my failing love, and the stupid lust that has left me so lost inside.

CHAPTER THIRTY-TWO

Despite my mental breakup and emotional cleanse of Max just hours ago, seeing him, and feeling his touch, makes this cut much deeper than before. I know he's a lying, disgusting asshole, but my heart still feels broken, and my brain like a fool. The attraction I've had to him has been so real, so unlike anything I've ever experienced before. What started as a chance meeting halfway around the world has ended with our lives crossing paths so many times. *Was it really all just one big lusty coincidence? No, it doesn't matter. I'm done with him.* This thought elicits the biggest sob of all, and I hug my knees in closer.

"Bella," I hear the voice of the one and only evil Mr. Lust. *Motherfucking son of a bitch. Can't a girl have a breakdown on her own?*

"Just leave me alone. PLEASE!" I shout to him. "Please."

"Jess, I just don't understand. That night in New York, I think about it all the time. About *you* all the time."

I shake my head at him. "Why, because I puked all over myself so you missed your chance for a threesome? Newsflash, no matter how drunk I was that wouldn't have happened."

"No. You don't understand. Yes, Lia was living with me then. But she is a family friend. We are not dating. I've never slept with her—I've never even kissed her."

"I don't believe you. You're lying. You're just a lying slut!" I lift my head only to shout at him then return it tightly into my knees.

"Jess. Believe me. I wouldn't lie to you." I feel Max drop down onto the ground next to me, and he places his warm hand on my knee.

"Jessa, please." Just hearing his nickname for me makes my heart skip a beat, remembering how strongly I've felt about him. Max's hand finds mine, and he gives it a gentle squeeze. The same touch that has lured me in all along doesn't fail now. No matter how angry I am at him, or how much I remind myself that I'm still with Jack, my body still craves his touch.

"Jessa, please talk to me." This time he scoops up my chin, forcing my head to turn in his direction. I turn my salty eyes away, not wanting to catch his. "Jessa, come on." He bobs his head around, trying to find my eyes, until I finally allow him to catch my stare. "My Jessa," his eyes have locked on to mine, and I see the concern seeping from his gaze. "Lia means nothing to me romantically. Her mother was my mother's dearest friend. I'm helping her because my mother would want me to. It's nothing more."

"Right. Then what about Emma?"

He lets out a big sigh. "I kissed her. That night at the St. Regis. But that was all. She means nothing to me. Please. Believe me. You know I could've left with her that night at your house, but I didn't want to. You are the only woman I want," he affirms. "But can't have." His last words are under his breath, but loud enough for me to hear given his proximity to me.

Oh, how I feel myself still wanting him, too. And I want to believe him. Believe that this is all one big misunderstanding, that our encounters aren't just a coincidence, and that his desire for me is as real as mine for him. *I want you, too. So, so badly.* My body won't allow me to forget this notion.

Max wipes away my tear, and I reach my hand onto his as he gently touches my skin. He wraps his arms around me, and for some reason this gesture unleashes the heaviest of sobs I had been holding back. He says nothing but holds me tightly, allowing me to finish the emotional cleansing.

"Here," he finally says, breaking the surprisingly comfortable silence. I look up to see a concerned Max offering me a handkerchief. *People actually still carry those?*

"Thanks." I try my best to dab the tears and mascara smudge from my eyes, seeing the dark smears on his previously pristine cloth. *God, I must look like hell. What do I even say to him now?*

"Come on, let's get you back inside. I think you could use a drink?"

I giggle at the thought, knowing I could use a full barrel of wine to wash away this day.

CHAPTER THIRTY-THREE

I stop into the ladies' room to apply fresh mascara, powder and lipstick. Amazingly, a five-minute touch-up has given my appearance some sense of normalcy. I blink back at my pale complexion, now decorated with rosy cheeks, compliments of my meltdown. My thoughts, feelings, and outlook on life have been pulled in every direction in the last twenty-four hours, and I'm not sure my brain has caught up to my heart. Even though I should be on the righteous path with Jack, my mind defaults to those same Lustful fantasies I've had since we met.

Max leads me back toward the festival, without a single word about what just happened. Thank god. My brain is spinning in too many directions to think logically, so I decide to simply be carefree for a moment. "Come! We'll have to wait forever if we don't cross now!" I shout at Max, and we race across the street from the bathrooms back to the festival area. My fingers are laced in his, laughing as we sprint across the lanes of traffic. We almost make it before the light turns, but a few taxis in the final lane must wait for us to cross, leading them to honk madly at us until we clear, and Max and I to laugh at the scene we've caused.

We catch our breaths at the side of the pier, leaning over to watch the shimmering waters between New York and New Jersey splash from the force of faraway boats. The sun is partially masked by a few clouds, leaving the spring day warm but far enough from the unbearable summer heat. "I almost lost you back there!" he says with a laugh.

"These aren't exactly my running shoes!" I say with a defensive laugh, nodding to my strappy leather shoes. I feel myself wonder where this afternoon may take us, until he opens his mouth again.

"So Jack is supposed to meet you here?"

"Yeah, with a friend. But I haven't talked to him all day so who knows when he'll show up."

"Well we are here. So, let's enjoy this day, while I have you." *Have me.* The same words he said not long ago. The irony is, despite me not being his, all I can think about is having him. I can't help but remember the night we came so close to having each other. I remember his strong fingers stroking me, readying my body to take his. His hot, fresh mouth taunting me.

"Let's do it," I say aloud, while affirming the double entendre to myself and subsequently feeling the guilt of such an adulterous thought. My Lust simply takes my hand again and escorts me inside the festival. His normal mysterious demeanor is notably absent today, and I'm even more drawn to this easy-going, divinely sexy man. He knows my boyfriend will be showing up at any time, but that doesn't stop him from this seeming display of affection. *It's just flirting, not cheating,* I think, temporarily placating my guilt.

"This way." He grabs my hand again and leads me through the growing crowd of attendees to a food station. The crowd forces him to pull me in close as we approach an oyster display. A look of horror covers my face as I look at the grimy dark oysters displayed neatly on a bed of ice. I've never eaten an oyster and have never,

ever wanted to. That is until this sex on a stick offered one to me. I listen as an older man with salt-and-pepper hair describes the various types of oysters and regions they're from. "Would you care to try one?" the oyster shucking man asks me politely. *God no, I don't want to put anything wet and slimy in my mouth. Unless it's coming out of him. Stop it, Jess.*

"I'll have a Prince Edward Island oyster," my Lust requests.

"And for the lady?" He turns to me anxiously, and I fret the words I'm about to say.

"I'll have the same." I gulp fearfully, while the thought of eating this disgusting food takes over my brain.

"What's the matter?" Max asks me, sliding his arm around my waist as though I'm his. "Don't you like oysters?" His comforting touch relaxes my fear a bit, and I decide to come clean.

"I've never tried them before," I admit, embarrassed to reveal that I'm not as worldly and cultured as he is. He lets out a laugh.

"Well now is a good time. You will like them. Trust me?" I nod my head wearily. "Just watch what I do." He holds up his oyster shell on display, then he raises the oyster to his beautiful lips, tilts it backward, takes a few gentle chews, then swallows. "Delicious!" he announces to the oyster man. "Salty and briny, just how I like them." *Did he just say grimy?* He picks up his glass of Prosecco and finishes his swallow with a sip of bubbles. "Now you try!" he says excitedly, motioning for the oyster man to give us another one. My uncertain stare gazes back at him and I begrudgingly accept the hard shell into my hand, wanting to embrace all of the adventure this day has brought me.

"So do you chew it? Or just swallow it?" I ask naively, soliciting a laugh from my Lust.

"Both. But you chew it first. If you swallow first it will be hard to chew it." *What?* It takes me a few seconds to understand his attempt at a joke. I giggle, appreciating that he's trying to be funny.

"Ok. Here goes nothing!" I smile bravely at him and look down to the slimy blob resting on a rock. It's then that I realize that I'm not sure how I actually get it into my mouth. Do I just suck? I begin to ask this question, but another giggle escapes when I think of the question in my head. *So, Max, do I just suck it, and then swallow the slimy stuff?* My juvenile and dirty mind foresees the parallels of doing this to him.

"What is it?" Max questions me, clearly amused by my repeated giggles.

"Nothing," I lie. *Here goes nothing!* I raise the little rock to my mouth and tilt it backward, watching and mimicking a nearby oyster connoisseur. The salty, gritty blob falls on my tongue and I let it roll there for a moment, feeling the strange texture in my mouth. I slide it between my teeth and take a slight nibble, not realizing my expression reflects my undignified and horrified state.

"Here," he says, handing me my Prosecco and laughing at my reaction. "This will wash it all away." I nod my head and force myself to swallow the slimy object. Thank God for delicious Italian bubbles.

"So what did you think?" the oyster man asks me.

"Umm," I pause, "I think it's probably an acquired taste?" He and Max break out into laughter.

"It's not for everyone. But we probably should have started you on something a little less briny. Do you want to try another?"

"No, thank you, I'd hate to spoil my appetite with so much other great food here!" We thank the oyster man for his time and walk into the crowd for more food exploration.

"So what is your favorite food?" His simple question is one that I don't have an immediate answer for.

"I honestly don't think I have just one," I confess. "There are so many great foods in the world that I couldn't live without."

"Ok, like what?"

"Cheese. With a baguette and fruit, with macaroni, on pizza… need I go on?" I purposely leave off grilled and on fries to not fully reveal my inner fat kid.

"Well I can see you have thought this through. And what comes second to cheese or cheese-related foods?"

"Chocolate!" I say without hesitation. As if anything could come close in comparison.

"Ok, then we shall find you some cheese, followed by chocolate," he instructs.

"Well what is your favorite food?"

Max looks at me, thoughtfully considering my question. "Anything I can share with you." His eyes burn into mine, overflowing me with lust for him. And I feel myself want him now more than ever.

CHAPTER THIRTY-FOUR

"*D*id you say this is Italian?" I ask my Lust about the red wine that rests in our hands.

"No, this one is from Napa," he says pointing to the bottle displayed behind us. *Come on, Jess, focus!* We've been wandering through the festival for nearly ninety minutes indulging in all things cheese, chocolate, and wine-related, and now I feel my buzz lightening me on my feet. I'm just buzzed enough to feel free with my flirtations, but not enough to be drunk. I promised myself not to let that happen again, I've already embarrassed myself around him once doing that.

"So where is this boyfriend of yours?" my Lust asks me, finally addressing the elephant who is not in the room. I realize I haven't even checked my phone to see if Jack has tried to contact me. I've been having way too much fun playing pretend with my beautiful Italian man to think of him. *Oops.*

"I'm not sure," I say, shrugging my shoulders. "I haven't thought about him in hours," I say honestly, looking for reassurance in Max's eyes, and feeling the guilt return.

"Well I will keep you company for as long as you like," he says with his signature wink. I melt a little inside and feel myself being even more drawn to this man. What a difference just a few hours can make. Since learning the truth about Lia, I'm filled with relief, and even hope. Maybe there's a reason why Jack and I came up here and got into a fight. I mean how many times do Max and I have to run into each other before our fate just cock slaps me in the face? I realize that this opportunity to explore what may have been, and may still be, has been handed to me on a silver platter. My daydream is quickly tempered by my own logic. *Remember his reputation, Jess, he's a manwhore. You're just another conquest to him.* I try to force the cautiously boring and judgmental keeper out of my brain.

"Hey man, what are you doing here?" Jack's voice interrupts my thoughts, and I instantly feel guilt spread inside me. Even though my body hasn't betrayed him, my mind certainly has.

"Hey, Jack," Max responds with a warm handshake. "Jess and I ran into each other, so we've just been sampling some food and wine. This place is great. Did you just get here?"

"About a half hour ago. I've been calling you, trying to find you," Jack says with a glare toward me, not hiding the agitation in his voice. It's clear that he's the one now trying to continue our fight from this morning.

"Sorry," I respond. "It's loud in here." His annoyance allows me to ease my guilt with my own remaining frustration toward him.

"I want to introduce you to my friend, Barrett." Jack motions toward a tall, skinny, overly preppy man with dark hair and green eyes. He's cute, dressed in a white polo and white jeans. His shirt is unbuttoned a bit too far, proving that exposing too much chest hair is never a tasteful choice.

"Nice to meet you, Jess. I've been hearing about you all day," Barrett says politely, extending his hand to mine.

"Hey man, I'm Barrett," he says, next introducing himself to Max.

"Nice to meet you. I'm Max."

"So how do you guys know each other?" Barrett asks skeptically, apparently trying to determine the circumstances that find me wandering around this festival with another man.

"We actually met in Paris when these two were on vacation," Max responds, "and now Jack is supporting one of my company's deals so we're working together as well."

"Small world," Barrett says, clearly still questioning why I'm really here with this other man.

"So what have you seen in the festival so far?" I ask, forcing myself to play nice.

"Mainly the South African wines. I figured if we started in the wine area I would probably find you." Jack says with a laugh, putting his arm around me, and touching me for the first time since yesterday. My body tenses with his touch, and I catch Max eyeing my body language, trying to read into our interactions.

"Well it is a wine and food festival, so it was a good guess," I say flatly. "Jack, they have an oyster station back there."

"Oh, awesome."

"Yeah, let's go check that out," Barrett says to him.

"You guys want to come?" Jack asks us. My Lust turns to me and gives me a slight shrug of his shoulders, indicating that he'll follow my lead.

"We've already been over there, so we might just keep working our way through," I say shamefully, realizing I'm trying to ditch my boyfriend for my lustfriend.

"Sounds good. Hey, thanks for keeping my girl company, Max," Jack says appreciatively.

"My pleasure," my Lust says with a gleaming smile toward me.

"Great. I'll text you in a bit," Jack moves in for a kiss and I turn my head slightly, forcing his lips to land on my cheek. Thankfully Jack thinks nothing of my averted lip lock, and he and Barrett go back to their festival exploration.

As soon as they're out of sight Max looks at me. "Come," he directs me, and takes my elbow leading me away. I frown that he hasn't reached for my hand again, but only hope that he's being respectful given Jack's presence nearby.

"Where are we going?"

"Somewhere that I can have you." *Oh. My.* I have no idea what he means by "have me", but my heart races and my body aches for the answer. I squeeze his hand to let him know my feelings match his. We walk through the exit, and Max does a quick glance to be sure we don't recognize anyone outside. The daylight is fading, and we stand on the edge of the pier, the waves splashing back and forth just a few feet away from us.

"So beautiful," Max says.

"I know, what a gorgeous sunset," I agree, feeling my heart race faster than my mind with anticipation. He lets out a little laugh and shakes his head. He then pulls my arm in, forcing me to push against him. I remember his fresh smell of Italian soaps and raw pheromones from months ago when our bodies were this close. Feeling his closeness overtakes any guilt I have for Jack, and I finally realize that this lust just might be more powerful than my love. This feeling is something I can't refuse any longer, and I decide I have to explore this truth.

"I was talking about you," he says with a smile, finding my eyes with his. I blush at the compliment, but find the sincerity behind his serious eyes.

"Oh, thanks," I say, glancing away from his intense stare. His warm fingers find my chin and they guide my face back toward him. I stretch on my toes and wrap my arms around his neck, my body feeling the carnal pull toward him. My mind tells me this would be wrong, but my body assures me it's only right. My heart pounds faster and faster as my lips finally meet his, a moment that I wasn't sure I would ever experience again.

I instantly lose myself into him, his soft lips rest against mine, and his tongue slides my mouth open, allowing our bodies to further connect. I crave closeness to him and I wrap my arms around him, letting my fingers run through his hair. I pull him to me and feel his body relax into me. We ravage each other's mouths, and the desires pull at every inch of my body, wanting and needing more of him. Everything inside of me is in a state of euphoria, and my body knows it's met its match.

His hands begin to explore me, starting at my waist, and then moving up and down a few inches at a time. I can feel his hands wanting to go down further, to caress my butt, but each time he inches closer down there he squeezes me tighter and moves his hands back up. He must be cognizant of our public surroundings, but for once I'm completely unafraid of PDA. Of being caught. It's all I can do to keep my panties on right now. I continue to melt into his arms, and electricity between us grows with each second that passes. Our lips remain locked for what seems like forever; I'm in no hurry to let this beautiful, lusty man go. I feel his manhood grow larger against me and my body aches to feel his skin against mine.

When we eventually pause to catch our breath, our eyes connect, and we wordlessly look to each other for a sign of what's next.

CHAPTER THIRTY-FIVE

"No, no, no! You must come back to my house with me. I won't take no for an answer," my Lust says to me, Jack, and Barrett.

"No, really, we don't want to be a bother. We can just head back to the hotel and have a drink," Jack responds. The four of us stand outside of the Tacos and Tequila event, trying to decide where to close out the evening. It's taking every bit of self-control inside of me not to jump on top of Max this evening. We've barely had any alone time together since our kiss—well, make-out session, rather—ended at the pier. Jack and Barrett found us shortly after we went back inside the festival and we've been hanging as a foursome ever since.

"I should probably get home, I've got a pregnant wife waiting for me," Barrett responds, indicating that he's leaving and I'll soon be stuck between my boyfriend and my lustfriend.

"Okay, dude, it was great seeing you. Hope it's not so long between the next visit!" Jack says giving a bro hug to his friend.

"Jess, it was great meeting you. Take care of this guy, don't let him get into too much trouble," Barrett says, giving me a hug.

"I'll do what I can, but no promises!" I say with a laugh. "You know what challenges I'm working with here!"

"Touché," Barrett laughs. "Max, great meeting you as well. You have my card now, so give me a shout if you want to grab a drink, or of course if my bank can be of service for you." He extends his hand toward Max.

"Nice meeting you as well," Max says, returning the handshake. "I'll be in touch." Barrett leaves us and my mind begins spinning, wondering if my evening of Lust will soon end.

"Well I don't know about you guys but I'm still game for a nightcap," Jack announces to us.

"Then it's settled. You will come to my home for another drink. You've hosted me at your house, so please, let me return the favor."

"Make yourselves at home." Max gestures for us to sit in his mahogany den. I sit gingerly on the chestnut tufted leather sofa, gazing at his book collections, which anchor a large window in the middle of the room. The view is of his small but private courtyard, housing perfectly sculpted evergreens that are lit by the soft glow of patio lights. I vaguely remember catching a glimpse of this room during my previous visit here.

"What can I get you to drink?" Max asks us.

"Well, what do you have?" Jack probes him.

"Virtually everything," he laughs. "Well most liquors, and a fairly deep selection of wine. Not much beer on hand right now though since I've been traveling."

"How about a Manhattan? When in Rome, as they say."

"Prego. I'll join you. And Jess, what can I get you?"

"Oh, just water please." After my full day of drinking I know I need some hydration. And I'm smart enough not to make the same mistake twice and end up throwing up in front of this beautiful man again.

"Gas?" Max asks me, catching me by surprise. *Did he just ask if I have gas?*

"Do you want gas in your water? You know, umm, bubbles?"

"Oh!" I say with a giggle. "No, still water is fine. Thank you." I feel my face blush, hoping he doesn't realize how amused I am by toilet humor.

"Of course," he responds with a straight face, thankfully either ignoring or oblivious to my childish humor. He gives a slight nod toward the back of the room and I see Enzo standing quietly and inconspicuously in the back corner, ready to dash off and make our drinks. *Wow.* I forgot that Enzo is not only his driver but also his butler. Having a man servant only makes him lustier. Lusty yet refined. Except when he slides his tongue against mine and I feel nothing but unrefined thoughts radiate from him.

"This is such a great place. How long have you lived here?" Jack asks, walking around the edge of the room and viewing the adjacent patio.

"Here, hmm, I've been in this house for maybe two years. Before that I just rented a suite at the Waldorf every time I came into town. It was nice, but I preferred having my own space. Somewhere I could make my own."

"We're actually staying at the Waldorf this weekend," I chime in. "I love the classic décor. It has an interesting old world feel to it."

"Oh I completely disagree," Jack says. I can't help but roll my eyes, wondering if Jack's just trying to pick at me. "It's too old school. I don't think they've evolved their décor over time at all."

"I have to disagree, Jack," Max says. "I think they are such a classic institution, and their look reflects that. They're staying true to themselves, and not putting loud music and mood lighting in the elevator, nor do they try to cater to twenty-somethings. No offense," he smiles, acknowledging the age differences between us.

"None taken, old man," Jack retorts, showing a bit of a wobble as he slaps Max on the shoulder, revealing his overindulgence of alcohol. That's just what I need, a drunk boyfriend to deal with while I stare at my lustfriend. On second thought, if he passes out then maybe I would have a chance to be alone with Max? *What happened to your weekend of reconciliation with Jack, your boyfriend? Don't be like your mother, Jess.*

Enzo enters the room with a silver tray and serves me first, placing a bottle of Evian on the table in front of me along with a napkin underneath. It's just like being at a restaurant and having wait service.

"Thanks, Enzo," I say quietly. He nods his head and gives me a slight smile, enhancing the deep wrinkles around his ageing gray eyes. He next goes to Jack and then lastly to Max to deliver their Manhattans. I watch him glance at Max, as if waiting for a command. Max simply gives a half shake of his head and Enzo understands the cue for his dismissal, quietly leaving the room and closing the wooden doors behind him.

"So where is Lia tonight?" Jack asks.

"Probably out with friends somewhere. I can't keep track of her whereabouts. She's just a party animal."

"And you're ok with this?"

"So long as she doesn't bring the party back to my house, it's fine. I think she'll be moving out soon, she's getting enough work now that she should be able to afford something."

"You just moved her in, and you're ready to kick her out?" Jack asks.

"Oh, no. She is staying here as a favor to her family. Our mothers were very close in Italy, and I promised to look out for her when she moved here. There's nothing more between us."

"Well, maybe not yet." Jack winks at him, raising his glass in a silent toast. I can't help but roll my eyes, but neither man catches my reaction.

"Buongiorrrnooooo," a drunken female voice rings through the apartment. *Good God is she right on cue.* "Ciao, Maxi," the voice calls as it nears us. I know instantly it's Lia, arriving home after a night of partying. I glance at my phone and see it's 1:15 am, surprisingly early for her to come back on a Saturday night. "Ciao," her voice calls again. This time she swings open the heavy wooden doors to his study. "Maxi!" she says excitedly upon catching a glimpse of him. I watch her face fall a bit as she sees that Jack and I are here. I'm not sure if it's because she wants Max all alone, or because she doesn't want to spend another night hanging with us. I can't exactly blame her, since the feeling is mutual.

I watch the scantily clad party girl skip across the room toward Max. Her white dress is akin to a sausage casing, squeezing in every inch of her perfect figure. I could never, ever, wear a dress like that, my curves would only look like sausage links. I reassure myself by remembering that she's not dating him. *But neither am I.*

"Ciao, Jessica!" Lia gives me a slight wave as she passes by me.

"Hello, Lia. Have fun at the club?"

"Ugh, no, it was filled with boys," she says, pausing to greet Jack.

"And this is a bad thing?" Jack asks, turning his head from side to side to accept her European greeting.

"No, I do not want boys. I want men! Like you and Max," she says. "You are both handsome men with good tastes. You appreciate women. These boys only want sex. God, it is the same everywhere! Roma was filled with boys. New York? Filled with boys. I do not need boy friend. I need man friend!" She raises her hands up dramatically to emphasize her point. "My darling, Max. Did you miss me tonight?" She gives him a kiss on the cheek and I watch him return the greeting, but his eyes catch mine and he shoots me a wink. I can't help but smile back at him, acknowledging the secret feelings between us.

Lia plops down onto the sofa that faces me, crossing her long, thin legs in front of her. At the end of her long stems are fluorescent green Manolos, with pencil thin, skyhigh heels. I'm 99% sure that if I stood up on those shoes they would simply collapse underneath me as they likely have a weight limit of 100 pounds. I'm insanely jealous of her tiny frame and how easily she can wear these tiny clothes and toothpick heels.

"What are we drinking?" Lia says loudly enough for Enzo to pop his head in the room. Before anyone can answer, she pulls Max's glass from his hands and takes a sip. I happily watch his expression become annoyed with her, but he doesn't say anything. "Manhattans? How obvious. What about you, Jess?"

"Just water."

"Booorrring. We need some tequila!" Enzo glances toward Max, who gives him a nod of approval, before running off to retrieve her request. It's reassuring to watch his interactions with her tonight, affirming everything Max claimed was true. She's just a young family friend, who even annoys Max a bit, but has no romantic ties to him.

"We need some entertainment. And music!" Lia jumps to her feet to take care of these needs. She grabs a remote from a drawer in Max's desk, and music comes singing through the speakers. The sound is classic, like an Italian opera, and her face immediately twists. "This is not party music. Make it stop." She hands the remote to Max, who plays along and changes the tunes to more contemporary music. "How about a game? Some poker?" She looks around gauging our interest. "Ohhh! I know! Strip poker!" I cringe at the thought. There's no way in hell I'm putting any more of my body on display next to hers.

"Maybe just a card game where we keep our clothes on?" I suggest.

"Uh, fine, but we will come up with a dare for the loser!"

I escape the third round of Scopa, an Italian card game that I'm way too tired to play, by slipping into the bathroom. My tired eyes stare back at me in the mirror, along with the sparkling reflection of Italian marble and silver patterned wallpaper on the bathroom walls. I'm now sober, the only one who is, I might add, and exhausted from the day. I resign myself to the fact that today's fun with my Lust is probably over, and push aside the painful realities of my relationship with Jack, especially after my shameful, yet oh so memorable, transgressions today. I pinch my cheeks and dab my shiny skin in an attempt to look more awake than I feel right now. *Time to force my drunk boyfriend back to the hotel. Hopefully he'll probably just pass out quickly and we won't have time to fight. At least not tonight, anyway.*

"Close the door," Max commands me, causing me to jump a little, just as I was about to exit the bathroom. My heart starts racing, uncertain of what's about to happen but excited by the racy ideas entering my mind. It's been hours since our hot kiss on the pier, and my craving for him has only gotten stronger with each second in his presence. I nod and quietly oblige, slowly turning the doorknob to silently close the door again. The door latch quietly clicks into place and a hopeful smile covers my face. *Deep breath, Jess.* Lust enters the bathroom from the adjacent bedroom, and I have a flash of memory from my last visit here. "My God, I've been waiting to get to you all night," he says excitedly. "We've had all these distractions. And all I've been able to think about is you." His eyes are filled with passion and longing, and I feel my body literally ache from the pull toward him.

"Me too. Today was great." I pause. "The time on the pier was…" I pause again, searching for the appropriate word to describe the mind-blowing, panty-wetting, overwhelmingly lusty make-out session that we had. I feel the heat in my cheeks, and everywhere inside me, as the memory returns.

"Magnifico!" he says excitedly but hushed. He walks closer to me and I feel my pulse quicken with anticipation. I inch back against the counter, using a hand to steady my weakening knees. Lust envelopes me in his arms and plants his warm, salty lips on mine. *Mmmmm.* I groan into his mouth and begin to scold myself knowing Jack's nearby, but I am immediately lost in his kiss. Everything inside of me turns to lust, feeling the chemistry through the pit of my stomach and the pit of my peach. My tongue explores his mouth, and our hands follow suit, finally having closed doors to touch each other freely. His body and his perfect bulge push against me, and I can't wait to dive in. Without thinking, I reach down for his pants, furiously unbuttoning them. I have no plan for what comes next, what I'll do with him, his body, or my fading morals. All I want is to have him, and all of him, touching me now.

Lust's hands slide beneath my dress, allowing his fingers to caress my skin. *Thank God I shaved today.* His fingertips begin to trace the line of my stretchy lace panties, and his right index and middle fingers alternate up and down my legs toward the exterior of my smooth peach.

"Should we really be doing this?" I ask, forcing my lips to pull away from him. My brain quickly reminds me of my intentions with Jack. To get us back on track this weekend, or acknowledge what our fate is. I look at Max and his caramel eyes to find reassurance but only see a man I'm desperate for.

"No. Probably not," he responds with a wicked smile, then quickly grabs my face again. I melt back into him, overcome with the need to feel his body on mine.

"Max? Maxi? Maxxximuuus?" Lia's voice creeps into the bathroom, indicating she's nearby, and approaching quickly. My heart races, wondering what she'd do or say if she saw us in here together. Or, more importantly, how Jack would react when she would inevitably tell him.

"Are we cursed?" Max whispers to me, dropping his forehead against mine.

"It certainly feels that way." I sigh, wrapping my arms around his neck.

"Stay here, I'll sneak out when I hear her down the hallway, and then you can give it a minute and come out. Ok?" I nod my understanding.

"Jess," he pauses, staring deep into me. "This is only the beginning. Promise me?"

"Promise," I say without real thought to what these words mean. I kiss him excitedly, my heart still pounding as he sneaks away. I take a breath and reflect on his words. *If this is really the beginning with him, am I really prepared for the end with Jack?*

CHAPTER THIRTY-SIX

> Are you sure you have to leave me? I don't think I can wait two weeks.

I smile wildly at the words on my phone from my favorite 212 phone number. My heart races every time I see a new message from him, which has been often since our mind-blowing make-out in New York. I recall his last words to me: "this is only the beginning." At the time they seemed so full of promise, hope, and Lust, but I had no idea where they could actually lead. Now they've brought us to the verge of exploring something more, which we have plans to do after we're both back in the US over Memorial Day.

The thought of spending Memorial Day weekend with my Lust tingles everything inside of me, but my heart can't ignore what it requires for me and Jack. The only man I've ever loved, who seemed so perfect for me, and who in many ways I do still love. Although things haven't been the same since I moved in with Jack, I'm still not quite ready to let it all go. But, I'm not a cheater like my mother, so I have to decide: do I end it all with Jack for a weekend of Lust? I know how strongly I feel for Max, but his reputation makes me question whether it would ever be anything more than that. *But will I ever get him out of my mind otherwise?*

"Jess, snap out of it!" Sarah commands me with a lighthearted smile. "We're going to China!" she shrieks in a purposefully muted tone, not wanting to disclose how we came to be sitting in these first-class seats, ones which nearby passengers have paid five figures for. *Come on Jess, be grateful for this opportunity.* I will myself to remember these words. The truth is, I am. I'm grateful for my job, this awesome opportunity, and for the great friends that I'm going on this venture with.

"Sorry!" I say, trying to mirror Sarah's excitement and disguise my distraction. I think I'm most excited about the shopping!" I volunteer, my mind consumed by the characters on my screen. *How should I respond?*

"Yeah, never mind the amazing new country we get to explore. We get to shop for knockoffs!" Ben says in a mocking tone, which makes both me and Sarah giggle.

"Be careful what you wish for, because I'm pretty sure I'm not getting on a flight home until we have done just that!" I proclaim.

"Ditto!" Sarah mirrors my sentiment. Oh, Ben, you thought you were here as a translator, but I think your true Mandarin test will come in the shopping mall."

Ben smiles and rolls his eyes at us. "Gee, can't wait. But remember," he pauses, "I'm here as translator *and* chaperone, so what I say, goes!" he attempts to say with authority.

"Bull shit!" I softly yell back at him. "You're here because you took a semester of Mandarin, which is far more than the two hours of Rosetta Stone that either of us have had."

I pull up the screen again, knowing we're minutes away from takeoff.

Will you miss me terribly? You can always change your meeting from Paris to Shanghai ;)

I quickly type the words, and after hitting send, I glance at my last conversation with Jack. We've barely spoken since our return from New York. His endless work trip has had him away since hours after we returned home, and now I'm off to China, forcing more distance and deferring any breakup, if that's our fated path, between us. It hurts my heart to even consider the end, but I can't ignore the strains we've felt in our relationship. *And dreaming about Lust has certainly distracted me from the thought of letting my love go.* My thoughts of him are confounded with guilt, but the fantasy of him, of us, has caused me to painfully consider the end of me and Jack.

I peer at my phone, knowing that technically it's supposed to be in airplane mode now that the plane is in motion, and stealthily check my messages.

Of course. Just bring me back something nice.

Anything in particular you want?

**Yes, I know exactly what I want
You**

His words excite me, embracing the feeling of how badly I want him too. These same feelings allow me to shrink the thought of his reputation, and if I'm really ready to end it with Jack. I feel the propulsion of the jet engines beginning, telling me we're seconds away from being airborne, and forcibly disconnected for the next fifteen hours.

The Shanghai airport looks similar enough to any other large, modern airport in the world, except that I can't read any signs, save the globally recognizable emblems of Starbucks, Burger King, and Pizza Hut. *Wow, no wonder people hate America, that's what they associate with us halfway across the world—fatty fast food and designer coffee.*

Thankfully, Global arranged for us to have a driver all week, and he quickly whisks us away to our hotel. We drive through the city and I enjoy the view of bright city lights as we approach our hotel, settled on a vibrant and affluent street, akin to a Rodeo Drive or Fifth Avenue in the US. Luxury stores, malls, and brands line the street, along with a full block of street vendors that sits within a five-minute walk from our hotel.

Ping, our sweet, wrinkly, and nearly toothless driver drops us off at the front of the hotel and brings our bags inside while we check in. "So what's on the agenda for tonight?" Ben asks, trying to stifle a yawn.

"I'm thinking we all need some room service and a good night's sleep. Any objections?" Sarah asks us.

"None from me," I say, catching Ben's yawn.

"Ok, I'll give you party animals the night off. But rest up, we have a country to explore tomorrow!"

After a quick unpacking, I venture into the lavish bathroom that I will call mine for the week. It has high-end stone and gold finishes, with ample space for a separate shower, two sink vanity, and soaker tub. Even the toilet has a separate water closet, which is a nice but unnecessary feature this visit, given that I'll be the only occupant of my room. Some fragrant bath beads catch my nose's attention, and I decide to try out the soaker tub before jumping into my spacious king size bed for a serious night's sleep.

I sink down into the warm water, too tired to wash my hair, so I pile it up in a heap atop my head. I cleanse my face twice, using my

Clarisonic to invigorate my tired skin and thoroughly remove any residual airplane germs and dried on makeup. Despite being unable to read the symbols, I find a button on the side of the tub and assume it's for the massage jets. Sure enough, warm water shoots out from all around the tub, giving me fresh circulating water, and gentle vibrations to further relax me.

I grab my phone to see how good my international phone service is here. No messages from Max. *Could it be lack of service?* I send Sarah a quick text as a test.

Trying out the soaker tub. Ahhmazing.

The conversation bubble quickly appears, and my heart sinks, realizing she's received my message and my service is indeed working. *Maybe Max is asleep. What time would it be in Paris?*

Oh good call! I'm reading the articles boss lady gave us.

Oops. That's probably what I should be doing. I recall her words to us just a few days ago. "Ladies, we need you on the ground in China now. Did you know that travel from the US to China will surpass that of the US to Europe next year? We need a marketing plan to grow in this market. Go see, eat, experience, and create. Learn the market and especially the consumers your age, and come back experts on China. Ok?" I recall Sarah and I nodding and hiding our squeals until she had left the room. A stroke of luck and opportunity hit at the right time. I have to remember this getaway isn't just a break to clear my head, but an opportunity to grow my career. *So give it a little focus, Jess.*

Good plan. Nightcap soon? I'm tired but could use something to put me to sleep.

My eyes are closing reading this riveting case study. Rain check?

I smile and nod at my friend, appreciating her focus.

Of course. Sleep well.

I soak for a few more minutes and decide to venture to the hotel bar alone. It wouldn't be the first time I did so in a strange city after all. Plus, no one knows me here, so I can throw on something comfortable and indulge in a company-funded nightcap.

I venture into the bar, and despite the late hour, notice it's still occupied by a few dozen patrons. I slide onto a barstool around the curved mahogany bar, choosing a seat which maximizes people-watching. My blonde hair is piled atop my head, my face bravely naked, and my body draped in a casual cotton dress.

I order champagne upon realizing Prosecco is absent from the menu. Not a bad way to start a trip. I pause for a brief silent toast to myself. *Here's to a new adventure in a new land. And to happiness. However, and wherever, it may come. I hope it finds me.* I lift my glass into the air and take a sip of the cool fizzing liquid grapes. As the coldness washes through my chest, I feel the shiver at the thought of ending things with Jack. God, it hurts to consider this, but I tell myself it's the right thing to do if I move forward with my Memorial Day plans with Max.

I turn my thoughts to the other man in my life. I relive the excitement of our last kiss, and wonder if anything will really come of spending a hot weekend together. I do know his reputation after all. I decide to use the upcoming week to make sure I know what I'm doing. That I'm breaking up with a man I love because we're not right together. Not because of a chance for Lust.

I fall into a conversation with a cute Canadian couple visiting China on holiday. We talk about travel, and our favorite places in the world, while sharing a bottle of wine and a near hour of conversation. I check the time on my phone, knowing I need to be semi-responsible, given the full day ahead. 11:45 pm. *Oh!* A new message from Lusty 212 rests on my screen and a smile fills my face.

Still awake? Good flight?

I see his message was sent twenty minutes ago.

Great flight! I was on Global after all. And where in the world are you?

He quickly responds.

Let me guess, enjoying a night cap? Must be almost midnight there.

You think a girl like me would venture alone to a bar in a foreign country? Surely that would only lead to trouble ;)

I flash back to our first night of trouble together.

I want to see you.

The words give me another fresh visual of him, and my body begins to feel the need for him, and the memory of his lips on mine.

I want to see you. Thirteen days.

I text with unfiltered candor, feeling less guilty about flirting knowing he's across the globe.

I need to have you.

Oh. God. How I need him, too. Need to feel his mouth, his body, his manliness against me. What I wouldn't give to have him here now. I shake my head at the fantasy, bringing my head back to the here and now, but the wish for him is too strong to shake the smile from my face.

"I need you, Jessa." *Holy shit. Is this the most elaborate trick my brain has ever played on me?* His voice is crystal clear, strong, sexy, and oh so Italian. And his familiar scent is as real as ever. My pulse races, and heart pounds, and my brain is fully taken over by my craving for his body. I take in the sight of him, oh-so-fucking hot with a hint of scruff and wrinkled linen suit.

"What? How?" I shake my head, unable to understand how he could be here, in the flesh right now.

"God, you're beautiful," he whispers into my ear, planting a hello kiss just behind my ear at the bend of my neck. I wrap my arms around him, and my body tingles as his warmth pushes against me.

"I missed you, Jessa. I need to have you. Now." *Oh. My. God. Did I just come?* I nod and slide out of my seat, wrapping my arms around his neck. He nestles his head into my neck, and my body is more alive than ever.

"Yes?" He poses his question again.

"Yes," I pant into his ear. In one swift move he tosses his credit card onto the counter, then scoops me into his arms, moving into a near gallop toward the elevator.

"Eighteen," I direct him to my floor. He presses the button and pushes his body into me as the elevator doors close. *Finally!* Our mouths meet, and I grasp his belt and tug it quickly while our tongues catch up like old friends. All thoughts of romance have left my mind and been replaced with impure, hedonistic, demanding, begging, needing thoughts of him inside of me. I slide my hand into his pants and smile into my kiss as I feel his greatness waiting for me. The elevator dings, pausing us for a moment, and he lifts me again, rushing out the door.

"Room 1812," I can barely breathe out the words. He hurries to the door and I pull the key from my pocket. He leans forward, allowing me to unlock the door, and we rush inside.

"Finally," he breathes for a moment, after placing me on the ground. "I've needed you for so long, Jessa. So fucking much."

I nod, the same feelings consuming me. "Me too. I want you. Now."

He groans in understanding and swoops me onto the bed. I stare into his dark, mysterious, and lust-filled eyes as I release his erection from his pants. I tug gently at him, feeling the enormity grow even more than I remembered. I push him backward toward the pillows and straddle him. His smile is that of a Cheshire cat, and I know my expression matches his. He pulls me closer, flipping me onto my back so he can take control. *Mmm, yes, please dominate me. Now.*

I feel his mouth running down my clavicle as he exposes my upper body. My already-on-the-verge-of-orgasm body can barely take the new flashes of heat he sends through me with every movement of his lips. All I want is Him. *NOW.* Inside of me. *NOW.* Fucking me. *NOW.*

"Uhhuh," is the only word I can manage as his perfection finally slips inside of me once and for all. *Oh, my.* He lies over me, his eyes intensely staring into me, revealing his need for me matches mine for him. This moment has been months in the making and it's everything I could've hoped for, wished for, and dreamed about. His rock-solid body plows into me at a measured pace. Not too fast, just the perfect speed to feel his tightened body slide against me with each perfect thrust. His hands don't stop moving. Up. Down. Around. Front. Back. Side. Tits. Ass. Clitoris. He's like a kid having a free-for-all in a candy store, eager to see and touch every inch that's before him. And it makes me feel unbelievably sexy.

I wrap my arms around him, mimicking his exploration, wanting to feel every muscle that curves throughout his strong body. I can't help but grab his ass. Taut and unforgiving, I feel it flexing over and over as his love stick moves inside of me. My body wants to let go all over him, and the ripeness of my peach forces a quiver with each rub of his skin against it. I pull his mouth to mine and allow the quivering to overtake me, forcing myself to continue on through it. He feels my release and grabs me tightly, pulling his lips to my neck, intensifying the sensation as parallel tingles run down my side. He continues sliding in and out of me as my quivering slows. He shows no signs of stopping, and continues on, wickedly smiling at the pleasure he can see that he's giving me. The intensity never leaves, and simply keeps building, while my body shudders throughout the torturous pleasure. My eyes stay shut, kissing him fervently, trying to stave off round two. I'm caught between that excruciating feeling of wanting to let go, yet fearing the all-consuming intensity of doing so.

"You're so beautiful, Jess," he says through panted breaths. "I've wanted this for so long," he admits. "Since I laid eyes on you in that bar."

"Me too. I'm so glad you're here," I say, looking deep into his eyes. The seriousness about him is so intense, until he breaks his gaze, closing his eyes as if to savor the moment as his body begins to tighten. Knowing what's coming next I begin tightening myself around him, trying to intensify his sensations. He responds immediately, wrapping his fingers into my hair, tugging my head into him. I take in the smell of his Italianness and feel my body give way to its need as his does the same.

The explosion of my mind matches that of my peach. We lie quietly for a moment, my mind overwhelmed processing my feelings for him. This man that I met months ago, have lusted over, dreamed about, nearly fucked, pseudo broken up with despite never having technically dated, is here. In my hotel room. In China of all places. He literally came to the other side of the world to see me. *This can't possibly be the world's most elaborate booty call, can it?* Even a man with this much money wouldn't need to come all the way to China just for sex. It has to be more than that. He's here for me. *For us.* A smile forms on my lips with this thought, and I'm immediately caught.

"What are you thinking about, bella?" he asks me softly, planting a kiss above my brow. His accent manages to saturate me all over again. I begin to clam up at the thought of expressing my feelings for him. *You just had amazing and ridiculous sex with him. You can be real, Jess.*

I giggle back at him. "Well, you, of course," I admit. "I just can't believe you're here! I mean, I'm so glad that you are, but I didn't think I would see you for another two weeks." He reaches his arm closer around me and pulls my mouth to his. Instead of using his words to explain why he's here, he lets his mouth show me why. Every bit of his kiss is filled with passion and emotion, and I'm overtaken by the fire in my stomach, and the fireworks that my new lover brings.

I crave every second of our endless make-out session. Our tongues slide easily into a rhythm, each almost taking turns guiding the movements in our mouth. I can't get enough of him, and him of me, and we both continue like teenagers with our hands and mouths exploring each other. His leg is wrapped around me, and we both lie on our sides on this king size bed, only taking up a fraction of space because we are so entangled with each other. Every second is as hot as the last and all I can think about is how amazingly much I want him all to myself.

I am too wrapped up in his lustiness to throw in the towel, so our lips remain locked until Lust finally pauses. He stops to gaze at me, and for a moment we just stare into each other without words. His left hand reaches above my right eyebrow, and he lightly strokes my skin, softly, sweetly, gently, allowing me to relax against his hand. "So beautiful," he says with his intense gaze. My already crimson cheeks can't redden any further, but I can't help but feel shy about my appearance. I lie naked on this bed, sans makeup, but covered by jet lagged, tired skin. I just smile back at him, noticing the slight creases around his eyes when he smiles.

"So how old are you?" I suddenly blurt out, verbalizing my curiosity. My Lust immediately laughs at my question.

"Well how old are you?" he retorts in a teasing tone.

"Guess," I say, raising my eyebrows.

"Hmm," he hums his lips together, eyeing me up and down. "Well this part looks pretty young and fit," he says, caressing my right butt cheek. "But this part, is, how you say, a little droopy?" he says poking playfully at my breast.

"Hey!" I shout defensively, moving my hand toward him to give a playful shove. He grabs my hand as it meets his chest, stopping my shove, and locking his fingers into mine.

"I'm joking! You are truly perfect, bella. Don't let anyone ever say otherwise." He gives my hand a squeeze, enriching his kind words with sincerity. I return a grateful smile and my own squeeze of his hand. "How old do you think I am?" he asks as I gaze back at him. I study him for a moment: his mouth has obvious smile lines, deep enough to show he's spent many years of his life smiling, but isn't a heavily aged man. The light is low enough in the room that his pupils are small, allowing me to notice the details within him. I memorize his brown eyes, noticing the dark ridges around the edge of his irises, and the gradual fade into a grayish green center around his pupils. He has a few lines in his forehead, likely due to the frequent raising of his eyebrows, one of his signature expressions, in addition to his winks.

The neck though, that's where one can typically tell age. Even people who barely age and have youthful faces often reveal their true age by the number of wrinkles found on their neck, or by the sagging where the ear meets the face. I reach my hand across his stubbly skin, to touch these telltale areas. I stroke him gently, and watch his eyes close to relish my touch.

"42," I say finally. His eyes pop open immediately.

"What?" he nearly shouts, clearly appalled. You think I'm how old?" he asks again, his incredulous but teasing tone getting higher with each word. I simply giggle at his response. "Oh, Jessa. So young and naïve," he says, looking over his shoulder as his worlds trail off.

"Naïve? I'll take young, but how am I naïve?" I ask a bit defensively.

"You know my English not good," he says with a mocking tone. "Is naïve the wrong word for a twenty-five-year old who just let a strange forty-year-old man into her hotel room to make love?"

Make love. Those beautiful words ring true in my ear. We're certainly not in love, but I do know I'm in lust with him. So I guess we technically just made lust. *Mmm I wouldn't mind doing that again.*

"I thought you were forty-two?" I giggle. "But naïve? I am not. Although you are a strange man," I affirm with a laugh. "Do you need a young American teacher to help you with your English?" I ask flirtatiously. He pauses, his smile fading into a more serious expression.

"No, I don't need *a* teacher. I need *you. Again.*" He rolls his body over against me and pushes his mouth on to me. *Oh, my God.* My still wet loins push the firework-filled knots into my stomach as I take his mouth against mine. I don't know how it's possible, but I want him even more now. My peach feels ripe and hungry, and it begs me to have him inside of me. I wiggle myself beneath his body, his erection pushing against my clitoris. I slide up and back against him, readying myself more with each stroke, and feeling his body respond to my touch. I continue for as long as I can, which can't be more than thirty seconds, before boldly taking what I want. I pull my hips up higher so that I'm raised above him, then quickly force myself down onto him, connecting our bodies once again.

We both groan as he fills me completely. So intimately. My body is still tight from my barely worn off orgasm, making his already large size feel even more powerful to both of us. "Fuck, Jessa," he says panting into my ear before nipping the side of my neck with his teeth. "I love having you."

"I love having you," I whisper in his ear, my body feeling carefree and carnal for him. We work in a slow rhythm, both barely able to tolerate each brush of our skin against each other. As my body slides up and down against his, my hardened nipples are teased by his smooth chest. I tighten my butt over and over, helping me move up and down his Italian pogo stick, forcing my eyes open to watch his reciprocated pleasure. "Baby, I can't wait," he says between near pained expressions. "Please. Jess. I need to feel you." He pants a few more breaths. "Now." His words are all that I need to realize how much I need to feel him again, too. I quicken the pace and within seconds we both let go, into each other's arms again, our bodies on fire, and our feelings for each other growing exponentially.

CHAPTER THIRTY-SEVEN

"I'm completely stuffed!" I exclaim, staring at the pile of plates stacked on the large desk. A combination of half-eaten Chinese delicacies and American favorites stare back at me from across the room.

"I think we better clear this out or we will wake up smelling like rubbish" Lust says, lifting himself from a leather armchair to his feet. I giggle to myself at his use of the word rubbish an indication of his schooling in England.

"I can get that," I say, jumping up from the other side of the desk.

"No, you sit," he commands me, placing his hands at my shoulders to push me back into my seat. "My mother didn't raise a helpless man." He kisses me on the forehead and begins piling the plates onto the service trays.

"Speaking of your mother, are you very close to her?" I ask, taking this opening to learn more about Sir Lustiness's family.

"Yes. Well, I was," he says, continuing his tidying. "She died when I was 19." *Shit, you knew that, Jess. Way to pay attention.*

"That's right. I'm so sorry. What happened?" I ask cautiously, hoping I'm not crossing a line.

"Cancer. I guess. It all happened once I went off to Oxford. She was not well, but never really told me how sick she was..." He pauses to shake his head. "If I had known, I would have left school to care for her. And she was so stubborn," he reflects with a sigh and a smile, "that's why she didn't tell me until the end. She was determined for me to have a better life. She didn't want me to lose the opportunity to have a world-class education. Sometimes I wonder if she was already sick before I went to school, and hid it. She was so selfless, my mother. God rest her soul." He turns toward me and plants another swift kiss on my cheek as he heads for the door. "Be right back, bella." I nod and watch him walk away from me, feeling guilty as I think about his tight butt, and how his perfect and most grandiose muscle perfectly plowed me not even an hour ago. *Come on, Jess, he opened up to you about his mother's death. At least get fucking him out of your brain for one minute.* The door clicks behind him and I turn to stare at him. "So what else do you want to know, bella?" He raises his eyebrow inquisitively, his dark eyes gleaming.

"Everything!" I proclaim.

"You'll have to be more specific," he says with a laugh. "Now come, talk with me," he pats his hand on the bed, indicating he wants me to come to him. I oblige, wondering if this will lead to conversation with our words or bodies. He slides backward on the bed until his back reaches the headboard. He spreads his legs out into a V position, then reaches his hand forward to pull me in. I slide up closer to him, and he pulls me in so my legs rest over top of his, our bodies roughly two feet apart. Oh my, it's hard to sit this close to him and not pull him into me. I can smell his fresh Italian soapy wonder from here, and my body begs me to draw in closer. *No, Jess. Talk to him. Slow down on the fucking and get to know him.*

"Ok, so what about your father? Are you close to him?"

His eyes lower to the bed, and he gives a slight shake of his head, combined with a big sigh.

"No. Never. I mean, I've never met him." *Holy fuck. Way to get deep, fast, Jess.* My heart immediately bleeds for him. This poor beautiful man who lost his mother and never had a father. *No wonder he's a womanizer, he had a fucked-up childhood. Oh, shit.* I stop our fantasy for a moment to remember who he really is. And what we've done. And that Jack is still my boyfriend. Fully cheating on him was never part of my plan. My heart begins to sink, but he quickly interrupts my thoughts.

"So, what about you?" my Lust asks me. Are you close to your parents? *Ugh, that's so not what I want to talk about with a half-naked man sitting in front of me.*

"Not really. Well, ok, in some ways I am, but in others not so much."

"Hmm. You make no sense."

"Well, I know I'm lucky that I grew up with two parents, and I certainly had lots of opportunities. So in that respect I do feel lucky."

"So you feel lucky, but not close to them?" *Oh. I guess my subconscious was hoping to avoid the question. Here goes nothing.*

"I'm not sure my parents really love me." *There. I said it.* Hearing myself verbalize the words pulls me back to the pains of my childhood. "They had their own issues, and I just fell to the wayside. Love isn't a word that is used in my house." I pause, meeting my Lust's eyes. He gives my hand a squeeze, reassuring me that it's ok to go on, so I do. "And my mother has this uncanny way of making me feel like shit all the time. Comments about my weight, what size clothes I wear, my hair, makeup, you name it. After two and a half decades it just takes a toll on a person. So, yeah. That's my family."

I look away, not wanting to recall the strain in our relationship, and Lust quickly picks up on my reflection. "Your mother is crazy. You are perfect, Jessa. Perfecto," he says again, this time gently turning my head so I have to look at him. His eager, caring eyes do their best to convince me and bring me back to here and now where I sit with him. "Perfect," he reaffirms, this time kissing my hand. "Here," he says rubbing his thumb across the top of my hand. "Here," he says kissing the inside of my forearm. "Definitely here," he says, planting his lips in the crease of my elbow. "Undoubtedly here," he touches my lips with his fingers, and I go from nearly unraveled to wanting to unravel the sheets with him again. His sexual aura begins to radiate, and mine lights up, sensing the possibility. "And here," he says, tugging me closer to him, placing his hand over my heart, forcing me to shift my body forward, my legs still resting on top of his. "And definitely here," he grabs my waist, this time pulling me fully against him, enabling me to wrap my legs around his body. I now sit fully in his lap, feeling his sex wand pushing against me. I feel that same pull, the sex ache, coming from deep within my peach pit. "And of course here," he brushes his lips ever so gently on my cheek, sending shivers through me. This ever so slight but astronomically sensual touch reminds me of the spark I've always had for him. That same movement would send me wild at our every encounter, and only now do I have him here, alone. Realizing the opportunity that sits before me, I don't hold back.

"I think my favorite spot on you is here," I proclaim, ever so slightly brushing my lips on his opposite cheek just as he did with mine. He raises his hand to my chin, but instead of kissing me he simply holds my face still, studying me for a moment. My eyes search his, and each millisecond of our staring contest has his eyes begging to have me again. He continues to hold my face, but moves his thumb to my lip. He ever so slowly pushes his thumb down the center of my top lip, then just as slowly down the center of my bottom lip, giving it a gentle tug between his thumb and forefinger.

"I *know* this is my favorite part of you," he says now, eyeing my lips after lustily fondling them. *Oh, fuck me.* I reach my hand in his hair, and as he wraps his arms around my body, I relinquish all self-control. He pushes his mouth onto mine, this time using his strong mouth to tug on each of my lips in between kisses. I want to explore his mouth with my tongue but he teases me, keeping his mouth closed just enough to keep it out while tugging at my begging lips. I break myself away from him, moving my mouth to his neck, tasting a tiny bead of saltiness stemming from the growing heat between us. I pause my mouth's trail upward toward his ear and sultrily use my tongue to lap the side of his neck, landing my lips on the edge of his ear. He lets out a deep exhale, his eyes closing as I let my teeth gently scrape the skin just below his ear. He moans again into me, burying his head between my breasts, which wiggles my robe partially open. His hands reach inside and my groans begin to match his. We both quickly forget our teasing game and let our lust carry us away into a semi-sweet and salty making of love.

CHAPTER THIRTY-EIGHT

I wake up still feeling completely exhausted, yet on a high, taking a minute to remember where I am. And who I'm with. I smile to myself, realizing how satiated I am from the overly awesome sexing last night. Sexings? *Geeze, how many times was it?* The bed is empty, but I know my Lust is nearby from the sound of his fuck-me-right-now accent commanding away on the phone. I lie quietly, enjoying the enunciation of his beautifully spoken Italian, but the pure sound of his voice gets my own ladyrection going. How is it possible to want to have someone again, when all I've done the past twelve hours is screw them every which way? I recall our lovemaking last night, how after the third session we both finally fell asleep in each other's arms, exhausted in the best possible way. I peer at the clock, realizing it's already 8:30 am local time, and I'm supposed to meet my coworkers in an hour for breakfast. I close my eyes, trying to work up the will to leave this warm fuckfactory of a bed to get myself in the shower. As hard as I try, that damn accent rings louder, and all I can think about is his perfect mouth. That perfect for kissing, perfect for fucking, soft, smooth and perfect-tasting mouth. It's all I can do not to tackle him and force fuck his mouth until I come all over his face. Again. And again. And again.

"Morning, bella," his voice is now louder, startling my face-fucking fantasy. He stands over me, his olive skin looking moist and refreshed from his shower. A towel drapes from his hips, begging me to pull it off of him. He leans over to give me a kiss on the cheek, and I feel the smoothness of his fresh shave on my hand. I breathe in as his lips linger on my cheek, relishing the refreshing oaky scent. It's more intense than usual given its recent application.

"Morning. How did you sleep?" I ask, propping myself up on my elbows.

"Never better. I was quite exhausted, after all. Must have been the jet lag…or someone." He gives me his signature playful wink. "So what's on your agenda today? Capturing the Chinese market one traveler at a time?"

"Something like that." I laugh, not wanting to think about work.

"Fantastic. That should keep you busy most of the day."

"Oh, are you trying to get rid of me already?" I tease him.

"Never," he says with seemingly genuine honesty. "That gives me time to get some work done before I ravage you this evening," he says playfully, planting his lips on my neck, tugging at my skin and my loins. I don't know how I can possibly wait an entire day without having him again. In fact, I know I can't.

I yank the corner of his towel, disrobing him into his birthday suit, revealing his morning salute. I quickly pull him into my mouth, enveloping each inch of squeaky clean flesh. *Mmm, nothing tastes better than a hard, fresh Italian sausage for breakfast.* He rests his hand on my head, sliding his fingers around my cheek, and grinning ear to ear. "Oh, God. Jessa." I watch his face twist with pleasure, and his eyes only leave mine when he closes them to process the sensation.

I make quick work of him, learning to synch the movement of my mouth with his expressions. I watch his body twinge in response,

Lost

and he grasps my hair into his fist. I slide his man muscle back as deep as it can go, and he lets out an audible sigh. Repeating this a few more times is all he needs to break free. His body begins to tighten, and I peer my eyes open and see his abs clench together in synch with his jaw as he fights off my victory. "Jessa, I'm so close." He pauses with a pleasured and pained expression. "What do you want me to do?" I pause for a moment, processing the question. At first I think he wants me to cheer him on to his grand finale, but then I realize he's being considerate of his, um, Italian delicacy.

"It's ok," I mutter through a mouthful of cock, eager to taste more of him. I draw him further into my mouth, grabbing his tightening buttocks and pushing him harder against my face. I use my right hand to caress his balls, and watch him nearly lose it.

"Fuck, Jess. You're unbeliev—" he stops, unable to speak, and I feel his salty warmth slide across my tongue and down my throat. I try not to giggle as I immediately have the thought of our oyster experience together—my first time swallowing salty objects with him. His body shakes for a few moments, and when he finally stills I pull my mouth from his body. He opens his eyes, and an overjoyed childish grin spreads across his face. He curls in his fingers and brushes stray hair from my face with an affectionate stroke. "You are quite full of surprises, bella." He grabs the towel from the edge of the bed, and twirls on his heel, flopping onto his back and next to me on the bed. He leans toward me, pulling me close into him, allowing my head to rest on his near hairless chest. I devour the smell of his Italian soap, and can't help but imagine the next time I'll get to devour him like this.

CHAPTER THIRTY-NINE

"Morning!" Sarah yells toward me from across the lobby. "Our driver is here. You ready to go?" I smile back at my friend, feeling obscenely tired but high on sex, and ready to conquer, or rather explore, China.

"Let's do this thing!" I smile. "Where's Ben?"

"Getting a coffee to go. We missed you at breakfast. I was beginning to think I'd have to drag you out of bed. But from the looks of it you had to drag yourself out," she laughs, waving her hand to my half-assed attempt to do my hair and makeup. My mouthfucking didn't leave me much time for gussying myself up, so my half-wavy sex bed head is pulled back, and mascara, concealer, and blush were a quick attempt to cover my horridly tired complexion and lack of sleep. I glance at Sarah's outfit, her standard casual jeans and a tight-fitting T-shirt, with her blonde hair pulled in a ponytail.

"Hey, Ben!" I greet him with a smile. He raises his eyebrows and gives me a hug hello while steadying his large cup of Starbucks.

"Thank God the best things about America have found their way over here," he says, lifting his coffee up triumphantly. "You want something before we go?"

"No, thanks. I'm good," I say cheerfully, patting my bottle of water that rests in my Longchamp. "Let's go explore!" I exclaim, walking toward the hotel revolving door.

"How did she skip breakfast, coffee, and still have this much energy?" Ben says to Sarah.

"Good question. The Jess I know doesn't function without a full night's sleep. And especially without breakfast." She pauses, thoughtfully. "Unless..." her voice trails off.

"What?" I probe her.

"Unless you're on a sex diet," she turns to me with a questioning stare. I know she's mainly joking, but I can see a hint of doubt in her eyes. My eyes widen, remembering the multiple orgasms that have given me the bed head and overly fucked glow. Ben laughs at her suggestion.

"Right. I bet she spent all night cheating on her boyfriend with some guy she just met here in this hotel. In the what, twelve hours we've been here?" he steps ahead of us to open the door, and my face falls for a minute. I haven't thought about Jack in hours. *Shit.* The guilt quickly overtakes me, knowing how badly I've cheated on a man I still love. And not just once. Not like the "oops I was drunk and his penis fell into me" kind of cheating. More like the "I knew what I was doing each and every time he penetrated me" kind. And I really fucking liked it.

"Jess!" Sarah yells at me in a forceful whisper. *Shit.*

"What?"

"Are you fucking kidding me? You so had sex last night."

"No I didn't!" I lie, also in an animated whisper, not wanting Ben to hear this conversation as we walk behind him.

"You're such a dirty liar. And a slut apparently!" She shoves me playfully.

"After you, ladies," Ben stops in front of our Mercedes, where our driver is waiting. I open my mouth to manipulate the truth, but I can tell from her expression that I've been made. I bite my tongue and feel my face redden. My friend knows me way too well for me to get out of this one.

"Where are we off to first?" I ask, quickly changing the subject. Ben peers over his shoulder from the front passenger seat.

"A Buddhist temple!" Sarah responds. *Great, maybe I can find an ancient Chinese prayer to forgive my cheating?*

CHAPTER FORTY

"Are you guys thirsty? I could go for a water." Ben squints at us through the afternoon sun, his deep green eyes filled with light.

"Yeah, I'd love one," Sarah responds quickly.

"Sure. Thanks," I agree.

"I'll be right back, don't let the paparazzi take you away," he laughs, pointing to our viewing public. Sarah and I plop down on a nearby bench inside the beautiful Zen gardens, just a few feet away from the home to centuries of Chinese royalty. The courtyard is filled primarily by Chinese tourists, and Sarah and I stick out like very blonde sore thumbs.

"I swear we've been photographed by like twenty people!" I laugh, turning toward Sarah. "Who knew we could be so exotic?"

"Well one of us has certainly been exotic," she snaps back as soon as Ben is out of earshot. "You totally had sex last night. Didn't you?" I stay silent, deciding what I should reveal. "Jess, come on. You can't play dumb, I know you far too well."

"Sarah, you come on. How ridiculous do you sound? So what, I fly over to China, and meet some guy in the bar to screw? You know I wouldn't do something like that."

"I do know that, which is what makes this even more intriguing! So spill it." She looks over her shoulder. "And fast, before our babysitter gets back."

"I would never screw some random foul guy from a bar."

"Well if you don't tell me I'll be left to assume that."

"Assume whatever you want. There's nothing to tell," I lie, not wanting to bring Sarah into my web of complexity and cheating.

"Fine. Ok. So you just happen to look like you've just had an all-night fuck fest when in reality you're just jet lagged."

I can't help but laugh out loud at her visual, knowing that the all-night fuck fest isn't that far from the truth.

"Yes. I never sleep well in hotels."

She nods, seemingly buying my story. "Can I see your phone? I want to see how far away our next stop is and my battery is dying."

"Sure," I oblige, handing it over, and feeling grateful that she's letting the subject go. I stare over my shoulder and see Ben posing for a picture with a group of Chinese girls, clearly enjoying his own bit of fame.

"Hey, Sarah, look behind us. Ben is totally eating up this attention!" She doesn't even flinch with my comment. "Hey, did you hear me?"

"Oh. My. God. You're such a whore!" she shrieks with excitement. "Who the hell is mister 212?"

"What?" I ask defensively, completely lost by her line of questioning.

"Umm, Mr. 212-538—"

Oh fuck. My heart stops, realizing she's reading my texts with Lust.

"No one!" I cry, grabbing for my phone. She jumps backward, flailing her arms to keep me from taking it back.

"This doesn't look like no one!

I can't wait to see you, and have you, tonight. Xo.

She pauses, looking up at me for an explanation. "Jess, I know this isn't Jack."

I let out a big sigh, knowing I'm caught and there's no point in lying to my friend. "Okay. Okay. It's a long story, though, and it's not what it seems."

"Ohhh kay, so you're not cheating on Jack with some dude while you're halfway around the world?"

"Not exactly." I shake my head, even though I know she's right. "This isn't just some guy that I met in a bar or something." I smile a little, realizing that in fact that is exactly how this all began, in the Sofitel bar in Paris. And then again in our hotel bar last night. "It's Max, you know, the Italian who causes me to make bad decisions?"

"Ohhh." Her eyes widen. "It seems I have some catching up to do."

"Yeah, it sort of came out of nowhere. After our trip to New York. This *thing*, or whatever it is I have with Max is recent. At least the sex part is. Last night was the first time we've slept together." I finish my spiel without realizing how broadly I'm smiling.

"Ok, I have a million questions about how you got from then to now, but we'll start with the two most important ones. Number one, how was the sex?"

I laugh at her boisterous tone, but am grateful to have someone to gush to.

"Unbelievable. He is so sexy. Like a walking sex on a stick that you just want to put in your mouth to taste."

"Well it sounds like you did!" She laughs. "So question number two is, how the hell did he end up in China?"

Oh. Right. That small little detail of how my lusty fuck buddy ended up here. "He just surprised me. I went for a nightcap in the hotel bar, and he was there." My smile is now contagious and Sarah's expression mirrors mine. I take a minute to realize how incredible it is he found me there. *Wait, how did he know what hotel I was staying in?*

"So he just flew halfway around the world for a booty call? Wow, you must be really good, Jess. Way to go, my friend!"

"It so isn't a booty call. I really, really like him. I mean yes, he's ungodly hot, but every time I see him I just want more of him. Want to know more about him, talk to him more, and make more and more love to him."

"Make love? Is that what you do with him?"

I laugh. "He's Italian, so he says expressions like that. If anyone else said them they would be completely laughable, but with him it makes him even more intriguing."

"So how incredible is his accent?"

"Ridiculously incredible. Why do you think I can't keep my panties on with him?"

"Now it's all starting to make sense." She nods. "So, what about Jack, though? How does he fit into your love affair?"

"Ugh. I don't know. Things haven't been great. Truth is, Max and I were planning a getaway for Memorial Day, and I knew if I were really going to have a weekend fling, I would have to break up with Jack first. I wasn't just planning to cheat on him. You know I'm not my mother." I pause with this realization that in this way I am in fact her. "I think we both know it's coming, anyway." I try to remind myself that Jack must suspect the end is near, too.

"Are you sure he feels that way? It seems like he's thinking of you." She passes me back my phone, and pulled up on the screen is a recent text from Jack.

Hey baby, hope your trip is off to a good start. Call me when you can. Love you.

What? Since when do I have sweet messages from him? I sigh with guilt-filled frustration. "This is seriously the first conversation he's tried to initiate with me all week. I don't get it."

"Maybe he realizes that you guys need to work things out? I mean this isn't some little fling with you and Jack. You live with him, Jess. And last I checked you were in love with him."

I consider her words for a moment, still confused by his message. "I know. I still can't believe I moved in with someone I'd only known for a few months. But things just haven't been the same lately. I don't know if it's his working so much, or something else, but I've been questioning if we're right together."

"Something else like a hot Italian? That might keep you from trying hard at your relationship."

I glance away, knowing she's probably right.

"Look, Jess. You know I'm not here to judge you. I just don't want you to get yourself in a mess you can't clean up."

"I know…I know you're right. But Jack doesn't get to send one 'I miss you' text and suddenly get to act like everything's fine, either."

"Well the good news is you don't have to figure it out today. For now, you enjoy whatever it is you're doing with Max, and you can settle everything when you get home."

"Thanks. You're right. For now, we have fun, and enjoy our trip!" I give her a hug, glad to have a friend who will listen without being overly motherly or judgmental. My own conscience is doing enough of that, after all.

CHAPTER FORTY-ONE

"What did you say it is called?" I yell toward Sarah as we saunter through our hotel lobby.

"Mint," she yells back. I nod my head, focusing on my texting and relying on Sarah to keep me from tumbling in my heels. Our day of sightseeing ended in an early happy hour, followed by pregaming in Sarah's room while we did each other's hair and make-up for our night out.

"So, is he coming to meet us?"

"Yeah he should be. He's at a work dinner but he says he's meeting us afterward!" I'm giddy with excitement, having spent all day away from my fucktastically wonderful Lust. It's not even twenty-four hours since our loins first met, but he's all I can think about. The anxious, eager butterflies dance between my stomach and my needy vagina, begging me to mate with my gifted Italian once more.

"Wow. You ladies both look amazing!" Ben says sincerely, standing up from his oversized club chair in the hotel lobby.

"Thanks!" we both respond in unison. No need for modesty when I agree with his sentiment. We do both look amazing. Sarah and her skinny frame look fantastic in a short, black silk romper. The sleeveless ensemble fits perfectly with a bright blue statement necklace, and her long thin legs look even longer with four-inch black heels, giving her a total of six feet of height. I decided to stick to a standard dress. The off-the-shoulder black fabric makes an X across my chest, cutting down just a touch to show my décolletage. The strips of fabric wrap around me, meeting in a V shape midway down my back. I too chose tall black heels, but added big gold earrings, borrowed from Sarah, for some flair. We both have our blonde locks curled, mine now falling into larger loose waves, but Sarah's still in shorter, more voluminous rings that fall just past her shoulders.

"So who is this you were talking about? Someone is coming out to meet us?"

"Oh, yeah. A, um, friend of mine," I say, purposefully omitting further detail. Sarah immediately giggles at my description, neither of our buzzes helping us to be discreet with my secret.

"Someone who lives here?" he asks, rolling up the sleeves to his white button-up shirt to his elbows.

"Something like that! Come on, let's go!" I urge them, excited to go explore the Shanghai party scene.

"As you wish." He steps aside and I watch him intently check out Sarah's backside as she walks away.

"Another drink?" Ben shouts in my ear. I nod my head in agreement, and raise my glass to Sarah, trying to determine if she too wants a refill.

"Yes, puhlease!" she shouts to him. He nods and walks away through the busy club. The dance floor of M1nt is crowded, but not completely wall to wall, so we have a teensy bit of room to waltz around. Their amazing DJ flips, mixes, and combines the best of American and European techno and hip hop into his own masterpiece creations that make it impossible not to jump onto the dance floor. Some tables of high-spending partyers sit nearby watching the likes of me, Sarah, and countless other buzzed patrons drinking in the scene. "So when will Max be here?" Sarah shouts to me.

"Soon, I think," I yell back, feeling a bout of anxiety and excitement run through me. It's only been half a day since I've seen him but my body wants him, and needs to feel him again. Ben walks up to us, holding a vodka gimlet for me, a rum and coke for Sarah, and a Tsing Tsing, a local Chinese beer, for himself.

"You two have more admirers," Ben says, laughing and handing over our drinks. I glance up and see that once again Sarah's and my blondeness has made us an easy target of people-watching in this foreign land.

"Looks like you have some yourself," Sarah says, pointing over to a table of girls staring toward us, waving eagerly at Ben.

"It's like they think we're celebrities or something," he laughs, giving his fans a shy wave back.

"Go say hi!" I encourage him.

"No, they probably don't even speak English."

"Even better! They don't have to speak English to speak the language of love," Sarah chimes in. "What do you always say?" Sarah encourages him further. "YOLO!"

"Fine. I'm really doing it for you, though, simply to keep you entertained!" Ben takes a drink then turns toward his group of admirers, a big smile plastered across his face. I give him a little wave as he walks away, and as I do, I see my Lust walking toward me. My heart begins to race with anticipation. I lean toward Sarah to alert her of his arrival.

"Sarah, that's him," I say nodding toward my approaching Lust.

"That's Max?" I watch her eyes move up and down him, her mouth forming into an approving smile. He looks incredibly hot tonight. Not unlike his usual appearance, but his confident stroll turns heads as he passes. He's dressed in a fitted khaki suit and white button-up, matching his gleaming white teeth. His naturally olive skin looks radiant against these lighter colors, and I can feel myself wanting to have him instantly. I give him a wave as he approaches, and a nervous smile covers my face. Despite how intimate we've been, I realize I still barely know more than where he's from and the size of his perfect penis.

"Nǐ hǎo," he says, the traditional Chinese greeting, along with his traditional European double cheek kiss hello.

"Nǐ hǎo," I respond back to him. "This is my friend, Sarah."

"Sarah, nice to meet you." Max leans in, giving her a warm handshake and a kiss on the cheek. Watching his mouth move toward her face gives me a tinge of jealousy, even though I know it's nothing more than a platonic hello.

"You ladies look fantastic! Do you want to take a break from dancing for a bit and have a drink with me?"

"Sure, I could use a rest," Sarah volunteers.

"Where's your table?" Max asks, looking around.

"Oh, um, we don't have a table. They were crazy expensive," I admit. Lust raises his eyebrows and nods his understanding.

"Ah, I see. I'll be right back," he says with a wink, heading toward the bar.

"Holy shit, Jess. He's totally fucking hot!" Sarah shrieks as soon as he's out of earshot. "Well done, my friend."

I giggle at her words. "I know. There's just something about him. I mean he's obviously cute, but it's something more than that."

"Yeah, I see what you mean. I think it's a combination of class and confidence. He just looks like a million bucks between that smile and that suit. And he looks well groomed. And endowed." She pauses with a sly smile. "Am I right?"

I laugh at her insinuation. "Sarah! I would never kiss and tell," I say slyly.

"Kiss? Oh please. We all know you've done far more than kiss him. You're going to go back and screw him again tonight, too. Not that I can blame you!"

"What are you ladies talking about?" Ben asks, interrupting our conversation. I turn bright red, unsure of how much he's heard.

"Nothing," Sarah responds before I can open my mouth. "Just Jess's *friend*." I make eyes at her, trying to shield Ben from the graphic details of my sexcapades.

"My friend Max is here," I volunteer, but quickly change the subject. "So how were your admirers?"

"Drunk!" he says with a laugh. "They spoke a bit of English, but between the music in here and how drunk they were, I caught maybe two words."

"Ladies, right this way." Lust returns with a young Chinese waitress. "Hi, I'm Max," he says confidently to Ben.

"Ben. Nice to meet you. You must be Jess's friend?" he asks, looking to me.

"Yes. Her *friend*," he says with a big teasing smile, raising his eyebrows toward me. *Hmm, what do you call someone who you've had sex with and cheated on your boyfriend with, who surprises you in China? Fuck if I know.*

"Join us, Ben. I was just about to show these ladies to a table." We follow our petite hostess to a booth toward the back of the club. It has a great view of the dance floor, but sits further away from speakers, making it slightly quieter than the other areas of the club. Ben slides into the round table, sitting alongside Sarah. I go in after her, then Max climbs in behind me, sitting so that he faces Sarah at the other end of the table. Within seconds a waiter delivers a bottle of Dom on ice with four champagne glasses. "Xièxiè," Lust thanks him in Mandarin using one of the few words I can recognize.

"A toast to new friends?" Max begins pouring the champagne into each of our glasses. Sarah catches my eye, mouth gaping open, and she mouths "oh my God" to his expensive gesture. Dom is by no means cheap in the US, but the overseas markup adds a 5x multiplier to virtually any label like this, easily making it a thousand-dollar indulgence. Ben stays quiet, and I can only imagine what he's thinking of me. I went from quickly moving in with Jack to having a wealthy fuck buddy in China. I silently start judging myself, allowing the guilt of my Jack situation to enter my mind again. I decide I should at least respond to his text and let him know I'm alive, and when I'm coming home. After all we'll have a lot to talk about when I'm back. *Good God, what will I tell him about Max? I don't even know what we are, or what our situation will be in a few days.* My semi-numb mind starts overanalyzing this situation. What could actually come of this? A relationship with a man who "lives" a plane ride away from me in New York, but is never really even there? *Shit.* I would never see him. Whatever fantasy I have allowed to dangle in my mind will need a reality check. And soon.

I peer over at Lust and see him chatting away with my friends. He's so good in these situations, I can even see that the ever-uptight Ben has begun to loosen up a bit. Max catches my eye and gives me a squeeze under the table. His hand gently rubs my knee, letting me know he's present and thinking of me. He's so damn good-looking. And mesmerizing. He continues the conversation with Sarah and Ben, while slowly inching his fingers up my thigh. With each gentle stroke of his hand on my skin I begin to feel more and more overtaken by seduction. I slide my knees a little further apart, giving him more access to the burning need growing between my legs. He slowly circles his fingers up my right thigh, moving them up a smidge, then back, allowing his taunting to continue in a painstakingly slow manner.

I grab his hand, still hidden beneath the table, and give him a reassuring squeeze with my fingers laced through the top of his, wanting to let him know it's ok to continue on his scandalous scavenger hunt. He squeezes my hand back, and I assume it's the signal for message received. I feel my bits wet for him, tantalized by his hand's movements, and eagerly awaiting their arrival. His fingers land on the edge of my panties and I silently gasp. He ever so gently slides his index finger beneath the fabric. *Holy shit, this is actually happening.* I breathe in shallow breaths, not realizing I've only taken in minimal oxygen during his alluring finger dance.

"So how did you guys meet?" Ben turns toward me and I nearly squeak with pleasure.

"Oh, he and Jack have been working on a deal together," I blurt out and then immediately regret my words. This is the first time the subject of Jack has come up around Max since we've started whatever this fling of ours is. Lust's hands pause, and I can see his smile fade. I glance around and realize everyone is waiting for me to elaborate on this revelation. *Fuck!*

"Jess, oh my God, I LOVE this song. Dance with me. Please?" Sarah gives me the "I'm trying to help you" eyes. I don't want to leave the beautiful man's hand stranded, but I know I've probably ruined the moment. Plus, how else would I elaborate on this story of how I know Max? "Jess. Come on! You can't leave me hanging!" Sarah prods me again, encouraging me to get up.

"Go on," Lust half whispers in my ear. The feeling of his closeness is like a drug, one that I am already addicted to. He turns his head further into my neck, this time his lips touch my earlobe and the electricity shoots through me from his slight touch. "I want to watch you dance. Go on." *Oh, God.* I would love nothing more than to climb on top of his lap, or face for that matter, right here and now. I give a slight nod of my head, acknowledging his words. "Go dance. Then I will come get you, take you back to the hotel and have my way with you. Yes?" He throws that final question in there making it sound like a command I can't possibly refuse.

Lost

"Ok, let's go!" I say cheerfully to Sarah, trying to force my legs into action. Lust stands up to allow me out of the booth, reaching his hand out to help me to my feet.

"Perfecto," he says quietly as I stand, just loud enough for me and only me to hear. He holds my hand until Sarah swoops up next to me, grabbing my arm to drag me away to the dance floor. He gives me a quick reassuring squeeze before she pulls me away.

Britney's signature sound, expertly remixed, blasts through the surrounding speakers. Sarah and I sing loudly to each other, both having a love for the Mickey Mouse club alumna from our childhood. We hold our hands together above our heads, dancing and swaying as one. Our half-empty glasses of Dom slosh over the side with each overly dramatic sway of the music. I'm lost in this sound, this moment, having the time of my life with one of my dearest friends. I've had a permanent smile on my face for the last hour, or however long it is we've been tearing up the dance floor. I glance toward our table and see Ben and my Lust, laughing and chatting together. I give my man, or lustbuddy, rather, a big smile, letting all insecurities about us and our unknown relationship status fall far into the back of my mind.

I see Ben rise to his feet and begin walking toward us. "Can I steal Sarah away for a dance?" he asks me as Britney's words begin to blend into the next song.

"But she's my dance partner!" I shriek.

"I'll be your dance partner," Lust's boomy voice rings into my ear as he sneaks up behind me, putting his arm around my waist. Feeling his body push against me shocks it into maximum arousal. I nod and let Sarah's hand go, and she turns toward Ben, joyfully spinning with him. Max stays behind me, but wraps his other arm around me so I'm pressed completely against him. I feel his arousal quickly grow into my back, and I can only think how desperately I want him. *Again.* I lift my chin up, looking over my shoulder to get a glimpse of him. This is the closest we've been all day and I can hardly wait any longer. His eyes lock into mine, him looking down into me and me staring up into him. "I missed you, bella. I thought of you all day."

"You too," I say honestly, pulling his arms tighter around me. He leans down and gives my neck a quick kiss, and I nearly fall apart, desperate for more. For a moment, any thoughts about judgment from Sarah or Ben disappear, and I can only think of him and me, together. *Now.* I whirl around on my heel and throw my arms around his neck. I thrust my lips onto his, and he gratefully responds, parting them so that my tongue can meet his. I lean into him, forcing him to walk backward a few steps to the nearby wall. I back him into a corner and continue kissing him with the desperation that seeps from my veins. My hands grasp his hair, unable to do anything but pull him into me.

"How drunk are you," he asks into my ear, pausing our make-out session for a quick second.

"Enough to dance in front of strangers," I laugh.

"But not like the night at Ware?" he questions.

"God, no!" I retort, reliving that embarrassing night for a brief second.

"Good. I just don't want to take advantage of you," he admits.

I shake my head at his words. "You're not. All I want is you. I have to have you again."

His mouth widens into a wicked grin at my forward words. My buzz has given me enough confidence to express my feelings, but not so much that I puke on myself or my handsome date.

"You have no idea," he says, and in one quick movement he twists me around so my back is now pinned on the wall. He pushes his body against me, one hand steadying himself on the wall the other pulling my hips into him. His mouth draws to mine like a magnet, and my knees weaken into him. We grab each other anywhere we can, our hands and mouths working nonstop. I feel his erection growing harder, and I can only think of having him inside me.

"I can take you to bed?" he asks, or states, through panted breath. I quickly nod my head, wishing we were already there.

Lust scoops his hands underneath me, startling me as my feet sweep off the floor. He carries me like a bride going over a threshold, or more accurately like a dominatrix about to get fucked sideways. I see surprise spread across Sarah's and Ben's faces, and my Lust pauses next to them. "Order whatever you want, just grab my credit card before you go," he instructs them as we walk past them and out of the club.

———

Lust carries me hurriedly through the hotel lobby, having only put me down for our quick taxi ride home. Our hands and mouths haven't stopped, and I've literally gushed through my panties at this point. We hop into the elevator and I rip apart the buttons of his shirt as quickly as I can. The doors open and he ushers me down the hallway, my hands pulling at his belt. We finally stop in front of the door to my room, and he fumbles with his wallet for a key. I use the opportunity to remove his belt and unbutton his pants. As soon as the door flies open I unzip them fully, tugging them down along with his boxers. His big, beautiful bulge pops right out and salutes me, and I hold my breath, beyond ready for this man to enter me.

He tosses me onto the bed and yanks my panties down as fast as he can, then pushes my dress up above my hips. He doesn't even pause to remove my shoes before he falls on top of me, and with one quick thrust our bodies connect once again. "Oh, Max," I nearly shout, the building attraction and teasing of the last few hours finally being released as our skin connects. The friction is all-consuming, and he moves his hips back and forth, thrusting hard against me, then retracting back until he's almost out of me. The sensation of his size sliding back and forth against my overly ripe peach is more than I can take. I grab his head and pull it to mine. As soon as his lips part I explode all around him, moaning into his mouth. He continues with only a few more thrusts before his body quakes with mine.

It takes a few minutes before the pulses slow, but he stays on top of me, arms extended, his eyes locked on mine. "You are unbelievable," he laughs, then buries his face into my neck. "Fucking unbelievable, Jessa."

CHAPTER FORTY-TWO

"Don't leave me," I protest, pulling Max's arm as he tries to sneak out of bed. "I'm not done with you," I tease him, trying to lure him to lie back down.

"Mmm, bella," he breathes into my ear. "You know I have to go. I already changed the meeting location, I can't stay." I smile at him, and myself, grateful that he changed his plans so that he could spend more time with me.

"You must be pretty important if you can just change a meeting location from London to Shanghai with a day's notice. A smile spreads across his face, enjoying my compliment. "Seriously, how did you pull it off?" He shrugs his shoulders nonchalantly at my question.

"Mmm," he says, swirling his head around so that his mouth nuzzles into my neck. "I pull it off just like this," he shows me, gently trailing his finger across my chest, tugging at the strap of my hot pink camisole. His touch gets me fiery in an instant, and I know I can't let him go just yet.

"Oh, is that right? Well let me show you how *I* pull it off," I retort, using my right hand to pull at the band of his boxers, popping them back against his skin.

"Careful!" he warns me. "I have a surprise in there you wouldn't want to ruin." My tongue wags at his suggestion, recalling the memory of his penis massage wake-up call, courtesy of my eager tongue. I stir at the idea of recreating the memory and, feeling frisky, I grab at his waistband again. "Jessa, I would love to stay in bed with you all morning. But I can't stand them up. I promise I will be all yours this evening. Ok?"

I give him my best sad face, trying to relay my disappointment that I won't be giving him a morning mouth-fucking. "Only if you make it up to me," I command him in a playful but naughty tone. He rises from the bed but leans over me, moving his mouth above mine.

"Je te promets, Jessa," he promises in French, leaving me swooning once again at that perfect mouth and delicious accent. The language doesn't matter, everything he says makes a girl's panties fall to the floor. *Especially mine.*

"So how was last night?" Sarah asks me as we sort through faux Tory Burch goods at the giant Shanghai mall, filled with designer knockoffs.

"Good." I smile. "Ok, great. Although I'm thoroughly exhausted again, but it's totally worth it."

"Yeah, I could tell by the way you left the club that you would be going straight to bed. And I don't mean to sleep!" She whirls around, and begins sorting through the purses next. "So have you had a chance to talk to him yet?"

"About what?"

"About, well, you know. What this is?"

I blink through the question. "I don't even know what it is. Or even what I want it to be, for that matter."

"Come on, Jess, you went twenty years without sleeping with a guy, then another five until Jack. You don't just give yourself to men that way. But with Max, well, I just want you to be ok with everything."

"What are you saying?"

"Look, I'm not judging you. You just don't normally move this quickly. And I don't want you to get hurt here. Her words redden my cheeks, forcing me to recall the same haunting thoughts I've twisted about in my brain for days.

"Come on, we're going to be late." I tug on Max's arm as we walk out of our lavish hotel suite.

"Almost...done!" he says triumphantly, holding his comb in his hand. I guess I shouldn't be surprised that someone this good-looking must spend a full two minutes combing his hair into the perfect position. And if that's his only flaw, I think I can learn to live with it. "You look beautiful, Jessa." He pulls me into his arms, and I close my eyes, slowly drawing in his smell. He nuzzles his mouth close to my ear, close enough that I can hear him inhale my scent. Thankfully I'm freshly showered and ready to be ravished. Well, not yet, but in a few hours once I have him all to myself. I look up into the grandiose mirror that hangs above a green marble vanity in our spacious suite.

"You know, we look quite good together," I acknowledge, realizing I've yet to really see us next to each other like this. He turns toward the mirror, getting a better glimpse of our coupled reflection. A big smile spreads on his face as he straightens the collar of his linen button-up shirt. His sleeves are rolled to the elbows, and he wears navy blue pants with a tan belt and matching leather shoes. A slight fringe of chest hair is visible beneath his shirt, but overall he's not a very hairy man, and I've come to enjoy his smooth, strong chest. Particularly in the post-coital spooning moments we've shared as of late.

"I think you're on to something," he purrs with a quick kiss on my cheek. I take a look at myself in the mirror and am pleased with my reflection. Thanks to the overwhelming number of sexings and out-of-my-comfort-zone food choices here, this dress is fitting better than ever. I chose my sexy red dress for tonight, a color similar to the one I was wearing when I met Max for the first time months ago. This dress has a straight neckline across my shoulders, with V-shaped cutouts at my waistline. I paired it with my tan heels, and despite their over four-inch lift, Max still stands at least five inches above me. Just add it to the list of reasons why I find him so incredibly sexy. "I would really like to ravage you right now," he admits in a matter of fact tone. "But you say we must go. So I must wait."

"Uhm," I squeak, feeling weak in the knees just at his suggestion. "Maybe we can be a few minutes late?" I suggest, feeling the pull for him between my thighs. He moves in to me, kissing me softly just beside my mouth, in the same torturous way he would before we were lovers. It sends tingles across my skin, and my lips pull toward his.

"No, you said we must go." He shrugs his shoulders. "We shouldn't keep your friends waiting." He pauses, looking at our reflection once again. "We do make quite the couple though, no?" His words electrify me as much as his lips did. *Couple?* Could he have possibly meant that in the literal sense?

※

"There you guys are!" I call out to Sarah and Ben, both seated at a modern, cozy bar just outside the hotel lobby. I notice the two of them looking cozy and relaxed together. Almost more date-like than friend-like. *But they couldn't be on a date. Right?* I tuck the thought aside for a moment. "Are we ready to go?"

"You betcha. Let me just pay for our drinks and we'll be all set," Ben declares. He waves a waiter over toward us and hands him his credit card.

"So how was your meeting today?" Sarah questions Max.

"Long. But worthwhile. Glad to be here now," he says to me, rather than Sarah, and his attention to me instantly makes me feel wanted.

"Let's roll," Ben says, jumping to his feet. He holds his hand out for Sarah, helping her off of her barstool. *Another check in the date column for these two,* I note.

"You guys make quite a handsome couple," Sarah says complimenting us.

"Thank you. I agree," Lust says with a wink. "And you two make a nice-looking couple as well," he comments, picking up on the same vibe that I'm sensing about them. I watch Sarah's cheeks redden, and our eyes dart to each other. She gives me a slight shoulder shrug and quickly looks away before acknowledging my growing curiosity.

⊱✧⊰

We head onto the large, crowded boat, ready to set sail upon the Huangpu River and the glowing city of Shanghai. "Why don't we get the ladies some drinks?" my Lust suggests to Ben.

"Of course. Any special requests?" he asks us.

"Surprise me," I respond, eager to talk to my friend.

"Me too," Sarah mimics me.

"Your wish is our command." Lust winks at me and walks off to the nearby watering hole.

"Ok. So what is *that*?" I ask as soon as they're out of earshot.

"What?"

"Um, this date that you seem to be on?"

"It's not a date," Sarah protests, her face turning red again.

"Well it sure looks like one," I tease her.

"I mean. Ugh. I don't know. There's something about him that I haven't noticed before. He's not so bad," she says with a smile.

"He's a great guy! I just never thought you would be into him that way. When did this happen?"

"Oh, I don't know. Somewhere between M1nt and this big boat, I guess!"

"Well that's exciting! But just be careful, you don't want to break his heart if you change your mind," I warn her, knowing how sensitive our friend can be.

"I know," she snaps. "I wouldn't try to hurt him," she says with a slight glare.

"Ok, sorry. I just don't want you to have some kind of vacation fling that's meaningless to you when we get home."

"Ok, pot."

"What?" I ask, fully confused.

"Pot," she points to me. "Kettle," she points to herself. I feel my defenses begin to flare up.

"That's not what I'm doing. I'm just…" I pause, not sure what I am actually doing.

"You're just having fun. And so am I. There's nothing wrong with that."

"I'm not just having fun," I blurt out. "It's more than that to me."

"Then what is it?"

"I don't know!" I say with exasperation. "I haven't exactly had time for a DTR since this afternoon. But it's real. And he called us a couple."

"So he said you're in a relationship?"

"Not those exact words." I shake my head, realizing how green I must sound.

"Jess, regardless, you realize someone is going to get hurt. You have Jack sitting at home waiting for you. He's your live-in boyfriend who you seemed to be in love with not too long ago."

"I know that!" I retort. "But it's not like that. He and I were barely speaking after our trip to New York."

"Let me see your phone."

"Ok, fine." I begin digging it out of my clutch. "What are you hoping to prove?"

She stays quiet for a moment, then whips the screen around to face me. "This." She slides her finger up and down, showing me the barrage of texts I have from Jack.

"Are you sure he's not trying to talk to you? Or have you been too busy fucking the Italian to notice?"

"Geeze. I don't know. I haven't seen these," I admit. I begin to read the words from my boyfriend, and I feel my heart sink.

Hey, how's your trip going?

Hey Jess. Thinking of you, let me know you got there ok.

Everything ok? Let me know that you're getting these messages.

Jess, I know you're probably mad at me. And I know I've been an ass. But we need to talk. Can you call me?

Babe. At least let me know you're doing ok. When will you be home? I miss and love you.

I swallow hard at this most recent message, the words drawing out the feelings I still have for him that I've pushed way down beneath the lust I've been having for Max the last few days.

"What are you going to do about this? Are you really going to leave Jack when you get home? You fell hard for Jack, and fell in love with him. And I know love isn't a feeling or word you toss around lightly. Do you really think you can have a relationship with a playboy who is never home, and probably has a lady friend in every city across the globe?"

I stand with my mouth open, still processing my thoughts. I watch Sarah's head twirl around, and I too see that our dates are heading back toward us.

"I just want you to be smart, Jess. I don't want to see you get hurt. I just think you need to have realistic expectations. And don't be an asshole to the man you're going home to, and maybe still love, unless you're 100% sure you're ready to leave him."

I nod my head, thoughts spinning around inside of it.

Lust moves himself next to me, resting his champagne glass on the bar height table adjacent to us. He hands me a similar glass, then slides his arm around my waist, sending the all familiar tingles through me again, momentarily quieting the love triangle that my brain is finally being forced to decode.

"Champagne," he says quietly, but with a wicked grin. "It always reminds me of the night we met." I too flash back to that exciting evening, where we wouldn't have even met if I hadn't been frustrated with Jack. "You wore red that night too. I'll never forget." His finger caresses the spot where my waist meets my hip, tugging gently at the fabric, and my sexual need for him.

"I can't believe you've never done this before," I say, turning my head toward Max so he can hear me above the clanking dishes and soft dinner music.

"I know. Despite all of my trips here I just never made time for it. I rarely have time for pleasure on these trips." Just hearing his beautiful accent say the word "pleasure" slaps images of me pleasuring him back into my mind. I peer backward and see the reflections of the very bright Shanghai in the distance, the image of the famous Pearl building, which used to hold the title of tallest building in Shanghai until another quickly popped up a few years later. "It's amazing how fast things move here. There are new buildings constructed faster than anywhere in the world."

"How do they do it?"

"They never stop working. They build twenty-four hours a day, seven days a week. It's unbelievable."

"Ah, sounds like your work schedule," I say, giving him a slight nudge.

He smiles and finds my eyes. "I manage to take a break every now and then. For the important things." He gives my hand a squeeze and leans in for a kiss. Tonight I'm less interested in a full PDA in front of my coworkers, feeling Sarah's judgment still lingering. She hasn't exactly been warm and bubbly the last few hours, and I'm struggling to keep the guilt of my infidelity from my mind with each of her glances.

"I think we're heading back to the hotel, do you guys want to join?" Sarah pauses us before Max's lips can reach mine. Max looks at me to answer Sarah's question. Given her mothering this evening I don't really want to waste my precious alone time with her and Ben. And I can't exactly have a serious chat with Max in their presence, anyway.

"We might just stay on the boat for a bit. I'll see you in the morning?"

She nods her head, and we say a quick goodbye before I catch her take Ben's arm and disembark from the boat.

"Ok, Jessa. What would you like to do?" He raises his eyebrows flirtatiously, and my normal smile is deflated by the thoughts Sarah has flooded my brain with.

Shit. I hadn't really considered how I might go about a serious conversation with him. We've been obscenely intimate with our bodies, but certainly not with our thoughts. *He's a playboy, Jess. And while he might be all yours today, that doesn't mean he will be for long.* I sigh, recalling the great memories and lust we've made; after all, when was the last time I felt this satisfied and desired?

"What is it?" He's attuned enough to realize something other than bedding him is on my mind. "Jessa. Are you having fun?"

"On the boat? Sure, the views are great."

He shakes his head to me. "No. With me. Are you having fun?"

I consider this idea for a moment. Of course I'm having fun with him. Who wouldn't consider multiple orgasms with a fucktastically hot Italian fun? The fun aspect is not the problem, it's the fear that it's *just* fun.

"What is it?" he asks me, and I realize my thoughtful expression became more serious than intended. "So you're not having fun?" he asks confidently, knowing well that I am.

"Of course I'm having fun," I say, trying to hide my nerves. *Shit. Maybe he's going there.* I fear the gravity of the words about to come. "But…" I pause, not wanting to turn the conversation serious quite so soon.

"But what?" he probes, his expression turning from confident to concerned in a blink.

"But I don't want this to be just some…thing," I say, lowering my eyes as I play my cards much quicker than expected, instantly terrified of how he may respond.

"Jessa," he says quickly, grabbing my hand. "This is not just a *thing* to me." He pulls at my chin, forcing me to look at him. "Don't you know that?" The butterflies in my stomach go from anxious to excited in an instant. I turn my eyes to his, and they meld, letting us each know how strong our feelings are. This is the first time I can remember sharing a glance that said "I want you to be more than my lover."

"You know this. Right?" He asks for my verbal reassurance.

"Well I hoped so. But I guess I just wasn't completely sure," I admit.

"I flew halfway around the world to see you," he says with near exasperation. "How else do I show you?"

"Well I don't know. You could've come here just for, you know. Having me," I say with a smile. This idea elicits a big laugh from him.

"Jessa. Let me be clear. I did not fly to China just to *have* some girl. I flew to China to see you. Yes, to have you. Because I could not, I cannot, stop thinking of you. Not since the day I met you." His serious expression melts me, and I feel more drawn to him than ever. Hearing his admission of his feelings floods through me. The pit of my stomach wants to touch him, and I can see from his stare that he feels the same. I simply smile at him, grateful for this admission. "You have no idea how wonderful you are. Do you?"

I blush at the question, uncomfortable by the idea that I'm something special. I stay quiet but let out a slight shake of my head. "I don't know. I've never thought of myself as that special," I admit.

"What?" he nearly shouts, raising his arms into the air. I laugh at his inner Italianness and his overly dramatic motions. "You're unbelievable. Ok? Don't doubt that. Ever." His words become almost angry with my self-doubt.

"Ok," I respond, embracing the vote of confidence from my beautiful man.

"Ok," he says, wrapping his arms around me and tugging me into his lap. My heart races at the warm, caring embrace. "Do I need to show you how I feel?" His quick change into a seductive tone flips my mind from serious to sexual thoughts in an instant. I simply nod my head, wanting him even more after our exchange. He leans into me, burying his head in my neck, then planting his lips just where my shoulders meet my neck.

The pull for him shoots through me and I pull his mouth to mine. Our tongues connect in a combined "I really like you and I'm really attracted to you" fashion. His hand runs up my outer thigh, having easy access beneath my dress. I want to be his, and have him now, but am unsure of where this can go, given our surroundings.

"Oh my God," he whispers into my ear, placing his lips on the edge of them, tugging gently. "Bella, I want to take you here and now," he says matter-of-factly, sending my mind racing at the idea. "But I know we can't. Not here." He has a red tone in his cheeks, and I'm quite pleased with myself that I can visibly see how much I've worked him up.

"I know," I concede, disappointed that I can't make love to him here and now. "Will you be able to wait until we get to our room?" I tease him.

"Not if you keep kissing me."

"You mean like this?" I plant my lips on him again, this time in a slow, sensual manner, using my teeth to lightly slide his bottom lip between them. I fall further into his kiss, and his arms for the beginning of another amazing and memorable night together.

CHAPTER FORTY-THREE

My eyes pop open, and I find myself wide awake and eager to get out of bed. Knowing it's my last day, and more importantly my last night here in China, I want to embrace every second of it. *Of him.* I peer over at my Lust, and see that he's sound asleep, sprawled out on his stomach and clutching his pillow tightly beneath his head. I couldn't have imagined that just days ago when I learned I was coming here, that I'd be spending a mind-blowing week with him. I tiptoe into the bathroom, hoping the sound from my white noise app is loud enough to mask my plans. I quickly hop in the shower, giving myself a quick scrub to wash away the city film I'm sure I absorbed the night before.

I towel myself off and tie a robe loosely around me, leaving about a gap of skin peeking out the middle. I glance in the mirror and notice the obscenely dark circles under my eyes. When lying in bed next to a man as delicious as Max, it's impossible to go to sleep, and now my reflection confirms both my lack of sleep and my attraction to him. I consider putting on concealer to cover my visible fatigue, but decide the bedroom is dark enough that he shouldn't notice. *And hopefully he'll be looking elsewhere than under my eyes.* I play with the tightness of the robe's belt, but then come up with an even better idea. I remove the belt, tying it tightly around my waist with a big bow in the front. The hotel-provided men's robe gives me enough slack to tie myself into the perfect present for unwrapping. I then pull the robe tightly around me, concealing my bow, and tiptoe back into the bedroom.

I hover over Lust for a moment before waking him. His heart-shaped lips are relaxed and ready for kissing, his eyes closed, looking peaceful and content. I lean forward and place my hand on the side of his face, feeling his morning scruffiness. I gently slide the outside of my hand against his skin, and give him a gentle kiss just outside the corner of his mouth. "Morning," I say quietly, in a near whisper, realizing I don't really know how he likes to be woken up, if at all.

"Mmm, good morning, bella." He slowly rolls over onto his side so he can face me. "You're up early."

"I wanted to get you something for your last day here," I explain.

"What?" He shakes his head. "You know I don't need any gifts. I have *everything* I want." He emphasizes the word as his eyes meet mine, and I can't help but start swooning.

"Well, in that case," I pause, letting go of the fabric and allowing the robe to begin to fall open, "I hope you like your present." I pull the robe off of me, leaving me naked and exposed, save my terrycloth belt and black heels. I don't know where this confidence of mine came from, but I'm embracing every ounce of it while it lasts. His eyes light up in an instant, going from just awake to ripe in a flash. His naughty smile covers his face, and I feel my loins excite for what's coming next. "Can I open it now?" he asks with apparent excitement.

"Consider your wish my command," I taunt him.

"Mmm. Bueno. Where should I start?"

I inch closer to him, and he places his hand on my waist, feeling the fabric of my bow and lightly sliding his finger beneath it to graze my skin.

"Can I start here?"

To my surprise, his eyes look down to my fuzzless peach, freshly shaved from my morning shower.

"As you wish," I giggle, uncertain of his plans for me down there. I fully intended on giving him a mind-blowing blowing, but I'll happily take any reciprocity.

"What's the saying?" he asks, looking to my eyes as he pulls me onto the bed with him. "Have your cake...and eat it too?" He raises his eyebrows in his famous expression, and I feel myself jump halfway to an orgasm before he's even touched me. He pushes me onto my back in a forceful, playful manner, and I scoot backward so my head pushes against the bed frame. He lowers his head between my legs and thrusts his magical mouth onto me.

"Ohum," I squeak, feeling the pleasure hit me with the first flick of his tongue. I wiggle my hips into his face, allowing him access to a full spread of me. He opens his mouth slowly, using his tongue just how I've felt it in my mouth. His lips move purposefully, and I hear him groan as he continues his work. He moves his hands beneath my buttocks, giving himself a lever to pull me in closer. He wiggles me forward and immediately devours my freshly shaven peach. "Ahh," I blurt out, his tongue working constantly, up down and around me, and I'm quickly two lashes away from the edge.

"Max, I want to have you," I beg him, wanting to feel him inside of me. He shakes his head no, and his tongue follows, sliding against me from side to side.

"No," he says in a low voice. "It's my gift. You have to give me what I want," he teases me.

"Ummhmm," I say between the beginnings of body twitches. "Ok. What do you want?"

He pauses his mouth massage and pulls his head up, his now widely awake eyes sparkling at me. "You," he says with a wicked smile. "To come all over my face." *Holy shit.*

His mouth dives back onto me, this time flicking his tongue harder, faster, and in varied movements back and forth. I know I can't resist what's coming, so instead I close my eyes and try to relax my tensing body, embracing the magic movements of his mouth. I unclench my buttocks, and my peach relaxes against his mouth, intensifying the pressure.

"Uhh, Max!" I squeal. He slows his tongue in a teasing manner, lightly and gently lapping against me. I twist my hips from left to right trying to stave myself off and enjoy this as long as possible. My arousal overtakes me, and the tide of convulsions ripples through my body. He grabs my hips and holds my body so I can't escape, moving his tongue against me as my limbs quake. "Stop," I beg him. "Please, it's too much." He gives me a few more seconds of divine sexual torture, before relinquishing his position. He moves his mouth outside of the pleasure zone, planting gentle kisses starting at my inner thigh and working his way up to my mouth. I have no hesitation about where he's just been when he plants his lips on mine for a sensual, desirous kiss. He rolls over next to me, resting his head in his hand. I say nothing, feeling a bit coy about how intimate we've just been. Lust is all smiles, looking equally as satisfied as I feel right now.

"I've never had a ripe Georgia peach for breakfast." He pauses, slowly sliding the end of his tongue against his tucked bottom lip. "It's fucking fantastic." *Oh. Dear. Me.*

CHAPTER FORTY-FOUR

Can't wait to see you tomorrow. Can I pick you up from the airport? I know we really need to talk.

I stare at this latest text from Jack. I'm still frustrated that he's been an ass the last few weeks and now he suddenly wants to talk. Nevertheless, I still feel guilty when I see his name, and I know it's because he still has a place inside my heart. I sigh at the thought of our breakup, knowing it won't be as easy or simple as my oversexed body wants it to be. But, I know it's the right thing to do. And, the exchanged promise of some future together with Max last night, whatever that may mean, helps to lessen the pain I feel when I consider the end with Jack.

I sort through my dress choices, looking for something memorable for my last night with Max. My excitement is dulled knowing that this adventure can't go on forever. The question that has burned in my mind all day is, where do we go from here? He said this "wasn't just a thing" to him, but what does that actually mean in the real world? The giant world that he's constantly traveling through, and rarely even in the same country as me?

My phone pings again, with another text from Jack.

I'm sorry I've been such an ass. I promise I'll make it up to you. Love you.

I take a deep breath, forcing myself to apply some logic to the situation, knowing I have to face him tomorrow.

Sarah will give me a ride, but thanks for the offer. I'll be at your house around 11:15 tomorrow night.

I purposely omit any loving sentiment in my response, not wanting to mislead him. I hit send and go back to outfit selection. I pull out an overpriced dress I picked up this afternoon, wanting to wear something special on our final night together. I don't know where we're going tonight, but I'm sure it's somewhere opulent, like him. I hear my phone ping again, and assume it's Jack again, but a smile covers my face when I see it's from my Lust.

Running late. Sending a car to pick you up. Be in the lobby at 8:00. See you soon, bella.

Shit! I force my thoughts of Jack aside and get myself ready for my Lust. I scour my makeup bag and find my bright red lipstick at the bottom of the bag. I run it over my lips, giving some much-needed color to my pale skin. My hair is straight, with the slightest curl at the bottom. I put on my tall black heels, with black lace panties and a matching bra. I give my eyelashes one last curl and an extra coat of mascara for an evening vixen look. *Here goes nothing.* I take a deep breath and walk out the door, hoping this isn't the last time I'll ever get ready for a date with Max.

Lost

The restaurant can best be described as high-end uber-trendy. It's location in the Bund 18 building allows for gleaming views of the sparkling night lights against the Huangpu river. A hostess leads me through the dimly lit, expertly decorated modern restaurant, each section packed from the intimate tables to the tall scenic windows.

She gestures across the room, and I see the subtle dark waves of my Lust's hair, his perfect body outfitted in a light gray suit and white button-up. He faces the windows, taking in the beautiful and well-lit backdrop of one of the busiest cities in the world. He lifts up his left wrist, wiggling his arm slightly to expose his exquisite and obscenely expensive gold Rolex as he checks the time. I take a deep breath as I near the table, eager yet anxious for what I hope will be a meaningful last night together. He must see my reflection in the window, as he quickly turns toward me as I approach, a big smile in tow. "Jessa," he grins. He quickly moves his eyes down my body, then gracefully grabs my hand, pulling me into him for a proper hello. I expect his lips to land on my cheek in his signature Italian greeting, but instead they skip right past the acquaintance greeting and onto my lips. I close my eyes as his warm, soft lips push into mine. *Mmmm.* I savor the moment, radiating from his simple touch. *God, I love how he makes me feel.* He extends my arm out to get another look at me, this time his eyes moving slowly up and down my body. He carefully studies me with a serious expression, and after his eyes fuck me up and down, he ends his viewing with an "I want to have you now" eyebrow raise. *Ohh. How the hell am I going to make it through dinner?*

"Hi!" I blurt out, his seductive stare nearly making me forget about my fears for our future.

"Bella. Please, sit." He slides his hand around my waist and I feel his electricity disperse from his hand right through me. I slide in to the intimate booth, which yields an impeccable view of the fast-paced kitchen, the restaurant area, and of course, the Pearl and the rest of the amazing high rises along the river.

"How did you get this table?" I ask, realizing we have the best seats in the house on the busiest night of the week. He winks at me then shrugs his shoulders, dismissing the idea that it's anything special. Before I can press him to respond, a waiter appears at our table with an iced bottle of Dom and two glasses.

"I ordered us some champagne," he explains as we both watch the waiter expertly remove the cork from the fancy bottle.

"Thank you. You know you spoil me," I say, giving his hand a squeeze under the table.

"There is no spoiling. I love making you happy." He gives my hand a squeeze back, then reaches over for a freshly poured glass of bubbly goodness.

"To our last night in Shanghai," I say before clinking his glass, and secretly wishing that we'll spend many, many more evenings together.

"I could barely focus at work today. I could only think of you," he admits directly. He leans into me, and I feel his breath dance on the edge of my neck. "I don't want to be a selfish man, but I'm hoping for another present from you," he whispers excitedly into my ear. "What you gave me this morning was just a tease. I need more." *Ahh.* The thought of his skilled mouth upon me has my loins instantly swooning.

"I think I can arrange that. But only if you behave."

"Ok," he laughs. "And what does that entail?"

"Letting me buy you dinner," I suggest. Between the Dom and what I can assume is an outrageously priced dinner menu, I'll be paying off my credit card for months, but I can't very well let my sugar daddy drop more money on me.

"Absolutely not. It's my treat."

"No!" I protest. "You've paid for everything. It's too much."

"No."

"Max, come on. I won't take no for an answer."

"Well neither will I."

"Fine," I sigh, knowing I won't win this battle, and I probably can't afford to. "But let me do something for you."

"Jessa, really. I don't need anything." He shakes his head before turning back to me with an eager grin. "Ok, there is something you can give me." He pauses, becoming serious. "You."

"Ok," I smile, knowing that I will gladly let him have me at the end of the night. Instead of using words I let my mouth give him a fantastically rich kiss to affirm his request. He smiles when I pull his lips away from him.

"No. Not like that. I want you. Not just in China. I want you in New York, Atlanta, Paris. Wherever I can have you all to myself."

"What exactly are you saying?" I ask, feeling my eager heart race. His serious expression quickly tells me the truth.

"I want you to be with me. *Only* me."

"As your girlfriend?" I blurt out the words before I've even thought them through.

"Yes. As my woman friend. You are all woman, not a girl, my bella." Goodness, he knows how to make a woman feel desired. I sit thoughtful for a moment, considering our situation here, how wonderful this week has been, and the reality that I'm going home to.

"I've had a great time this week, but—"

"No butts!" he interrupts. "I've watched enough American movies to know that phrase is followed by disappointment. And you can't disappoint me on our last night together."

"Max, I know your reputation. And it's not just that. My situation at home is…complicated."

Max sighs and looks away, and I wonder if I've said too much. I never planned to call out his reputation, but my spinning mind was computing too fast to filter my direct words.

"I know. I know." He shakes his head after a few moments of silence. "What you've heard about me. It's true." *What? No denial?* He quickly continues. "It's true because I've never met anyone like you. Someone who's company I crave, that I've wanted to see day after day. Someone who has challenged me, and confused me the way you do. Someone that I can laugh with, and make love to. Someone that I've truly cared about the way I do you. There's something about you, Jessa. Something I can't let go." His eyes hold mine again and I feel overwhelmed by his words, allowing myself to finally wonder if this is more than just lust.

But is this really what I want? To extend this lovely affair into the real world back at home? To move out of my boyfriend's house, break up with him, and really try this relationship out? Concern begins to creep upon my Lust's face while I silently analyze. My heart overtakes my head and I simply blurt out my emotions.

"I want you too." *There. I said it.* The thoughts that I've had since I met him in Paris. I want him. I want more of him. I want to be with him in more ways than one. I want him to be only mine. I reach over and grab his forearm, giving him a reassuring squeeze. "I want to see what will happen with us."

The slight wrinkle in his brow begins to relax as he hears the words he's been waiting for. I record his rare moment of vulnerability, a side I've not see until now. Beneath the layers of expensive soaps, fabrics, and labels is a man who just wants a chance at what…love? *With me.* A deliciously desirable, rich, charming man who wants me. I smile giddily at the thought. I look up at Max as my fingers slowly trace swirls across his arm. He grabs my hair, twirling his fingers through it as he pulls my mouth to his. It only took months and countless strokes of fate, but here we are together, on our own wills, ready to give this thing a shot.

His tongue wrestles with mine, our bodies electrified from the words we've exchanged. I kiss him hard, my feelings growing stronger by the minute. All of the things I've thought, and hoped for, are finally coming true. We will have our chance to be together. Actually together as a couple. I taste his mouth for what feels like forever, only pausing when I sense a shadow lurking over us.

Lost

"Excuse me, sir, are you ready to order?" an older Chinese man with perfect English inquires. The normally cool Max looks flustered, our exchange of feelings clearly being new territory for him.

"Are you hungry?" Max asks, turning toward me. My body is nearly heaving from having locked lips, but my only hunger is for him. I turn my head over his shoulder and slide my hand between his legs. His Italianness is at a full salute, and it's the only thing I want to taste.

"Not for food," I manage to say with a straight face.

"Actually, we have to go," Max informs the waiter. "You have my card."

"Yes, sir." The water nods, and moves the table outward, allowing us an easier exit. Max slides out first, then offers me his hand to help me out. He grabs the open bottle of Dom with his free hand, whisking me away for an incredible evening of Lust.

CHAPTER FORTY-FIVE

The hotel room is quiet. Eerily quiet. I consult the clock and see it's only 7 am in Shanghai, still hours before we have to leave for the airport. The sheets beside me are empty and cold, and I strain my ear for sounds of Max. *He must be in the bathroom?* I blink my tired eyes, forcing them open just enough to further survey the room. I glance toward the bathroom and see no lights beneath the closed door. *That's odd.* I flop out of bed and walk quietly up to the door, again listening for sounds of life. *Nothing.* I knock quietly before opening the bathroom door. Upon further silence, I swing it open and my eyes confirm he's not there. *He must've gone to get us some breakfast*, I sweetly think of him. *Wait, where are his toiletries?* My eyes and mind are fully awake now, processing what I'm seeing.

My heart races as I whirl around back into the hotel room and feel my fears further confirmed. All of Max's things are gone, except for his shiny gold watch on his nightstand. My phone is without any texts from him, and there are no apparent notes explaining his absence. *But he's always wearing his watch—unless he was in such a hurry to leave me that he forgot it. Oh, God. I'm such an idiot.* The tears begin falling down my face, faster than they've ever fallen before. I fall onto my knees, curling up in a ball, holding onto my only tangible memory of him: his shiny gold watch.

I replay last night's conversation in my head. He clearly said he wanted me. Wanted to try things with us. That this wasn't just a fling. But now he's gone? *I'm such a fool. An idiot. Why would I suddenly be the girl he would fall for? There's nothing special about me. He could have anyone.* My sobs grow louder, but not loud enough to mask the knowing voices in my head. *I was never his, and he was never mine.* I was simply another girl, another fling, another meaningless conquest. Everything he said was bullshit. The only thing real between us was the chemistry we had. But it was just sex. Just a fling. Just...Lust. *It's over, Jess. Your trysts with Max. Your relationship with Jack. Oh, fuck. What have I done?*

I knew his reputation. I knew better. *And now I have to say goodbye to Jack, too.* The one I've loved and have lost as well. It's all my fault. Love was never enough for me. I thought I needed this lust. This is my karma. I should have trusted in what I had with Jack, allowed my heart to have faith, to take a chance and fight for love. But now it's all gone. Everything.

No more love. No more Lust. Just me. Completely Lost and alone.

CHAPTER FORTY-SIX

"So what are you going to say to Jack?" Sarah asks me, staring straight ahead as she navigates us through the dark and quiet highway that takes us from the airport into the city.

"I don't know. The truth I guess?"

"That you had an affair with Max?"

"Well no, not exactly. What's the point? It's over." I shake my head at the words, finally able to say them without tears because they've all been cried. There's nothing left inside of me. "Everything is over."

"Is that what you want? Even after, well, what happened in Shanghai?"

"Whatever happened with Max is over. Clearly. But that doesn't change anything with Jack. When I decided to cheat, that's when it was over. Now we just have to make it official." Despite the sinking feeling inside of me, I am numb. My heart is shattered, pained into a state of shock, which graciously brings a glimmer of numbness to my broken soul. I never should have taken a chance on Jack. And definitely not on Max. I should've stayed alone and unloved, then I would've never had to feel the pain of losing it. Him. Them.

"So will you talk to him tonight?"

I glance at the clock, seeing it's near midnight. "I think I have to. I'm totally exhausted, but I can't let this go on. I need to be fair to him."

"Jess, are you absolutely sure? Sure that you're done with Jack?"

"It's not my decision. I mean I do still love him. It's not that the feelings disappeared, they just changed when our relationship was strained. He's not the same Jack he was even a month ago. He's not the guy I fell in love with. That guy seems to have vanished. If he hadn't, who knows what would've happened with Max."

Sarah leans her right hand over and gives mine a reassuring squeeze.

"And either way, I've made my bed. No pun intended." I sigh, realizing how poignant my words are.

"You're doing the right thing, Jess. You'll get through it, I promise."

"I know. I'll be fine," I lie, willing the numbness back to protect my fractured soul. "So tell me about Ben. Was this just an international fling?"

She shrugs her shoulders. "It's too early to tell. But he's more gifted than I would've guessed."

"Really! Wow. Our boy Ben. Good for him. And for you, I guess! So how gifted is he? Is it just a gift, or is there talent to back it up?" We both laugh at my ridiculous metaphors, and Sarah keeps me preoccupied with the PG version of their trysts in China, until we finally turn down Jack's street. *My street?* My former street anyway.

"You sure you're ready to do this? You can always stay with me tonight and talk to him tomorrow."

I stare at his house up ahead, and begin to feel the nerves churn my stomach. "I'm good. Really."

She pulls into his driveway, and I climb out of her Jeep Cherokee, grabbing my bag from the back. I hear a door swing open and Jack bounds from inside the house, wearing a nervous smile as he approaches me.

"Let me get your bags, Jess." He passes me by and I shrug at Sarah.

"Good luck," she mouths to me. I nod my head, grateful for her concern.

"Call you tomorrow," I say leaning in to her window, feeling my heart begin to pound inside my chest. She nods, and leans her head out the window toward Jack.

"Goodnight, Jack." She waves to him, then switches into reverse, quickly leaving the two of us alone in the driveway. I look to Jack, who is filled with nervous excitement, not exactly the emotion I was expecting of him tonight. Jack hurries my bag to the front porch then quickly jogs back to me.

"Come with me." He grabs my hand and hurries inside. Resting on the kitchen counter is a bottle of Prosecco on ice, with two glasses next to it.

"I thought you wanted to talk?" I ask, confused by this setup.

"I do. I need to explain myself to you. Jess, I know I've been an ass. Unforgivably so. I haven't made time for you, and I wasn't making you a priority. I realize that now, and I'm truly sorry," he says with sincerity. "We can talk about everything, but I just need to get this off my chest first." He glances nervously at me, and the remnants of my feelings for him trickle to the surface. I give his hand a reassuring squeeze, encouraging him to finish whatever this is.

"I love you Jess. I nearly fucked things up with you earlier this year, and now I've done it again. I'm an idiot. I know that. And I don't want to lose you. I promise I'll never shut you out like this again. You're the one person I need. I just wasn't as quick to realize it as I should have been. But now it's crystal clear. I love you. I need you. And I want to be with you forever."

What? My head begins to spin out of control. He grabs my hand and leads me through the kitchen toward the deck outside. *Oh my God.* I see the flickering candle lights and flowers covering nearly every square inch. *He can't be serious. Can he?*

He leads me through the open door and lets out a deep exhale before dropping onto one knee.

"Jessica Marie Bauer, I love you so much. And I know I haven't appreciated you the way I should have. I promise I'll spend the rest of my life making it up to you and giving you everything that you deserve." He pauses, retrieving a box from his pocket, and my breath escapes me. The candle lights flicker against the sparkling diamond and the shiny gold watch as I breathlessly await his words. "Will you marry me?"

ABOUT THE AUTHOR

Jennifer Davis is a native of Georgia. Like a true native, she received a Bachelor of Science from the Georgia Institute of Technology and a Master of Business Administration from the University of Georgia.

Jennifer's favorite season is fall, and she loves watching her teams play college football. She enjoys spending time with her family, traveling, and baking. Jennifer aspires to learn Italian, largely due to her love of Italian food and wine.

Her stories stem from an adventurous imagination and vivid nightly dreams. Jennifer began writing her first novel, *Lost*, in 2013 as a way to unwind and give life to her stories beyond the confines of her own mind.

Jennifer resides in Atlanta with her husband, son, and big shaggy dog.

Made in the USA
San Bernardino, CA
03 May 2017